FIVE SECONDS

Running blindly; lungs working furiously.

Not enough distance. Not enough time to get away.

Three seconds.

A concussive wave at his back. Early. The terrorist had miscounted.

He felt himself being lifted in the air, thrown forward.

Something flashing in his peripheral vision. Hands windmilling. Slicing furiously at air. Chiun. And in that sliver of airborne time at the hellish forefront of a consuming wave of raw explosive energy, Remo finally noticed the Master of Sinanju's costume. In his altered police uniform, the old man looked like Korea's answer to the Keystone Kops.

Remo made a mental note to ask Chiun about the outfit when they reached the Void, for there was no doubt in his mind that they were both going to die. And as this final thought flitted through the mind of Remo Williams, the wave of intense heat from the powerful blast overwhelmed them.

Other titles in this series:

Created by Murphy & Sapir

THE Destroyer™

FADE TO BLACK

A GOLD EAGLE BOOK FROM
W⊕RLDWIDE®

TORONTO • NEW YORK • LONDON
AMSTERDAM • PARIS • SYDNEY • HAMBURG
STOCKHOLM • ATHENS • TOKYO • MILAN
MADRID • WARSAW • BUDAPEST • AUCKLAND

First edition April 2000

ISBN 0-373-63234-7

Special thanks and acknowledgment to
James Mullaney for his contribution to this work.

FADE TO BLACK

Printed in U.S.A.

To Tom and Marsha

And a special caveat to everyone in the entire universe who reads The Destroyer: Remember, all of Chiun's opinions are his own.

STOP THE PRESSES!

What of my opinions? Of course they are my own. This, O readers of trash, is the last straw.

A Proper Dedication

For years at the start of these Korea-insulting Destroyer things there have been names placed in dedication. After almost three decades I must break my silence and ask: Who are these people? Be warned that most of them are total strangers to me (except for this Marsha who is a lovely woman whom the Master is quite fond of). The rest are doubtless there because the authors were indebted to them in some vice-related way and so, rather than surrender their kneecaps when the bill came due, cooked up this scheme in lieu of pay. It is unsavory and beneath even these dirty little Remo books.

And so I wrest control of this page until further notice and rededicate this book to a very special man whose patience, kindness and beauty are boundless. Namely me.

I am told also to further dedicate this book to the Glorious House of Sinanju (which should go without saying by now) and to say that we can be reached by something called e-mall at "housinan@aol.com." However, since I haven't a clue what an e-mail is, if you don't get a response, blame the cheap white help, not me.

I remain,

Chiun

Prologue

Excerpt from The Annals of the Glorious House of Sinanju:

> To all later generations that they might learn
> truth!

The words you read have been inscribed by the
awesome hand of Chiun, unworthy custodian of the
present history of our House and trainer of Remo
the Fair, who, though not technically of the village
proper, was deemed an adequate receptacle by the
Master in spite of his pale complexion, strangely
deformed eyes and near total lack of gratitude for
the greatness bestowed upon him by the most be-
nign and patient Master Chiun. But there is no
sense in complaining about things one cannot control, especially the ingratitude of a thankless found-
ling, so why bother?

The History of Sinanju

AND LO DURING THIS portentous time, the Master
of Sinanju did venture to the most distant western
shore of the current Rome. It was called America.

So vast was this nation that it took many days over-
land to travel from its cold and barren eastern
shores to the warmer climes of its west. But because
of his special status as royal assassin to America's
mad yet generous Emperor Harold I, the Master did
not have to waste his time on common ground
transport. A flying machine of Korean design (see
The Thieving Wrights: Where They Went Wrong)
did spirit him to his destination in mere hours, thus
sparing him prolonged contact with the dregs and
castoffs who did populate this land.

The Master of Sinanju did travel in secret in the
dead of night. This he deemed necessary, for
though the Master was acting in the interests of
Sinanju, he was not acting directly on behalf of his
emperor. However, he was on a mission that would
ultimately bring glory to the House and, as a result,
glory to he who had contracted with the House. For
this reason, when the veil of secrecy was at last
lifted, Harold the Generous would rejoice in the
Master's secret actions. Of this, the Master of
Sinanju was certain.

And the Master's airship did travel to that region
of America known as California—named thus de-
spite the fact that it was not ruled by a caliph, but
by a governor (see *White Nomenclature: the Case
Against*).

As promised by those who had summoned him,
a carriage awaited the Master. The coach was a kind
reserved for only the most revered individuals in
this nation. Called a limousine, it was, and not even

the Master's emperor of the time did have one of
these special carriages.

The Master was ushered into this regal chariot
and was driven in haste to the preordained meeting
place. His destination was a wondrous province of
this Caliphless-fornia. A place of magic and wonder, the name of which was known in the four corners of the world. Hollywood it was called, even
though no woods of holly were immediately visible
to the naked eye *(ibid)*.

When first he had ventured there, this province
had presented an enigma to the Master. For though
the word *studious* was trumpeted from every building, no evidence of current study or past education
was visible in its inhabitants. Only upon closer inspection did the Master realize that the word was
actually *studio*, which in this tongue was roughly
equivalent to the atelier of the French.

Once in the Woods of Holly, the Master's limousine did speed him between the heavy castle
gates of Taurus Studios. There he was met by those
who had summoned him.

The first was called Hank Bindle, the second
Bruce Marmelstein. Makers of magic they were.
Illusionists were they. Theurgists of the highest or-
der who did transform paper into moving images.

"Hey, babe. How you doing? Looking good,"
did the first magician, the one called Bindle, pro-
nounce as the Master alighted from his sleek black
chariot.

The prestidigitator Marmelstein, not to be outdone, did intone, "Looking great, but what am I talking? It's got to be—what?—a hundred in the shade out here. I'm sweating my mazurkas off. Let's go up to the office."

This they did, Bindle and Marmelstein flanking Chiun, toadying respectfully to the Master.

The air within their fortress of glass and steel was cool, controlled by machines built for men who could not control their own bodies. Only when they were secure in their inner sanctum did the two address the Master.

"The picture's gonna be great," Bindle insisted.

"Gangbusters." Marmelstein nodded, seeming to agree. As was his wont, he employed an odd colloquialism that the Master had not before encountered.

"Boffo," Bindle pressed, seeming to agree with the agreement.

Their confusing use of language did not distract the Master. For it was written in our histories by the Lesser Wang that "there is a time to endure the braying of jackasses and there is a time to talk turkey."

Although the Master had partly ventured to this land because of difficulties with their mutual project, there were also problems with a contract between the Master and the wily sorcerers Bindle and Marmelstein.

"I have been contacted by barristers who claim that you are attempting to rewrite our original agreement," the Master intoned seriously. His piercing hazel eyes searched for deception. With Hollywood producers this was like looking for water in a swimming pool.

"Lies," lied the crafty Bindle and Marmelstein in unison.

"They have informed me that you wish to cut my percentage down from the agreed-upon amount."

"Would we do that?" Bindle squeaked.

"No," Marmelstein answered his partner.

Now, the Master of Sinanju was not a fool. He knew that these two conjurers were attempting to deceive him. And though telling falsehoods to a Master of Sinanju was, under ordinary circumstances, an offense punishable by death, the Master did have need of these two. In his wisdom did Chiun the Brilliant take a new tack.

"I have heard rumors of production delays," the Master said craftily.

"It's a little behind," the worm Bindle confessed.

"More than a *little*," the spineless Marmelstein muttered, with a furtive eye on his partner.

"A couple of weeks behind," the slimy Bindle admitted.

"What we were wondering..." Marmelstein ventured.

"If you could, you know..." offered Bindle.

"Move things along," Marmelstein finished.

There it was. The mendacious magicians had spoken aloud that which the Master already knew.

They needed the Master of Sinanju to move their production forward.

"It would be a pleasure to aid you, O wise Bindle, O learned Marmelstein," the shrewd Master said magnanimously.

With the words of the Master ringing true in their ears, there was much relief in the private halls of Taurus. Their faces—brown from the captured sunlight of coffinlike booths—did brighten with pleasure.

"Great," the sorcerer Bindle sighed.

"Perfect," the toothy Marmelstein exhaled.

But before relief overwhelmed them, the Master of Sinanju held up a staying hand. "*When* certain contract provisions are met."

Smiles melted into suntanned skin. The round white eyes of the two magicians belonged to animals in an abattoir.

"But..." Bindle spoke.

"B-but..." Marmelstein stammered.

The Master cut them off.

"Our contract will be reopened. I have learned much these many months since first I signed. It will be rewritten in such a way as to make impossible any attempts to deprive the Master of that which is rightfully his due. Plus ten points. *Gross.* This for my *agita.* Only when this new contract is processed will I agree to aid you with your difficulties."

The tricksters Bindle and Marmelstein were at a loss, thwarted by the superior skills and mighty bargaining position of the Master of Sinanju. They conferred among themselves, but only briefly. Finally, Bindle spoke.

"You can have it all," he said, choking on the words.

"Everything you want," Marmelstein echoed.

"You will give points?" the Master asked craftily.

"Everything's negotiable," the defeated Bindle stated.

"Whatever you say," agreed the dejected Marmelstein.

"I have heard a rumor that a film starring the foulmouthed jester Edward Murphy was said to have lost money. This in spite of domestic grosses exceeding one hundred million dollars and a production cost much lower than this," said Chiun the Insightful, who had studied the habits of these Hollywood cretins and was aware of the sly manipulations they were known to make on paper. "This so that the makers of the film did not have to pay the writer."

"A *lie*," Bindle insisted.

"A mistruth," Marmelstein interjected.

"And if it *was* true, we would *never* do that to you," Bindle stressed.

"Wouldn't *dream* of it," Marmelstein agreed.

"That would be prudent." The Master of Sinanju nodded sagely. "For if I were to ever learn again that you have attempted to cheat me, I would be forced to deal with you thusly."

And in demonstration, the Master of Sinanju did raise a single fearsome fingernail.

The Master did draw this lone Knife of Eternity along the center of Bruce Marmelstein's heavy desk. He expended no effort and when he was finished, a single sharp line—more precise than any manufactured edge could produce—bisected the gleaming piece of mahogany furniture. As Bindle and Marmelstein watched in fear, the Master did slap both hands flat on either side of the line. In the wake of the thunderous clap, the desk did separate in twain, dropping open like the petals of a blooming flower. The rumble of the crashing fragments shook the fortress to its very foundation.

When the Master turned back to face the magicians, he did detect a scent displeasing to him emanating from the lower garments of the wizards. They spoke in haste to him.

"You'll get everything you want," the sorcerer Bindle gasped.

"I'll *personally* guarantee it," Marmelstein the Magician agreed quickly. His eyes were filled with terror.

"The new contracts will be ready for you to sign in an hour," Bindle insisted.

"Half an hour," Marmelstein said rapidly.

"We'll courier them to your hotel."

"That reminds me," the Master said, stroking his beard thoughtfully. "I wish you to pay my hotel expenses, as well."

"Done," agreed Bindle.

"I'll call the limo," said Marmelstein. Pulling at his trousers, the magician went off to summon the coachman who would take the Master to his lodgings.

"I'll get the ball rolling with legal," Bindle said, heading for his telephone.

"I will wait outside," said Master Chiun, the brilliant negotiator, for the odor in the inner sanctum of the titans of Taurus was more than he could bear. He left the conjurer Bindle to talk to legal.

Thus did the Master of Sinanju, in the earliest days of what Western calendars inaccurately deemed the twenty-first century (see *Pope Gregory XIII: Calendars, Carpenters and the Confusion They've Wrought*), arrive in and conquer the province of Hollywood.

1

On the evening of his murder, Walter Anderson steered his Ford Explorer up his driveway at the usual time. A hint of the summer Walter would never see wafted through the open driver's side window, carried on eddies of warm spring air.

Commuting through Washington that morning, Walter had been surprised to see that the cherry blossoms were just beginning to peek from their buds. Since he hadn't noticed them on Friday, they had to have started coming out over the weekend. No matter how lousy his mood, the sight of those tiny pink buds always made him feel a little better.

Walter drew slowly up the slight blacktopped incline from Clark Street in suburban Maryland, stopping his truck tight behind his teenage son's red Camaro. He cut the engine.

Walter paused for a moment, staring at the closed garage door beyond Mike's sports car. The weak 1950s-style overhead bulb that hung next to the frayed, unused basketball net threw amber shadows across the weathered beige garage door.

He was late again.

Penny would be mad at him. Again. But that

seemed to be a given lately. This just happened to be one of the busiest times of year for the construction firm he owned. What did she expect him to do—sell the business? The whole argument was stupid and was always the same. But Walter never heard her complain about the money. Oh, no. Sometimes he'd point this out, but it only provoked more yelling. Tonight he just wasn't in the mood.

Walter let out a sigh that reeked of his three-pack-a-day Marlboro habit and climbed wearily from his truck.

The flagstone path had been installed in the 1960s and was showing definite signs of age. Walter noted dozens of cracked stones between the slowly disintegrating mortar as he trudged toward the front door.

She'd been on him to fix the walk for at least five years. "You build *buildings,* for Christ's sake, Walter," Penny berated him with clockwork frequency. "With dozens of men working for you, you can't spare *one* mason to patch the goddamn walk?"

Heading for the front door for what would be the last time, Walter decided to fix the walk. Just like that. Walter Anderson—a man who hadn't gotten his hands dirty in construction for more than a decade—would go to the hardware store and get a couple of bags of concrete mix. He would personally rip up and redo the walk this weekend.

A spark inside him wanted to be nice. To do something decent for the mother of Mike and little

Alice. But mostly he was just tired of hearing her nag. He wouldn't get one of his guys to do it. He'd do it himself.

She'd probably find a reason to complain about that, too. They'd look destitute in the eyes of the neighbors if he did the work himself. They weren't paupers, after all.

He didn't care. His next weekend's plans already set at nine o'clock Monday night, Walter happily slipped his house key from the others on the ring in his hand and brought it up to the lock on his front door.

At just the slightest pressure, the door popped open.

"Damn kids," Walter muttered as he pushed the door open all the way. "Least it's not January."

He took one step across the threshold—his hand still on the brass knob—when he felt a sudden blinding pain shoot through the side of his head. He reeled in place.

The living room was swept in dark maroon shadows. Penny was there. So were the kids, Alice and Mike. On the couch. Gray electrical tape across their mouths. Eyes pleading. Hands and feet bound tightly together.

The pain again. Powerful. Overwhelming.

A second to realize he'd been attacked.

He lunged at his assailant. Or wanted to. But something had changed. Penny and the two kids were lower now. On his level. Terrified.

No. He was on *their* level.

He had fallen. Hands reached up to ward off the next blow. Something struck his fingers, slamming them against his own skull. A shotgun butt.

Fresh pain. Fingers, broken.

Blood on his fingers. His own blood from the gaping wound in the side of his head.

The room was spinning. Ceiling whirling high above him. Cracked plaster. He'd promised to fix that, too.

This weekend. Along with the walk. Hell, he'd even clean the garage. Everything this weekend. If only he could live. If only God would spare his beautiful wife and precious, precious children.

The room, and the world around it, was collapsing into a brilliant hot flash of light. Coalescing into a pinprick explosion. Flickering once, then vanishing forever.

One final blow to the head, and Walter Anderson collapsed in a bloody heap to the floor, never to move again. The front door slammed shut behind him, cutting off the view of the cracked flagstone walk, the repairs of which would now be left to the new, future owners of the Anderson house.

"GET THOSE DAMN CAMERAS *out* of here!"

Lieutenant Frederick Jonston had yelled that three times already, growing angrier each time. No one seemed to want to listen tonight.

One of the uniforms disengaged from crowd control and headed over to the cluster of reporters. A few other officers followed his lead. Together, they corralled the members of the press back behind the yellow sawhorses.

It was a zoo. At first Jonston had wanted to string up whoever had alerted the media by their eyeballs, but the detective found out after arriving on the scene that the press had received a cryptic phone call from the hostage takers themselves. Just as the police had.

"They still not answering?" Jonston asked the sergeant on the radiophone in the car next to him.

"Nothing, Lieutenant."

Leaning on the open door of the squad car, Jonston looked at the house. Upper middle class. Neatly tended grounds. Nice neighborhood. He frowned.

Lights from the roofs of a dozen cruisers and the dashboards of as many unmarked cars sliced through the postmidnight darkness.

This hostage drama had gone on for four hours. If Jonston had his way, it would *not* go on another four.

He turned to the sergeant.

"How long's it been?"

"More than twenty minutes."

That was the last time they'd heard from the men holding the Anderson family.

One of the hostage takers' victims was already dead. They had let the son—maybe seventeen years old—get as far as the front door before shooting him in the back of the head. There had been a lot of screaming inside after that.

Crouching low, Kevlar-outfitted officers had dragged the boy behind police lines. But he was a lost cause. Jonston's concern right then was the rest of the family. As far as he knew, the other three—father, mother and daughter—were still alive inside. He intended to keep them that way.

"It's been too long," Jonston mused.

Cameras whirred all around. Some were network. The curse of being so close to Washington.

A few men were clustered around him. SWAT-team members, hostage negotiators and other detectives. The microphones were far enough away that they couldn't pick up his words.

"Let's do it," Jonston whispered gruffly. "Take them out if you have to. Whatever force is necessary to save the family. I don't want any more dead. Understood?"

There was not a single questioning word.

The assault began less than three minutes later. Tear-gas canisters were launched through front and side windows. A split second later, doors were kicked open simultaneously in kitchen, garage, basement and front hall.

Two men went in through the shattered living-room picture window, rolling to alert crouches on the glass-covered floor.

Though their timed movements were textbook perfect, none of the efforts made by police were necessary.

The first men in the living room found the Anderson family. The father was piled in a corner, dead from an apparent beating to the head.

The mother and eight-year-old daughter were on the couch. Each had a clear plastic garbage bag over her head. The mother's had been tied with a bathrobe belt, the daughter's with a short extension cord. Warm mist from their last, desperate breaths clung to the interior of the bags. Their sightless eyes gazed in horror at the vacant air before them.

Across the room, the television played; silently turned to a channel covering the hostage story. Although the power to the home had been cut, the TV was plugged into a black battery box. A retractable silver antenna wobbled in the smoky air.

The tear-gas haze cleared a few minutes later. Lieutenant Jonston was ushered into the living room. His face contorted in disgust at the sight of the dead family.

"Where are they?" he demanded, his voice a low growl.

In reply, a shout issued from the basement.

"Down here!"

Dozens of boots and shoes clattered on the old wooden staircase as the men hurried downstairs.

Several SWAT-team members were gathered before an area at the front of the cellar that had once been sectioned off for use as a coal chute in the old house. Jonston bulled his way through the men into the narrow alcove.

Stones and mortar that hadn't been disturbed in

a hundred years were collapsed in a pile near the foundation wall. A black tunnel extended beyond.

Jonston heard the radio squawk of officers within the depths of the burrow.

"Where does it go?" he demanded levelly.

"We don't know yet, Lieutenant," replied a heavily armored officer crouching before the opening. "It's pretty deep. Looks like they might have been tunneling it for days. Weeks, even. Must have just broken through tonight."

Jonston glanced up at a small window above him. It sat directly over the tunnel. The dirty panes faced the street, blocked by a thick evergreen. Blue squad car lights swept the window.

The killers had slipped out beneath his own feet.

"I want them found *now!*" Jonston snapped.

The escape tunnel led to the sewer system. Fanning out, the police discovered a cap had been loosened on a street near some woods three blocks away from the Anderson house. No one had seen any suspicious vehicles or men on foot. No one had seen a thing. The killers got away scot-free.

After the police were through combing the home, and relatives were finally allowed inside, it was learned that the only things missing were the Anderson daughter's Girl Scout beret and sash. The killer or killers had left both cash and jewelry.

In a further bizarre twist that capped the whole macabre affair, a small independent film entitled *Suburban Decay* was released three days later. In the film, a family with the surname Anderson was terrorized and finally murdered by a psychotic neighbor. The film's killer—an antihero who was eventually successful in his efforts to elude authorities—used a tunnel to escape.

Because of the real-life similarities, the movie was elevated above the art houses and film festivals where such films generally languished. It was bought by a major distributor and went on to make 14.8 million dollars, a box-office take almost 250 times the original cost of the film.

When it was suggested by a print reporter that the mild success of the movie was based solely on public fascination with the real-life Anderson case, a studio spokesman was quoted as saying, "We are saddened by the loss of the friends and family of the Andersons. It is a loss that we, too, feel. We cannot, however, let bizarre similarities to current events compromise the artistic integrity of this studio. Life goes on."

Reading this report from the comfort of his den, Lieutenant Frederick Jonston made only one bitter comment. "Yeah. It goes on for some."

Afterward, he wadded the newspaper and threw it in the trash bin next to his cluttered desk. He missed.

2

His name was Remo and he had stopped trying to pretend he was interested in what his employer was saying five minutes before. He had stopped actually listening to what was being said four minutes and fifty-eight seconds earlier. What he had gleaned in those first two seconds before his eyes glazed over and his mind wandered had something to do with bombs or guns or some other things that went boom. At least he thought that's what it was about.

Remo didn't like bombs. They always took the fun out of everything. He thought about bombs for a little while. Ticking, exploding. Sometimes, when they went off they were very bright. Almost pretty. Like fireworks on the Fourth of July. Remo watched a bomb explode in his mind. He yawned.

"Remo, are you paying attention?"

The voice creaked like a rusted hinge on an ancient door. It yanked Remo from his reverie.

When he blinked, he was once more sitting on his living-room floor of his Massachusetts home, legs crossed in the lotus position. From the chair above him, the pinched face of Dr. Harold W. Smith looked down, irritated.

"Yeah, I heard every word, Smitty. Ka-boom. End of the world, all the usual stuff. You hungry?"

"No," Smith replied tightly. "And this is serious."

It had to have been. At least in the mind of Harold Smith. The gaunt old man generally didn't approve of face-to-face meetings. His sharp features were somber. The gray-tinged flesh around his thin lips formed a taut frown. A battered briefcase was balanced carefully on his knees, which were stiff in the neatly pressed gray suit. Confident he had Remo's attention focused once again, he resumed speaking.

"I have found a disturbing sameness to these cases. I am not certain what the underlying connection is—if any. It *is* possible that they are merely coincidences. Perhaps even copycat incidences."

"Yeah. Copycats," Remo sighed. "Can't have them."

Smith's frown deepened. "You cannot tell me two words I have spoken since I arrived, can you?" he challenged.

Remo's bored gaze suddenly found focus. "Sure I can," he said. "Um…" His dark eyes flicked around the room, as if the clues to Smith's briefing were buried in the wallboard. At last he snapped his fingers, struck with a sudden burst of inspiration. "You said 'Hi, Remo' when I let you in. There. Two words."

"Actually, I said 'Hello,'" Smith said thinly.

"Oh. Well, I got the 'Remo' right." Dejected, he sunk in on himself, a balloon deflating.

"And could you please turn off the television?"

The big-screen TV had been on since Smith's arrival. On it, four creatures with frozen plastic faces and teardrop-shaped bodies cavorted around a surreal landscape. Each was a different color: orange, maroon, blue or pink. Geometric shapes jutted from the tops of their heads.

For some reason Smith could not fathom, the costumed characters spoke in insipid baby talk while they buttered muffins and bounced balls around the TV screen.

"Don't tell me you've got something against the TeeVeeFatties, Smitty?" Remo asked. He had been staring blankly at the program through most of Smith's briefing.

"Please, Remo—" Smith began.

"That's Poopsy-Woopsy," Remo interrupted knowingly, pointing to the pink creature. "Jerry Falwell says he's gay."

"Yes," Smith said flatly. His lips pursed. "Where is Master Chiun?" he asked suddenly.

It was the one question Remo had hoped Smith wouldn't ask.

"Chiun?" Remo said innocently, his spine growing rigid.

"Yes. If you insist on ignoring me, I would like to share this information with both of you at once. I do not wish to have to repeat myself a third time for his benefit."

"I'll pay attention," Remo promised. "Honest."

He clicked off the TV. Poopsy-Woopsy, Tipsy, Wee-Wee and Doh collapsed into a single bright dot and were gone.

To Smith he seemed suddenly too attentive. The older man's eyes narrowed suspiciously. "Is Chiun at home?"

Remo missed a beat. "He's not here," he admitted vaguely.

"When will he return?"

"I'm not sure. He's been keeping kind of odd hours lately," Remo said. "I haven't seen him in days."

Smith's eyebrows slid almost imperceptibly higher on his forehead in an expression of mild curiosity. "That is not like the Master of Sinanju."

"Trust me, Smitty," Remo muttered. "It's more like him than you wanna know."

Remo was being deliberately unresponsive. The two Masters of Sinanju—the only true practitioners of the most ancient and deadly martial art in the history of mankind—had probably had some kind of fight again.

Smith let the remark pass.

"As I said, these cases I mentioned are similar."

"A bomber?" Remo asked, now genuinely interested.

"There have been no bombs involved in any of the incidents," Smith replied, puzzled.

"Didn't you say something about bombs?"

"No. Remo, please pay attention. There have already been seven people killed."

Smith took the battered leather briefcase from his lap and set it on the floor between his ankles.

Another man would have extracted files from the valise in order to more thoroughly brief his field operative. Not Smith. He didn't like to rely on paper. Paper was a physical link to the secret work that had occupied virtually all of his adult life.

As director of CURE, the supersecret organization charged with safeguarding the constitution, Smith's desire for secrecy approached paranoia. Although he had used computer printouts in the earlier days of his stewardship of CURE, that habit had waned with the encroachment of the pervasive electronic age.

Telephone briefings were the norm, although at this stage of their decades-long relationship a meeting with Smith was the exception to the rule. The odd nature of this assignment had flushed him out of his office in Folcroft Sanitarium in Rye, New York. For this reason alone, Remo tried to concentrate on what his employer was saying.

"There were two bodies found approximately one month ago in a wooded area in the Florida panhandle. Both were college juniors. Roommates at the same university. They had been hung by their ankles and sexually mutilated. According to police experts, they were tortured for a number of days. Eventually their throats were slit."

Remo's attention was focused now. Smith's dry

recitation of the case's facts seemed only to add to the horror of the incident.

"Did they find out who did it?" Remo asked.

"Not as such," Smith admitted. "But there *is* a pattern." Smith shifted uncomfortably in his chair. "A seemingly unconnected murder took place a few days after this incident. A torso was found in a box near a waste receptacle at a condominium complex in Boise. Authorities are still unable to identify the victim in this case."

"The same killer?"

"Possibly," Smith hedged. "Are you familiar with the Anderson case?"

Remo shook his head.

"It has gotten a great deal of coverage on the news the past few days. A family of four was murdered in their Maryland home."

"Oh, yeah. I think I might have seen something about that," Remo nodded. "The guy dug a tunnel out or something?"

"'In' would be more accurate. This was how the killer or killers gained entry to the Anderson home. They merely used the same route for egress."

"Wasn't there something about it being in some dip-shit movie?" Remo asked. "That's why it was on so much."

"Yes," Smith replied. "A film dealing with much the same themes as the true-life Anderson case has opened to critical praise. It is currently doing well in art houses."

"What's wrong? Outhouses all booked up?"

"That would be a more appropriate venue," Smith agreed humorlessly. "But be that as it may, the Anderson case is only part of a larger picture. In the other two incidents I mentioned, films were also released with themes similar to those murders. Like the Anderson film, these did better than expected in large part because of an apparent public fascination with the true-to-life incidents. It is my belief that the fictitious events on-screen are directly linked to those in real life."

Remo shook his head. "Smitty, this seems like kind of a nothing assignment. I know the FBI can't find their ass with both hands and a fanny map lately, but it doesn't sound like they'd need to pull Efrem Zimbalist Jr. out of mothballs for this one. Can't we just take a break and let them do their jobs for once?"

Smith sat back in his chair. His steely gray eyes were mildly accusatory. "You have been taking a break for the past three months," he advised, voice level.

"It hasn't been that long," Remo said dismissively.

"Yes," Smith said, nodding, "it has."

Remo raised an annoyed eyebrow. "Okay, maybe. But can I help it if the bad guys have been in a slump?"

"I had an assignment for you one month ago. The survivalist group in Utah. There was also the potential Islamic terrorist cell in New Jersey the month before that. In both instances you refused to go.''

"Been there, done that,'' Remo said. "Survivalists and Arab terrorists are yesterday's news. Say, the Russian Mafia's big these days. Or killer viruses. Can't we do something with those?''

Wordlessly, Smith removed his rimless glasses. Tired fingers massaged the bridge of his patrician nose. "Remo, CURE does not exist to alleviate your ennui. Frankly, I have been a little concerned by your attitude of late. Ever since your encounter with Elizu Roote in New Mexico—''

Remo's tone hardened. "You don't have to bring that up.''

During his last assignment a few months before, Remo had encountered a man unlike any he had ever met in all his years as CURE's enforcement arm. Surgically enhanced with biomechanical implants, Elizu Roote had offered unexpected resistance. And nearly killed Remo.

"I believe I do,'' Smith pressed. "Twice in the past six months, your abilities have been put to the test by abnormally dangerous foes. Most recently Roote, and before him, Judith White. I have noticed a creeping apathy in your attitude since then, which I believe is a direct result of these experiences.''

"Apathy schmapathy,'' Remo grumbled. "Maybe I've just learned not to sweat the small stuff. Life goes on, Smitty.''

Smith replaced his glasses. His gray eyes were

level. "It does," he said, tart voice even. "For some."

Remo sighed. "Okay, okay, I'm in. So these crummy movies hadn't been released yet when these things happened?" he asked, his tone anything but enthusiastic.

"No."

"Could still be a copycat. Some screwball's getting into sneak previews and then getting his rocks off staging the scenes before the movies are out."

"That is a possible scenario. Also, there is much information contained in studio press kits—promotional material mailed to critics before the films come out. It is also possible that prints of the films are being stolen before they are released for general distribution. The movie company is claiming that any of these scenarios is a plausible explanation."

"Wait a minute, Smitty," Remo said, a sliver of concern in his voice. "*Studio?* All of this shit's being shoveled by *one* company?"

His thoughts turned to Chiun. The Master of Sinanju was in Hollywood right now working on his top secret film. Before he'd left, Chiun made Remo promise he wouldn't breathe a word to Smith about his film.

Remo had seen the bozos who ran the studio that was making the Master of Sinanju's movie. The stuff Smith had described was so appalling that it could be right up Bindle and Marmelstein's alley. For a sudden tense moment, he held his breath.

Smith was nodding. "The studio responsible is

called Cabbagehead Productions,'' the CURE director said.

Remo exhaled silent relief. Not Taurus Studios.

"Okay, this seems pretty cut-and-dry to me. Nimrods make lousy movies, kill people to boost ticket sales.'' Remo nodded. "And at this point, by the way, I think we should all breathe a sigh of relief that this never occurred to Chevy Chase.''

Smith had already stood to go, collecting his briefcase from the floor. Remo rose to his feet, as well.

"If this is a for-profit venture, I want it stopped,'' the CURE director said.

"Can do.'' Remo nodded. "Just call me Remo Williams, Wrestler of the Mundane. Say, Smitty, this place isn't in Hollywood, is it?''

There was something in his tone that caught Smith's attention. It was almost guilty.

"Cabbagehead Productions is a small independent company located in Seattle,'' Smith said slowly. "Why?''

"No real reason,'' Remo replied vaguely. "Bad memories from the last time I went to Hollywood.''

Smith knew what he was referring to. Nodding understanding, he said, "Do you want me to set aside two tickets to Seattle?''

"Not necessary,'' Remo said quickly. "I can handle this one on my own.'' He ushered Smith to the front door.

It was tempting to let the potential headache slide. After all, Smith had had more than his share when dealing with the Master of Sinanju. But in the foyer, dread curiosity got the best of him. As Remo held the door open, Smith paused.

"Remo, is there something going on with Master Chiun that I should know about?"

The bland veneer of affected confusion on Remo's face faded to weary resignation. His shoulders sagged.

"Do you trust me, Smitty?" he asked tiredly.

The question surprised the CURE director. "I suppose," he said slowly. He was already regretting asking.

Remo locked eyes with Smith. "Then trust me now. You do *not* want to know."

The tone was somber, deadly serious. His expression could have been carved from stone.

For an instant, Smith opened his mouth, about to press the issue further. He thought better of it almost at once. Mouth creaking shut, he stepped out the door.

Remo clicked it shut behind him.

As he descended the steps to the sidewalk, the CURE director thought of times in the past when Remo had worn that same expression in regard to the Master of Sinanju. As he hurried down the sidewalk, Harold Smith decided that it might be prudent to stock up on Maalox and Alka-Seltzer on the way home. Just to be on the safe side.

3

Shawn Allen Morris's résumé boasted five years of "intimate experience at the frazzled edge of the film industry." In a forum where truth was always subjective, Shawn had raised the art of inflating one's personal experience on a résumé to gargantuan proportions.

The implication was clear. He was claiming that, like many young men in Tinseltown, he'd spent years toiling on low-budget "indie" films. Even by résumé standards, this was an utter lie. The truth was, the closest Shawn had ever come to the film industry was working on a canteen truck on a vacant tract of land near the Paramount lot.

The high point of that job had been the day John Rhys-Davies—Sallah from the *Indiana Jones* movies—had stopped by for a cheese danish.

When he had first arrived in Hollywood, Shawn spent his evenings attending film school. For 175 bucks per class per semester, he and his classmates would sit in the dark watching Ingmar Bergman movies and pretend to find meaning in them.

At night, he'd talk for hours with his fellow would-be auteurs. And though the arguments were loud and frequent, Shawn and his friends did have some common ground. They all agreed that *they* were intellectuals and visionaries while the rest of the world was comprised of nothing but *Independence Day*-watching troglodytes. When day came, these underappreciated geniuses would emerge bleary-eyed from their coffeehouses only to go back to their jobs parking the cars and busing the tables of the aforementioned troglodytes.

Shawn was no different than his classmates. His years of experience in night school left Shawn Allen Morris qualified for one thing: running a canteen truck.

Graduation came and went, and still, after five long years of school, each daybreak found Shawn wiping down the same cracked Formica counter with the same smelly rag and selling the same putrid egg-salad sandwiches to the same sweaty, hairy teamsters.

He would have languished there forever—his genius never recognized—had fate not finally dealt him a movie-inspired chance meeting.

Business had been slow that fateful afternoon. Shawn was about to close up shop when the fire-engine-red Jaguar squealed to a desperate stop in the lot beside his ratty old canteen truck. A frenzied young man sprang out. Wild-eyed, he raced over to Shawn, who was in the process of collapsing the supports to the trapdoor above his counter.

"I need a blueberry bagel with cream cheese!"

The customer's intent face was borderline frightening. His cheekbones were high and pointy, jutting out almost as far as his bizarrely elongated chin. His lower jaw extended out, as well, putting his lower teeth in front of his uppers. His face was contorted in a perpetual half grimace, half smirk.

At first, Shawn assumed the man was an actor in creature makeup for some bad sci-fi movie. It was only when he was smearing the cream cheese on the bagel that the customer removed his pair of heart-shaped red sunglasses. Shawn's mouth dropped open.

"You're Quintly Tortilli!" he gasped.

"That's the name on my Oscar," the customer snapped urgently. He waved an angry hand at the bagel. "Give it here, asshole."

Shawn hesitated. He knew of Quintly Tortilli all too well. The man was a hero to every failed filmmaker. Although he was now one of Hollywood's most famous directors, only a few short years before, Tortilli had been employed as an usher in a theater. This in order to be closer to the films he loved so much.

According to all the bios, Quintly devoured films. When he'd made the transition into movies, the young director had borrowed heavily from everyone and everything. Sometimes he regurgitated whole scenes and plots from obscure *B* movies in his own loud, ultraviolent films. In any other industry this would be seen for what it was: stealing. In Hollywood it was "homage." Quintly Tortilli was a true Hollywood success story. And now he was displaying some of his famous impatience at the canteen truck of Shawn Allen Morris.

As Tortilli flapped an angry hand, Shawn hesitated. He held the precious bagel away from his customer.

Shawn had tried to break into the motion picture business in every legitimate way imaginable. He had nothing more to lose. As Quintly Tortilli waited testily beside the truck, Shawn raised his hand. Fingers uncurling, he allowed the bagel to plop to the truck's floor. For good measure, he ground a heel into the smooshy cream cheese.

Tortilli's already demented eyes widened. "What the fuck did you do that for!" he screamed.

Shawn's voice didn't waver. "I want a job in film," he said softly.

"What?" Tortilli snapped, his knotted face twisting into a caricature of human anger. "Gimme my fuckin' bagel!"

"A job for a bagel," Shawn insisted. "Quid pro quo."

"Quasimodo *what?*" Tortilli ranted. "What the fuck is this? All I want's a fuckin' *bagel,* for fuck's sake."

"And *I* want a job in film," Shawn replied calmly. "Get me one and I'll give you your bagel."

Tortilli's voice had been growing in volume and pitch. By now it was a woman's whine combined with a high-pitched shriek.

"What the fuck!"

"That's my offer. Take it or leave it." Shawn

crossed his arms firmly over his chest. For added emphasis, he made a show of grinding his foot further into the flattened bagel.

Tortilli fumed for a moment. Finally, his twisted alien's face split apart at a point between his curled, jutting nose and his witch's chin. "You start tomorrow," he hissed. "Now give me my *fucking* bagel!"

That was that. In two days Shawn was two states up the coast, sitting behind a desk in the Seattle offices of fledgling Cabbagehead Productions.

Cabbagehead had been established by a group of wealthy backers who were hoping to break into the independent end of the film industry. The company was supposed to produce the types of counterculture art movies that invariably got good word of mouth at Academy Awards time.

The motivation of Cabbagehead's anonymous benefactors didn't matter to Shawn. He was home at last. In the motion picture industry. It didn't matter that in his job he had to act as location coordinator, producer, wrangler, set designer, assistant editor, occasional gaffer and—due to his experience on his canteen truck—caterer. Thanks to Quintly Tortilli's lust for instant bagel gratification, he was finally where he belonged.

In the eight months he'd spent in the dreary Pacific Northwest, Shawn had overseen the production of thirty-eight motion pictures. Most were barely above the amateurish level of college films. But that didn't matter because no one here was into big-budget Hollywood glitz. They were making "serious" films. All of the wretches who drifted in and out of the Cabbagehead offices knew it was only a matter of time before a dozen gold statuettes lined the empty shelf above Shawn Allen Morris's cheap lobby desk.

During his eight months in that tawdry office, only two people had ever seemed unimpressed by all they were trying to accomplish there. The first was the mailman. That bourgeois bastard always had a smirk on his face whenever delivering the bizarrely wrapped and addressed packages sent to Cabbagehead from would-be filmmakers. The second undazzled visitor walked through the front door one afternoon as Shawn was reading a screenplay entitled *Hate Like Me,* written by a lesbian Black Panther California university professor named Tashwanda Z.

Cabbagehead couldn't afford secretaries, so Shawn was sitting at the tiny desk in the main waiting room when the man entered. Shawn could tell straight off that he was a prole. Probably thought *Back to the Future* was great cinema.

The man looked to be somewhere in his thirties. He wore a white T-shirt and a pair of tan chinos. His leather loafers seemed to glide across the floor without touching it. Unlike the bemused expression of the mailman, this bumpkin's dark face was somber. Almost cruel.

Although possessed of a slight build himself, Shawn was not particularly intimidated by the thin young man as he crossed the lobby to his desk. Shawn didn't even put down the script he was reading when the man spoke.

"You in charge?"

Shawn sighed with his entire body. Delicate hands closed the script. "I am *President* Shawn Allen Morris," the Cabbagehead executive replied disdainfully. "And you are?"

"Remo Valenti, MPAA."

Shawn snorted. "In that getup? Yeah, right. Look, if you're here to pitch a script, forget it. I've got four films in production even as we speak, two more green-lighted for next week that I haven't even *read* yet and, to top it all off, I just found out one of my shit-head lead actors got called for jury duty and was too stupid to weasel out of it, so my people have to recast. So unless you're good with a bullwhip and a chainsaw, there's the door."

Testily, Shawn reached for another script. He was dismayed to find a hand pressed on the cover. The hand was attached to the thickest wrist Shawn had ever seen. The Cabbagehead president looked up into the dark eyes of his visitor. They were like tiny manhole covers, opened into utter blackness.

"Listen, Sam Goldwyn," Remo said, "I don't want to be here—you don't want me here. Why don't you just tell me what I want to know and I won't slap you with an NC-17."

"You don't even know what NC-17 means." Shawn smirked.

It was Remo's turn to smile. "Sure, I do," he

said. "It means No Crap or I Break 17 Bones. First one's a freebie."

The hand flashed by faster than a single movie frame.

Shawn felt a horrible, crunching pain at the ball of his right thumb. The brittle crack of a lone metacarpal filled his horrified ears. He gasped in pain.

As Shawn pulled his broken hand from his desktop, Remo waggled a cautionary finger.

"Now tell the truth," he warned, "or you'll get an NC-17 *and* a PG-13. Give me the who and where on whoever's killing people to make these junk movies of yours sell."

"That's why you broke my freaking thumb?" Shawn demanded. He stuffed the injured digit under his armpit. "I already told the cops a million times. I don't know what the hell's going on. At first I thought it was just a lucky coincidence, but now I think maybe someone's out to sabotage us. And it's really too bad," Shawn added. "When I heard about that first body I thought...whoa! My ship's come in. The press was fantastic back then. Rode the crest of that wave straight into Telluride. But it's gotten crazy lately. That Anderson thing was too much. One body, maybe two helps a movie. But four? That's overkill."

Remo's eyes were flat. "I'll show you overkill in a minute," he promised. "For now, there has to be some kind of connection."

Shawn tried to shrug. It was hard to do with his thumb jammed under his arm. "That's what I thought," he agreed. He quickly added, "Not that *Crating Sally* wasn't an Oscar contender even before that torso showed up in the orange crate. But the press coverage didn't hurt to keep us fresh in the minds of voters. We only missed that one by a couple of votes," he added bitterly.

Remo had seen the *Crating Sally* poster on the wall on the way in. A woman's frightened face peered out from the shadows of an ordinary wooden crate. It was clear from the size of the box that there wasn't room for any arms or legs inside. A pool of blood formed in front of the box.

It was part of an overall theme. On all of the posters around the room, blood, mutilation and kinky sex seemed to be a recurring motif.

"Don't you make anything with talking pigs or cartoon bugs around here?" he asked, amazed.

"We'd never sell out for monetary success," Shawn sniffed in reply. "Cabbagehead is about creating art."

Remo shook his head. "This isn't art," he informed the youthful executive. "Art is a statue in the Louvre. Art is the ceiling of the Sistine Chapel. Art is a painting of the Virgin Mary that looks like the Virgin Mary."

"We did a movie about her." Shawn nodded. "Updated the whole Christ mythology. Mary was a whore in Canada who wanted to get an abortion. We almost got the jury prize at Sundance for that."

He had hardly finished speaking when he felt another sharp pain. This one in his ring finger. As the sound of yet another cracking bone filled his ears, Shawn swore he saw a flash of movement this time.

Remo's hand returned to his side.

"What the hell was that for?" Shawn cried.

"All the nuns at St. Theresa's Orphanage," Remo said. "Okay, so you don't know who's behind this. You the owner?"

"No," Shawn answered quickly, hiding the rest of his fingers below his desk. "We're sponsored by a consortium of investors out of Hollywood. I don't even know who they are."

"You don't know who your own boss is?" Remo asked doubtfully. "How'd you get the job?"

"I—" Shawn stopped dead.

A look of inspiration. Almost delight. Shawn shot to his feet. He winced at the pain in his hand.

"I'll show you," the independent film executive enthused. He bounded from behind his desk. As he headed for the door, his face held all the enthusiasm of a Roman centurion who was about to shove a Christian into the mouth of a ravenous lion.

THE BUTCHER, THE BAKER AND THE CANDLESTICK MAKER was the type of film no one would ever see even after all the major film critics in America placed it on their year-end ten-best lists.

As Shawn Allen Morris guided him onto the *Butcher* set, Remo was first surprised by the lighting. He doubted anything being shot in the shadowy Seattle supermarket parking lot would be visible once the film was developed.

A grisly orgy was taking place on a pile of rotting garbage. Softly chugging pumps spurted red goo from nozzles buried under latex in the faux-mutilated corpses of five deathly still actresses.

Guiding the actors off-camera was a thin figure in a purple polyester suit. His back to Remo, he was hunched beside a camera watching the scene play out in all its lurid glory. As Remo approached, the man raised a hand, slicing it down sharply.

"And...cut! Fucking beautiful! Perfect! That's a wrap everybody! Dailies at my place by midnight. And don't lose them in the fucking cab."

When he spun around, triumphant, Remo saw that he was wearing a flowered disco-era shirt open to the navel. Gold chains hung in layers over his mottled black chest hair. Surprise bloomed full on Quintly Tortilli's knotted face.

"Morris, you idiot, this is a closed set," he barked.

"He's with the MPAA, Quintly," Shawn Allen Morris confided, aiming an unnaturally crooked finger at Remo. The oily rag from the car that he'd wrapped around the digit unspooled. On the cloth, the yellow, grease-smeared image of Wee-Wee the TeeVeeFattie beamed at Tortilli. Wincing, Shawn rewrapped his makeshift bandage around his broken fingers.

"What the hell happened to you?" Tortilli didn't wait for a response. He wheeled to Remo. "And since when do you MPAA ratings fascists kamikaze a movie that's still in production? You go back to those fossilized dictators in Hollywood and tell them they can shove their butcher knives. Every single instance of the word *fuck* in this film is artistically essential. I'll release it without a fucking MPAA rating if I have to. I'm holding a fucking mirror up to society, man. Deal with it.'' Eyes wild, Tortilli's pointy chin trembled with passion.

Once the diatribe had reached its passionate conclusion, Remo extended a single, uninterested finger at the panting Quintly Tortilli. He looked at Shawn Allen Morris. "Who the hell is this?"

Shawn gasped. "That's Quintly Tortilli," he hissed. When Remo's expression failed to change, Shawn pitched his horrified voice low. "*The* Quintly Tortilli. Only the most famous director in America Quintly Tortilli."

"Oh." It was clear Remo still didn't know who on earth the director was. "He ever do anything good?"

Shawn's nervous eyes grew wider. He glanced at Quintly Tortilli, who was now glaring more than enough hatred for both Remo and Shawn.

"He won an Oscar for *Penny Dreadful*," Shawn instructed hoarsely. His eyes pleaded with Remo to recognize Tortilli. Even if he had to pretend.

It was the movie title that finally sparked recognition in Remo's eyes. "You mean *he's* responsible for the piece of garbage that revived Jann Revolta's movie career?"

Shawn Allen Morris felt his stomach collapse into his bowels. "Is that the phone?" he announced abruptly. And with that, he turned and ran for all he was worth. As he bounded back to the highway, his filthy bandage flapped a TeeVeeFattie flag at the air in his wake.

Turning from Shawn's retreating form, Tortilli crossed his arms over his chest. "Okay, storm trooper of the Hollywood thought police, what do you want?" he demanded.

"For you to promise me you're not going to resurrect Gabe Kaplan, too," Remo said. "Barring that, a list of Cabbagehead's backers will do."

Tortilli snickered loudly. "Fuck you," he offered.

He turned and walked away from Remo. Or tried to. When he attempted to take a step, his foot froze above the ground. Something held him firmly in place.

When he looked down, he found a hand wrapped around his neckful of gold chains.

"Look, I don't even want to be here," Remo said.

As he spoke, Quintly Tortilli felt himself being lifted into the air. Remo was using the director's necklaces like a handle. A knot of linked gold jutted from Remo's hand.

"I wanted to stay home," Remo continued, not a hint of strain on his face. "But I'm being punished because I've been too picky about boring assignments."

Tortilli stretched his toes. They didn't reach the

ground. Arm extended, Remo was holding him a good six inches off the damp parking lot.

"On top of that, I've gotta make sure my boss doesn't find out about any of this freaking hush-hush movie junk."

"Chkkkkkggghhh…" said Quintly Tortilli.

"What?" Remo asked, distracted. "Oh, yeah."

Reaching over with his free hand, he swatted the director in the shoulder.

Tortilli felt the entire revolving world screech to a halt. As the Earth stopped, he alone began to spin.

It was like an amusement park ride gone wild. He twirled and twirled and twirled in place until his brain felt as if it would spiral out his ear. The parking lot around him turned into a smeared horizon of indistinct blots.

He was moving too fast to even vomit. Centrifugal force kept his bile-charged food in his stomach.

It seemed that he was spinning forever. After an eternity of twirling, the blurs around him finally began to coalesce back into recognizable shapes.

Quintly dangled woozily above the ground. Distant buildings rolled in waves.

"Not that I should really care one way or the other about his stupid movie deal," Remo continued without missing a beat. "Smith'll find out sooner or later."

Remo was still holding Tortilli's necklaces. The chains bit into the director's neck. His face was purple.

"Ghhhhkkhhhh..." Tortilli gagged. The choking pressure made his head feel it was about to burst. Vomit was trapped in his throat at a point just below the gold knot.

"What?" Remo asked, annoyed.

"Gggggghhhhhkkkkkkkkkkkkkkkkkk..." Tortilli begged.

"Oh. Save it for after the return trip," Remo advised.

Another swat to the shoulder. Tortilli felt himself spinning back in the opposite direction. The pressure at his neck lessened as the chains uncoiled. In less than thirty seconds, he'd twirled back to the starting point.

"Now," Remo said, dropping the reeling director to his feet, "same question as before. Cabbagehead's backers. And this time, try to limit gratuitous use of the *F* word."

Quintly's answer was distinctly nonverbal. Grabbing his stomach, the director doubled over. He promptly vomited the churning contents of his stomach onto the pavement. Bile and half-digested Cocoa Puffs splattered the outdoor set.

"Ew!" shrieked an appalled actress, whose naked torso was decorated with oozing rubber stab wounds. Quintly had discovered her behind the counter of a local pharmacy. Long legs smeared with artificial blood recoiled from the vomit.

"Darn," Remo complained. "I always forget the second part."

As Tortilli continued to heave, Remo reached out

and pressed two fingers against a spot behind his left ear.

The director's throat froze in midvomit.

At Remo's touch, the retch caught in Tortilli's throat. He waited for a second, expecting it to come. It didn't. Not only that, but the desire to vomit was gone.

Panting, he looked around. The fuzzy world was beginning to take firmer shape. As he swallowed a gulp of sticky saliva, the bitter tang of bile burning in his mouth, one word croaked up his raw throat.

"Schoenburg," Tortilli hissed.

"Huh?" Remo asked.

"Schoenburg's a Cabbagehead backer." Tortilli's voice grew stronger. "He's one of the biggest." He massaged his neck where the links from his chains had bitten into flesh. A flash of misplaced enthusiasm sparked in his bugging eyes. "Man, that was some trip."

"Stefan Schoenburg?" Remo asked. "The director?"

Tortilli nodded. "And George Locutus. Damn, you're strong. But you don't even look it. Can you do that thing again?" he asked hopefully. A long finger twirled the air.

Remo ignored him.

Stefan Schoenburg was arguably the most famous director in the history of film. And George Locutus was one of the most successful producers. Together, these two men nearly had a lock on the top-ten most profitable movies of all time. It didn't make sense that they'd have anything to do with a backwater company like Cabbagehead.

"Those two guys must be multimultimillion-aires," Remo said. "What do they want with a dippy operation like this?"

"That's nothing," Tortilli boasted. "They're just the two biggest investors. There are dozens more."

Tortilli quickly rattled off a few more names. If they weren't immediately familiar, most at least tweaked at the back of Remo's consciousness. Since he wasn't exactly up on all things Hollywood, they had to be famous. The Cabbagehead backers list was like a Who's Who of filmdom.

"Don't they make enough with their own bad movies without leeching off other people's?" Remo said. "What are they doing here?"

"Prestige," Tortilli explained. "Schoenburg was a box-office king for two decades but he wasn't happy till he finally got an Oscar. All of those guys are the same. Some want their first award, some want their tenth. That's Hollywood. It's all about the statue, baby."

Remo frowned. No matter how cutthroat the movie industry might be, he doubted that a man like Schoenburg would kill to extend his fame. That left few other options.

"Do you know of anybody who might have a grudge against the company? A fired employee? Maybe someone who actually paid good money to see one of your movies?"

"I don't handle that shi—" Quintly paused. After Remo's *F* word comment, he wasn't sure if another curse might incur his assailant's wrath. "That stuff. I'm creative."

"Tell that to somebody who didn't see your big hit."

Tortilli bristled. Then he remembered who he was talking to. "All the critics agreed *Penny Dreadful* was a great movie," Quintly pointed out meekly.

"It was a *lot* of great movies," Remo agreed. "I counted about ten before I pulled the tape out the VCR and heaved it out the window. And that was only in the first twenty minutes. You make a guy like Schoenburg look creative."

Skipping around the director, Remo headed back for his rental car. To Remo's great irritation, Tortilli hurried to keep pace with him.

"You've killed people, haven't you?" Tortilli ventured abruptly, bug eyes growing crafty.

"Not today," Remo replied sweetly.

"Wow! You're a real-life natural born killer!" Tortilli shouted, jumping with enthusiasm. "Man, that's so cool."

"I never said that," Remo said, glancing over his shoulder. The people back at the pathetic movie set hadn't heard. Most of the actors were already gone. Judging by their pupils, the apathetic attitude of those actors and crew that remained was chemical in nature.

"You didn't have to say it, man," Tortilli continued, his voice enthusiastic. "It's written on your face. In your eyes. Man, those are the deadest eyes I've ever seen."

As they walked, Tortilli began reaching toward Remo's face. Remo slapped the hands away.

"Wowee! I didn't even see you move," Tortilli squealed, his tone a mixture of excitement and awe.

"Keep watching."

Remo doubled his pace. Tortilli jogged up beside him.

"You know, you never asked me if I, you know, actually knew the killers," the director said slyly from Remo's elbow.

Remo stopped dead. The killer's eyes that Tortilli had so admired a moment before became as frigid and menacing as the icy depths of space. "Talk fast," he said coldly.

Quintly registered his tone with some alarm.

"I'm not sure I actually do," the director said quickly, raising his hands defensively. "I just hear talk sometimes. I didn't tell the cops, 'cause I don't trust them. But I trust you. Killers are always a lot more trustworthy than regular stiffs. It's a recurring theme in my movies. I can steer the way if you don't mind the most brilliant director in the history of film riding shotgun."

Remo considered this for a moment. He hated to admit it, but Tortilli could be helpful.

With a resigned sigh, he reached out and grabbed a cluster of Quintly Tortilli's chains. "If your voice gets any louder than your clothes, you're riding in the roof rack," he warned.

Pulling the director like a dog at the end of a leash, Remo headed for his rental car.

4

His head was little more than a skull covered with a barren sheet of ancient parchment pulled taut. Gossamer tufts of yellowing-white hair above shell-like ears bobbed appreciatively with every birdlike movement of his neck.

Chiun, Reigning Master of the House of Sinanju, the most ancient house of assassins on the face of the planet, was being given a tour of his movie's soundstage.

The finishing touches had been put on the various sets weeks before. To the tiny Korean in his triumphant saffron kimono, they all looked authentic. And beautiful.

"All of the interiors are being shot on this stage," Hank Bindle said to the beaming figure at his side.

"What of locations?" Chiun asked, adding knowingly, "This is a term I have heard many times. It is when a movie goes outside. My film takes place largely in the province of New York in the filthy city of the same name."

"We've got a New York mock-up on a back lot here at Taurus," Bruce Marmelstein explained.

"We've already gotten some pretty good shots there."

"But we've shot in New York already, too," Hank Bindle said to his partner, the cochair of Taurus and the studio's business-affairs manager. Bindle was the creative member of the team. "That part of production wrapped two weeks ago."

"That's right," Marmelstein agreed. "We're all set there."

"Maybe a little second-unit stuff," Bindle cautioned.

Marmelstein turned to his partner. "This late? Did the A.D. tell you that?"

"This morning."

"That's gonna cut into time and production costs."

"Not my department," Hank Bindle said with indifference.

The Master of Sinanju wasn't listening to their insane prattle. The two of them talked incessantly without ever saying anything. After a trip to the men's room, they could sometimes blabber for hours nonstop. At least until the sniffling wore off.

"Two weeks," Chiun trilled. The very air around him seemed alive with joy. "Then it is nearly complete."

Neither Bindle nor Marmelstein disputed the assertion.

Chiun's shoulders shuddered visibly as he considered the implications of completed location work. His dream was that much closer to fruition.

He was a wizened figure who appeared to be as old as time itself. Anyone meeting him for the first time invariably assumed him to be nothing more than a frail old man. Bindle and Marmelstein knew better, which was why the cochairs of Taurus Studios were willing to take time out of their schedules to give a personal tour to the lowly screenwriter.

"The squad room," Hank Bindle pronounced. He swept his hand to the left.

The interior of a New York police precinct had been reproduced in meticulous detail. All that was missing was the ceiling and the side wall through which they now looked.

Chiun's radiant face beamed pure joy. "It is as if my words have come to life," he enthused, hazel eyes tearing.

"Chiun, baby, didn't you know? We're in the business of making magic," Bruce Marmelstein confided.

The three men walked onto the set. Paper-strewn desks were arranged haphazardly around the room. Behind the desks sat actors dressed in the familiar blue of the New York City Police Department.

Chiun frowned as they walked between a pair of desks. The two men nearest him seemed bored. They stared blankly into space. The phones atop their desks were silent.

The old Korean stopped so abruptly Bindle and Marmelstein almost plowed into him. The Master of Sinanju appraised the two men a moment before turning back to the studio cochairs, his wizened face perturbed.

"I do not believe these two are constables," he intoned.

"Constables?" Marmelstein whispered out of the corner of his mouth.

"Cops," explained Bindle, sotto voce.

"Oh," Marmelstein said aloud. "Well, that's 'cause they're not contribbles. They're just actors."

"Actors?" Bindle scoffed. "Not even. They're just extras. Walking props."

Chiun turned back to the nearest man. The uniformed extra had been drawn from his boredom by the conversation. He looked up to find the three men hovering above his desk. He seemed uncomfortable at the attention.

"I—I *am* Juilliard-trained," the man offered, knowing he had been insulted but not wishing to upset the studio heads.

"Give me your diploma," Bindle snorted. "I have to go to the can." He snorted loudly, glancing to his partner for support. Marmelstein choked at Bindle's wit.

The Master of Sinanju ignored the idiots. He tipped his head to one side, as if listening for something. After a moment, he reached a single long finger toward the actor. His nail—like a sharpened talon—pressed into the muscled shoulder of the man.

The flesh beneath the uniform was warm. Frowning, Chiun spun from the confused young man.

"This is not a prop," Chiun said. "It lives."

"Barely," Marmelstein mocked. "Uncredited, nonspeaking, union-scale drone. He might as well have a tattoo on his head saying, 'Hi, I'm the least important thing in this picture. Ignore me.'"

The young actor seemed crushed by the harsh assessment.

"It is being compensated for its time here?" the Master of Sinanju demanded.

"Compen-whazzat?" Marmelstein asked Bindle.

This time Hank was at a loss, too. Most four-syllable words that weren't the names of prescription drugs were beyond him.

"Paid," the seated actor supplied.

"Ohhh," Bindle and Marmelstein nodded in unison.

"Of *course* it's being paid," Marmelstein continued. "The union would have all our asses on a silver platter if we didn't pay the scene fillers."

Chiun crossed his arms over his tiny chest. "If it receives remuneration, why is it indolent?"

"Union-mandated break," Bindle explained.

The young man was growing more and more perturbed as the conversation went on. With his acting skills, it was bad enough accepting a nonspeaking role to begin with. But to be continually referred to as little more than a chair or a mop was too much.

"Excuse me, sirs," the actor sniffed haughtily, "but I am a human being, *not* an 'it.'"

Sitting at his desk, arms crossed, face a mask of self-righteous anger, the young man almost dared the three of them to dispute him. He expected an argument. He expected more verbal abuse. He expected to be fired on the spot. He did not, however, expect what happened next.

The hand flashed out faster than any of their eyes could follow. Five bony fingers smacked with an audible crack into the back of the actor's head. The man's teeth came alive. They clattered like rattling dice inside his mouth. A filling in one molar popped out from the vibrations. And with that wash of sudden, blinding pain, all thoughts of self-righteous actor's anger died a Method death.

The Master of Sinanju wasn't even looking at the man he had just struck. It was as if the actor didn't exist.

"This brotherhood you speak of," Chiun said to the Taurus cochairs, "who are they that they would dare meddle in my wondrous production?"

Bindle and Marmelstein frowned in unison.

"He means union," the seated actor offered timidly. Fingers and tongue searched his mouth for his AWOL filling.

"Oh, the union. Everything's union in this town," Bruce Marmelstein explained. "Bastards tell us what to do and what to pay everybody. Hell, they practically time the shitting schedule." His brow furrowed, genuinely confused. "But you must have joined the screenwriters' union."

"*Ixnay, ixnay,*" Bindle whispered to his partner.

"Ah, this is familiar to me." Chiun nodded, remembering now an early conversation he'd had with Hank Bindle about his union membership.

"Mr. Chiun doesn't believe in unions, Bruce," Bindle whispered.

"Of course not," Chiun sniffed. "A Master of Sinanju does not pay dues. He accepts tribute."

"I admire your integrity." Hank Bindle nodded.

"In-gritty what?" Marmelstein asked his partner.

The definition of the unfamiliar word was never explained to the Taurus financial expert. Kimono swirling, the Master of Sinanju spun away from the two executives.

"You!" Chiun announced, aiming an imperious finger at the man he'd just assaulted. "Resume your work!"

The Juilliard graduate wasn't sure exactly what was expected of him. But his skull was still reverberating from the blow Chiun had struck. Flinging his filling to the floor, he grabbed up the prop phone from his desk. His weak smile sought approval.

But Chiun was no longer there. The old Korean had already whirled on to the next extra.

"Return to your duties, player!"

When the confused young actor hesitated, the Master of Sinanju's hand found a cluster of nerves at the small of his back. To the extra, it felt as if someone had poured boiling acid down his spine. Screaming, the man leaped obediently for his own desk.

The commotion brought the attention of everyone on the set. Chiun stormed into their midst.

"Hark, unimportant playactors!" he intoned to the gathered extras. "You are charged with the awesome task of breathing life into a story written by me! A more glorious duty you will never have in your pitiful lives of make-believe. Therefore, you will allow this joy and honor to sustain you, breakless, throughout the duration of filming."

There was muttering from the crowd.

Most of the actors merely seemed confused. A burly man at Chiun's elbow who understood exactly what was being said tapped the Master of Sinanju on the shoulder. His beefy face wore a surly expression.

"Or *what?*" he challenged.

Later he swore he'd gotten both words out before he became airborne. Most of the other extras told him he only got as far as the first syllable before he went sailing over their heads.

The rest of the cast and crew watched in shock as the 240-pound extra sailed over the mock-up walls of their squad room. He landed with a heavy thud somewhere distant. Judging by the ensuing hail of shrimp and finger sandwiches, he'd touched down in the vicinity of the craft-services tables.

As food rained down, the men and women on the set nearly plowed over one another in their haste to return to work. The soundstage exploded in a frenzy of activity. For the first time since Chiun's arrival, it looked like an actual police station. Standing amid the chaos, the old man beamed proudly over at Bindle and Marmelstein, who were standing near the edge of the set.

When Chiun looked away, Bindle elbowed Marmelstein in the ribs.

"What do we do?" Hank Bindle muttered nervously. His lips didn't move. Though his heart raced excitedly, he dared not even smile.

Bruce Marmelstein was equally unemotional. "We shut up and tell the A.D. to roll 'em," he whispered in reply. "This production is *finally* back on track."

Plastering on the phoniest toothy smile he could muster, Marmelstein strode across the chaotic set to the Master of Sinanju. Hank Bindle trotted to keep up.

5

"I don't know if I know anything," Quintly Tortilli cautioned. As they drove through Seattle's suburban streets, a light mist collected sullenly on the windshield.

"You don't," Remo informed him blandly.

Tortilli missed the sarcasm. "It's just that I hear things," he persisted. "Some true, some not. People confide in me 'cause I'm at the vanguard of the new culture."

"You look just like the ass end of the old one," Remo said. "And what was our rule about annoying Mr. Driver?"

Tortilli instantly dummied up.

The last time he'd spoken out of turn, Remo had followed through on his roof-rack threat. Tortilli had spent fifteen minutes up in the rain clutching on for dear life as Remo tore down the highway.

His ugly purple suit was stained dark with water. He never thought polyester could absorb so much. On the floor, water pooled at his soles. His Skechers were soaked through. Dead bugs filled the gaps in his teeth.

Thankful to be in out of the cold and rain, the

young director remained mute as Remo headed into
a less reputable part of town. He offered directions
with a pointed finger.

Along the street on which they now drove,
squalid tenements scratched at the joyless early-
morning gray sky. The tiny front yards were pools
of rain-spattered mud. In spite of the deteriorating
neighborhood, the sidewalk seemed fairly new. The
street itself was in good repair.

Remo suspected that the bombed-out look was
affected. It had as much to do with Generation-X
atmosphere as anything else. In the new counterculture, disrepair was chic.

"Mmm-mmm-mmm," Tortilli hummed
abruptly. His bugging eyes were frantic. He tapped
the dashboard.

"I told you to go while you were on the roof,"
Remo reminded him.

Tortilli shook his head violently. "Mmm-mmm-
mmm!"

When Tortilli began to nod and point desperately, Remo realized they'd reached their destination. He pulled to the curb between a pair of matching rusted Ford Escorts.

"Okay, limited talking privilege is restored," he
said to the shivering director. "Which one is it?"

Quintly Tortilli scrunched up his already over-
scrunched face. It resembled a tightly balled fist.

"The guy I called said it was that one," he said.
His pointed chin singled out a four-story building
down the block. "But he could be wrong. He's just

some guy I met in a bar who likes my movies. He said the group in there bragged about doing the sorority girls in Florida, the ones they found hanging from that tree. But they weren't in on the others. At least not according to my source."

Remo popped the door. "Then they'll only pay once," he promised thinly.

His tone made Tortilli shiver all the more.

As Remo rounded the curb, Quintly Tortilli opened his own door a crack. He jutted his protruding lips through the narrow opening.

"You gonna be okay?" Tortilli asked in a whisper. "My boy says there's a whole gang in there."

"Stay here," Remo said in reply. He slapped the director's door shut.

Tortilli had barely enough time to pull his pursed lips to safety. Just in case, he crossed his eyes and did a rapid inventory. He was relieved to find both lips still attached below his drooping, broad nose.

Trembling at the damp and cold, he glanced back up.

In both directions, the sidewalk that ran before the row of crumbling tenements was empty. Remo was already gone.

"Shit, a guy moves like that ought to be on film," Quintly Tortilli muttered, impressed. Suddenly recalling Remo's objection to his cursing, he bit his lip. "I hope his freakin' puritanism don't make me lose my knack for gritty, true-to-life urban dialogue," he said worriedly.

Frowning across every unnatural angle of his

twisted face, the famous director began patting his soaked suit jacket. He needed a cigarette.

LIFE SUCKED.

Leaf Randolph knew it with certainty. He'd come to this drear conclusion during a single, drug-inspired epiphanic instant on his fifteenth birthday.

Until that moment of insight nearly ten years earlier, Leaf had been so consumed with the mundaneness of life that he hadn't really been aware of its pervasive suckiness.

Back then Leaf's father programmed for Macroware—the software giant based in Seattle. The Randolph patriarch was always too busy trying to eliminate the bugs du jour from the company's latest behind-schedule software to notice anything about his son's life. The fact that Leaf had become a junior high-school junkie wasn't even a blip on his radar.

Even though Leaf's mother had to know something was amiss, she turned a blind eye to his drug use. As his habit worsened, she retreated further into blissful ignorance. Whenever he was exceptionally stoned, she'd take to polishing the furniture. By the time Leaf was thirteen, the Randolph family had to wear sunglasses to Thanksgiving dinner in order to dull the glare from the credenza.

On that fateful day that would alter his outlook on life forever, Leaf and his two closest friends, Ben "Brown" Brownstein and Jackie Farris, had scored some Scandinavian Mist from a dealer who'd just smuggled it back from Europe. The stuff was powerful.

"Man, no wonder them Vikings, like, kicked the Pilgrims' ass," Brown commented as he exhaled his first puff of the extrastrong European marijuana.

He was perched on Mr. Randolph's tidy workbench. An electric guitar lay behind him.

Since it was Seattle and they were teenagers, the three of them were just expected to be in a band. Brown had gotten the expensive instrument two birthdays ago. He had yet to figure out how to tune it.

"Dude, don't Bogart it," complained Jackie when Brown started to take another hit.

Grumbling, Brown passed off the joint to him. "Try not to drool all over it this time," he muttered.

Only when it came time to pass the marijuana back to where it had started—the soft, uncallused hands of Leaf Randolph—did the other two boys notice something was wrong.

Leaf was staring into the corner of the garage where his untouched drum set had been gathering dust for the past five years. But as they studied the expression on their friend's face, they realized that Leaf was looking at a place far beyond the confines of the two-car garage.

Since Leaf had been first to try the weed, his eerie silence and glazed expression were troubling to the others.

"Dude, what's up?" Jackie asked, afraid this

Euro-junk was some kind of secret Russian pod-people plot to hollow out the brains of America's youth. He didn't realize that for years MTV had been doing a more effective job at this than the most diabolically inspired Communist mad scientist.

When Leaf spoke, his words were a croak.

"It sucks, man," he said.

Jackie and Brown relaxed. Their brains—such as they were—were still their own.

"Are you shittin' me, dude?" Brown scoffed. "This shit is, like, the best."

"Not this, dude," Leaf said, accepting the joint in his clammy hand. *"This."* As he took a massive toke, he swept his hand grandly. "The whole suck-hole world."

"Oh," Jackie said, the light of understanding at last dawning in his glazed eyes.

The three of them pondered the implications of Leaf's remark for several long seconds.

Finally, Jackie broke the silence. "Your mom got any Twinkies?" he said, scratching his nose.

Leaf didn't try to press his revelation any further. The implications were clear to him. That was enough.

The knowledge that life was grim and pointless made the following few years even more miserable for young Leaf. He was the only one who understood. *Truly* understood.

Life was just one bleak minute after another.

Stretching into hours, crawling into days, oozing into years, collapsing into decades.

You died young, you died old. Whatever. It didn't matter. No matter what you did, you still died.

Only single moments of pure intensity broke up the endless, tedious minutes between his fifteenth and twenty-fourth years. Some of these were caused by drugs. If life was a dotted line, his drugged moments were the dots that broke up the empty sameness of the rest of the page.

The only other moments for Leaf that most approached happiness were those of greatest agony. Pain—like any drug—was intense. And Leaf found that he liked to inflict pain. On himself, on others. It really didn't matter.

The razor-blade scarification he practiced on himself and on his strung-out girlfriends inevitably led to murder. A slit arm, a slit throat—what was the difference?

The first girl had been a whore. He was underage at the time. Circumstances were such that they hadn't even bothered to try him as an adult. He walked when he turned twenty-one.

After that, Leaf had picked his moments more carefully. There were other bodies, but they weren't as likely to be traced back to him as the first. Like that pair he and his buds had been hired to take out in Florida.

That one had been sweet. Two girls, tons of screaming and—best of all—money. Leaf was about to enjoy the last of the dough he'd made on that weird job.

He was sitting on the damp floor of his dingy basement apartment. A couple of hard-core friends—he'd long outgrown Jackie and Brown—had just returned with some brown gold.

Grimy needles were passed around. Leaf was lifting his syringe to his scarred forearm when something caught his eye.

A flash of movement.

A small rectangular window at the top of the foundation wall looked out on the backyard. When he looked up, Leaf saw a pair of legs glide past.

The other four men weren't paying attention. In the corner of the shadowy room, the TV hummed softly. Looking at the bright colors on the screen, a pair of the men muttered unintelligibly to one another.

"Shh," Leaf hissed.

When they glanced at him, the others saw that he was looking toward the window. All eyes turned that way.

As he strained to listen, the only noise Leaf could hear was dull music from the TV. Otherwise, all was silent.

Maybe he'd imagined the legs.

"What?" one of the other junkies said.

Leaf shook his head. "I guess it was noth—" he began.

All at once a horrible wrenching sound came from the rear of the room. Whipping his head around, Leaf briefly saw something big and flat sail past the window. He swore it had the wedge-shaped contours of the entire bulkhead assembly—concrete base and all. The crash was far away.

The garish gray light of dawn spilled down the wet stairs. Carried down with it came a voice.

"Surprise! You've been selected a winner in the official Marion Barry Needle Giveaway Sweepstakes!"

Leaf saw the legs again. They seemed to melt down the backstairs. They were attached to a lean young man who screamed "trouble" with every confident step. In the shadows of the basement, his eye sockets were black and menacing.

The five men scrambled to their feet.

"Oh, there's five of you," Remo lamented as he came across the basement floor. "Sorry, but according to contest rules, you can't *all* be winners. We have to save some drug paraphernalia for our sponsor. Who's in charge here?"

"Who the fuck are you?" Leaf demanded.

"That answers that question." Remo nodded.

The druggies had fanned out around him. Each carried some sort of weapon, but judging by the way they walked, only two of them had guns. Remo singled out one of those.

"In the spirit of tobacco companies paying for antismoking public-service announcements, I am required by the official terms of the Marion Barry Needle Giveaway Sweepstakes to offer a live PSA on the evils of drug use."

The men clearly didn't know what to make of this strange intruder. When they glanced to Leaf for instructions, Remo was already sweeping his arm up and around.

He clapped a cupped hand on the top of the head of one of the gunmen, creating a vacuum. Shocked, the man tried to pull away but found he could not. It was as if Remo's hand were welded to his head.

"This is your brain," Remo intoned somberly.

Remo pulled up. The resulting tug of air pressure popped skull bones that had been fused since childhood. Weak flesh surrendered to a force more powerful than a fired cannon ball. With a sucking sound, three pounds of gray matter launched out of the top of the man's head. The brain landed with a fat wet splat at the feet of the four surviving drug addicts.

"This is your brain on the floor," Remo continued. He looked at the others, eyes dead. "Any questions?"

For lifelong drug addicts, the reactions of the remaining four were remarkably quick. Three switchblades snicked open. One of the men whipped a revolver from the back of his waistband, swinging it at Remo's face.

Remo concentrated first on the gunman.

"Here's another PSA for you," Remo began.

As the young man's finger tightened on the trigger, Remo's hand flashed out. With a quick tug, he pulled the man forward, steering the barrel of the gun into the open mouth of another junkie. With a muffled pop, the gun took off the back of the startled drug addict's skull.

Clouding eyes wide, the dead man joined the first body on the concrete floor.

"Guns don't kill people," Remo concluded to the startled gunman. His voice was cold. "*I* kill people."

As the gunman tried to take aim a second time, a slap from Remo steered the barrel of the weapon deep into the man's own forehead. He collapsed with a life-draining sigh.

Beside Leaf, the last junkie tried to run. Remo snagged him by the scruff of the neck, flinging him back absently.

Soaring backward, the drug addict hit the foundation wall at supersonic speed. Every bone in his body was crushed on impact. As the gelatinous body slipped to the floor, the cracked concrete veneer revealed a man-shaped silhouette.

With a horrible sinking feeling, Leaf realized that he was alone. He dropped his knife and threw up his hands.

"I surrender!" he pleaded.

"That's not how this works," Remo replied, voice hard. "What happens now is I ask you questions in exchange for mercy points. Each question answered truthfully brings you a step closer to the mercy you don't deserve. Each lie erases a single mercy point. Understand?"

Leaf had fallen to his knees. Tears welled up in his bleary eyes. He knew that he was minutes away from death. And in those moments that he now knew would be his very last on Earth, Leaf had another realization—in its intensity much like the one he'd had back in his parents' garage so many years ago.

Life was worth living.

"Please," he begged, sniffling.

Remo ignored him. "The girls in Florida..."

Leaf sucked in an involuntary mouthful of air. Guilt flooded his fearful eyes.

"The ones you mutilated and hung from a tree," Remo persisted. "Give me the who, how and why."

Given the surroundings, Remo expected to hear that they'd been influenced by the Cabbagehead movie that depicted a similar scene. Since Quintly Tortilli had said that this group was involved only in the Florida murders, Remo assumed that Leaf and his cohorts were part of some larger gang that got off on mimicking the violence depicted in the low-budget films. But Leaf Randolph's response surprised him.

"We were paid."

Remo blinked. "Paid?" he said.

"Yeah." Leaf nodded. "This guy called me on the phone one night. Told me what we should do and where we should do it." He glanced at his dead compatriots. His frightened eyes grew sick. He closed them, hoping full disclosure would buy him some of Remo's promised mercy points.

Remo's thoughts were beyond Leaf and his companions. He was right back to his own suggestion to Smith that this was a scheme to enrich Cabbagehead's backers.

"You recognize his voice?" he pressed.

"No. He said he knew about me, is all."

"If he paid you, how'd you get the money?"

"He mailed it here."

Remo glanced around. The place was a shambles. Empty fast-food wrappers and dirty laundry were spread everywhere, interspersed with a multitude of used needles.

"I don't suppose you filed the envelope?" Remo asked.

Leaf bit his lip. "That was weeks ago. I tossed it somewhere. But my mom's come to clean once since then. I guess it *could* still be here." Leaf hugged himself for warmth. "Weird about that Cabbagehead flick that came out after. It was like seeing myself on screen."

Remo turned back to him. "You didn't know about the movie beforehand?" he said.

Leaf shook his head. "No way. When those other ones happened—like that family in Maryland—I thought, wow." He tipped his head. "You think someone got paid there, too?"

As he leaned his head to one side in a questioning pose, Leaf's exposed neck was too tempting an invitation to refuse. Remo dropped his hand against the drug addict's throat.

A short, meaty buzz, and Leaf's head thudded to the floor. His body joined it a split second later.

Hands on hips, Remo surveyed the grisly scene, a troubled frown across his dark features.

There hadn't been a lone group of killers. In spite of Tortilli's source, Remo assumed this would be the case. But now this seemed too organized to be the work of any of the dolts he'd seen at Cabbagehead. Something was going on here. Something that somehow seemed bigger than either he or Smith had originally suspected.

Turning on his heel, he headed back up the mossy stairs to the backyard. On the flickering television, the warm pastel colors of Tipsy and Doh reflected against the dull plastic surfaces of the many scattered syringes.

As REMO REACHED the sidewalk out front, a thought occurred to him.

"Dammit," he muttered suddenly.

"What's wrong?"

Quintly Tortilli was standing next to Remo's car, a cigarette hanging desperately from his lips.

"I probably should have asked how much they got paid," Remo said. "Oh, well. Let's go." He rounded the car.

Tortilli stayed on the sidewalk.

"You did more than talk, didn't you?" he said knowingly over the roof of the car, an excited gleam in his eye. "You kacked them, didn't you?"

Remo popped the driver's-side door. "Remo leaving," he warned. "Is bad director coming, too?"

"No way, man," Quintly Tortilli said, shaking his head excitedly. "You've got real-live dead bodies piled back there and you expect me to leave? I only get to see fake violence in my line of work. This is like a fu—" He caught himself. "It's like a dream come true."

Flinging his cigarette to the mud, Tortilli spun away from the car. He fairly danced down the street, a gangly figure in a soaking-wet leisure suit.

As Tortilli disappeared around the alley beside Leaf Randolph's tenement, Remo climbed behind the wheel.

For a moment, he considered waiting for Quintly Tortilli. After all, the director had already given him a lead. And this was a dangerous neighborhood. On the other hand, Remo would be doing the entire moviegoing public a favor if he abandoned Tortilli and allowed the natural savagery of an area like this to take its course.

In the end, it was no contest.

"That movie was *really* bad," Remo said in justification.

He turned the key in the ignition.

Remo drove off into the mist, abandoning the young auteur to the mercy of the mean streets he loved so dearly.

6

Polly Schien didn't like the way the men looked at her.

There were a lot of them. All dressed in the same bland gray jumpsuits with the same logo on the back—GlassCo Security Windows of New Jersey, Inc. For most of the past week, it seemed as if the offices of Barney and Winthrop had been taken over by the men in GlassCo gray.

Polly had decided on day one that she could have done without them. This tired thought flitted through her brain for what seemed like the hundredth time as yet another one of the workers passed her desk.

The black stubble around his mouth cracked into a leer as he glanced at her chest. Even though she'd been wearing turtleneck sweaters the past few days, she still felt naked.

Polly used one hand to gather the wool more tightly at her neck. It was a move she was all too familiar with.

"Do you mind?" she demanded angrily.

"Not at all. Just gimme a time."

The comment brought a rough cackle from the

other jumpsuited men nearby. Polly's coworkers—
especially the women, but even some of the men
of Barney and Winthrop—looked on in mute sym-
pathy.

It wasn't a very nice atmosphere. The window
people were horrible. Gross. Totally unprofessional.
The only one that seemed like a human being was
their supervisor.

He was English. Polly always had a thing for
Englishmen. If an American male had had the same
pasty skin, unmuscled body, overbite, big nose and
awkward hunch as the GlassCo supervisor, Polly
wouldn't have given him the time of day. But on
this man the whole package somehow seemed regal.

It was the accent, of course. Polly knew it was
her one true weakness. In Polly Schien's mind, all
you had to do was slap a British accent on a man
who was a hillbilly in every other discernible way
and suddenly Jethro Bodine became Prince Charles.
But she couldn't think about that right now.

The rude GlassCo worker wasn't leaving her
alone. He was still standing beside her desk, holding a tube of that special caulking he and his coworkers had been using to further cement the windows in place. For what reason, Polly had no idea.
None of the windows on the thirty-second floor of
the Regency Building in Midtown Manhattan so
much as rattled, let alone popped out of their
frames.

"What time do you get off?" The man leered.

Beyond him, near the huge gleaming panes of glass that overlooked the busiest city in the world, some of the nearest GlassCo men on ladders paused at their work. They, too, held tubes of the same caulking. They rested them on the top tiers of the collapsible steps as they watched the drama at the desk below. Farther down the line of windows, bright midmorning sun beat in on other similarly dressed workers, still busy at their pointless task.

"Leave me alone," Polly said, annoyed. The scruffy man had made advances before, but this day he seemed particularly aggressive. She had already considered a sexual-harassment suit, but dismissed the idea. The guy looked like he drank everything he ever made. Going after GlassCo itself was out of the question. She dared not risk upsetting you-know-who.

"Edward, would you please return to work? I'd like to finish this morning."

The voice came from behind Polly. It was the purest, most flawless upper-crust British accent she had ever heard. The English language distilled. *Him.*

The GlassCo worker—whose jumpsuit patch identified him as Ed, not Edward—glanced behind Polly in the direction from which the voice had come. A frown blossomed. Reluctantly, he left the desk. With the party over, the rest of the GlassCo workers turned back to the panes.

Polly felt her heart trip in her fluttering chest as she heard the precise footfalls on the drab carpet behind her. A moment after he had spoken, he slipped gracefully around before her, a silhouette carving a noble shadow from the flaming yellow sunlight behind him.

"I am most dreadfully sorry," Reginald Hardwin purred.

"That's al—"

Polly never finished the sentence.

He took her hand. Actually took it in his!

His hands were soft. Not a callus on them. Not like those of the American lunkheads always working out at the gym, pumping iron to prove how macho they were. Here was a real man. Soft skin, yellow teeth and all.

Polly felt her face flush crimson.

"This has been a trying week. For all of us." Still holding her hand, Reginald sat on the edge of her desk. "These creatures that I am forced to work with are oafs."

"Oh, they're not—" She swallowed hard. "They're okay."

Reginald smiled. "You're too kind."

She was disappointed when he released her hand. A moment later, he was back on his feet. As he turned to walk away, Polly Schien leaned toward him.

"I hope I'm not being too forward, but..." She seemed flustered. "Are you a lord or something?"

Pausing before her, Reginald smiled sadly. "While the aristocracy has fallen on difficult times of late, things have not gotten so bad for the royals that they must work for GlassCo Security Windows of New Jersey. No, I'm afraid I am just a simple expatriate doing a simple job.''

"Oh." Polly seemed embarrassed. "It's just your use of language. It's so precise. We don't get much of that here."

"You really are too, too kind." Reaching out, he brushed her cheek with his velvet fingertips.

And with that, he was gone.

The GlassCo men finished whatever it was they were doing half an hour later. They—along with Reginald Hardwin—left ten minutes after that.

Polly cursed herself inwardly the entire time they were cleaning up and climbing aboard the elevators.

"'Are you a lord?'" she muttered sarcastically after the gleaming elevator doors closed on her Prince Charming for the last time. "Was that the best you could do? Dammit, how stupid can I get?" She slapped herself in the forehead.

Her one chance at landing a real man, and she'd blown it. Horribly.

Polly had been unable to approach him as he was packing to go. She was too embarrassed. Now that he was gone, she replayed the moment over and over.

"Stupid, stupid, stupid."

The embarrassment lingered for a time, but as the minutes wore on, it was rapidly eclipsed by anger.

Her mother used to say that no opportunity was a lost opportunity. Maybe she could still turn this around. Maybe he'd think it was funny. Maybe the two of them could laugh about it over dinner at her place.

Maybe, maybe, maybe.

Before his elevator had reached the lobby, Polly Schien had made her decision.

One of the workers had said that GlassCo was located over in Jersey City. She had a few Jersey phone books on her desk. Finding the right one, she scanned the business white pages for GlassCo.

It wasn't there. Nor was GlassCo listed anywhere in the Yellow Pages.

She had already decided on a course of action. There was no turning back now. Boldly, she picked up her phone, stabbing in the number for information.

"Yes, hello. In Jersey City. The number for GlassCo?"

An electronic voice told her that the number had been disconnected.

Polly slowly replaced the phone.

Her face a puzzled frown, she slumped back in her chair, trying to think of a possible explanation for why the GlassCo company would just up and disappear.

As she stared out the windows her dream man had refurbished, the late-morning sunlight seemed to take on a brighter, more dazzling hue. It was as if the rays had broken up and taken flight, soaring brilliantly toward her.

Polly didn't have time to think about the beauty

of it. The split second after she'd noticed the breath-taking optical illusion, shards of glass from the ex-ploding windowpanes ripped mercilessly through her face and chest. Her body was shredded to pâté. The shock wave followed, picking up the raw meat of Polly's corpse and flinging it backward.

Heavy desks were thrown through cubicle walls. At the same time the plastique on the windows was detonated, dull explosions at the interior of the building blew the debris back outward.

The offices of Barney and Winthrop, as well as the entire thirty-second floor of the Regency Build-ing, were wiped out in a matter of seconds. Dust and powdery glass exploded through the gaping holes all around the building.

Glass panes above and below the blast zone sep-arated from their frames. They broke away in sheets, like ice sheering from the side of a massive glacier. And as the Manhattan skyline trembled, enormous deadly shards soared down toward Mad-ison Avenue.

THIRTY-TWO FLOORS BELOW, Reginald Hardwin re-placed the retractable silver antenna of his portable detonator with a single crisp slap of his palm.

"'Are you a lord?'" he mocked. "Daft bint."

The other trucks had already gone. His was the last.

He watched in satisfaction as the windows around the thirty-second floor began separating from the building.

As the huge slabs of deadly glass began raining on Manhattan, Hardwin climbed quickly behind the wheel of the final GlassCo truck.

"And we did it all in one take," his smooth-as-butter English voice commented proudly.

On the sidewalk beside him, a smartly dressed woman was impaled through her upturned face by a sheet of glass.

While numerous screaming pedestrians met similar ends, Reginald Hardwin drove calmly away from the scene of carnage.

IN A DINGY APARTMENT in Queens, a solitary figure watched the news replay the shaky footage of the events in nearby Midtown Manhattan.

Video cameras were ubiquitous these days; a tourist visiting New York had caught some of the initial blast.

At the sound of the explosion, the camera whipped up the side of the Regency just in time to film the windows blow into empty air. The glass rushed out, seemingly in tiny fragments. Catching sunlight, the fragments fell like pixie dust onto the crowd far below.

The news edited out much of the resulting gore. A little blood here, a staggering pedestrian there. And a lot of screaming and running.

In his tiny room, the man smiled. Behind him, a ragged American flag had been slung across the water-damaged pressboard wall. On a rusted hook next to the door hung Alice Anderson's green Girl Scout beret and sash. Dark circles indicated where the merit badges had been removed.

"And Act One goes off without a hitch," Captain Kill announced proudly to the squalid room.

Leaving the TV on, he focused his attention back on his typewriter. He scrolled another sheet of crisp, clean paper into the carriage.

As the television murmured softly in the background, the sound of two-fingered typing clacked slowly and methodically, rebounding against the stained walls of the tiny apartment.

7

Harold W. Smith watched the aftermath of the explosion in Midtown Manhattan on the small black-and-white television in his office at Folcroft Sanitarium.

The old TV sat at the edge of his gleaming high-tech desk, the sole modern intrusion in the otherwise Spartan office. Hidden within the depths of the onyx slab on which the television rested was a computer screen, angled so that it was visible only to whoever sat behind the desk. The familiar alphanumeric arrangement of a keyboard was buried at the edge of the slab. Smith's gnarled fingers drummed swiftly away at the keys.

The computer monitor also functioned as a television screen, but the director of CURE was already using his system to monitor both police and press reports of the incident.

The blast had occurred no more than twenty minutes before, so there was little information beyond the immediate hysteria that normally accompanied such an occurrence.

Smith was certain only that there had been an explosion and that, as yet, no one was taking credit for the blast. His tired eyes were scanning lines of text, hoping to learn something new, when a familiar jangle sounded at his right ankle.

Continuing to read the latest data, Smith reached into the bottom desk drawer. Removing the cherry-red phone from its eternal resting place, he tucked the receiver between shoulder and ear.

"Yes, Mr. President," he said crisply.

"You hear about New York?"

The hoarse drawl would have been familiar to all Americans. In the past two years, it had become an irritant even to the those who had twice installed him in the highest office in the land.

"I am monitoring the situation even as we speak," Smith replied.

"And?"

Smith paused in his work, the telephone receiver balanced in the crook of his neck. His fingers rested at the edge of his desk. "And what, Mr. President?" he asked.

"What the hell's going on?" the President demanded.

"Very little," Smith admitted. "You *are* aware that this happened only twenty-two minutes ago?"

"Dammit, I know that," the President said impatiently. "But this isn't like those African embassies two years ago. This is goddamn New York City, Smith. That and Hollywood are my two fund-raising cash cows. If they're pissed at me in Manhattan, it could seriously impact my legal-defense fund."

Smith's fingers dropped from his keyboard.

He wanted to be appalled. After all, there were bodies at that very moment still oozing warm blood on Manhattan sidewalks, and the President of the United States was more worried about how a domestic terrorist attack could affect his fund-raising apparatus. Yet, though he wanted to be shocked, Smith could not be. That sharp edge had been dulled by this particular President a long time ago.

"Plus the ball-and-chain's still got her eye on a Senate seat there," the President pressed. "Now. Six years from now. She won't even tell *me* for sure. Whatever you have to do to nail this thing down, do it fast. I didn't squeak out of that impeachment thing only to have something like this overshadow my last year in office."

Smith considered letting it pass. After all, they'd been down this same road more times than he cared to remember over the past two years. Yet a response was necessary.

Worn leather chair creaking in protest, Smith leaned forward. He touched a firm hand to his desk.

"Mr. President," he began, as if reciting by rote. "I will take this opportunity to remind you once more that CURE is not here as a quick fix to any passing political crisis. Your seven predecessors all understood that. For nearly four decades, this has been the arrangement and it will remain thus as long as I am director."

The President's reply was preceded by an angry snort of air. "Get off your high horse, Smith," he growled. "They bombed New York, for Christ's sake. Stuff like this is right up your alley."

"Yes," Smith agreed, "but if CURE is to get involved, I want you to be clear why. It will be because I have determined that there is a threat warranting our attention. It will not be to protect your reputation with your donors or to aid your wife in a political campaign. Is that clear?"

There was a pause during which Smith expected to hear the President hang up the phone. That had happened a few times lately, as well. But the Commander in Chief remained on the line. When he spoke, it was as if he were biting off every sour word and spitting them at Smith.

"Do I still get to suggest assignments?"

"Suggest, yes," Smith admitted.

"Then I *suggest* you move the hell into New York and find out what's going on. And I *suggest* you put those two guys on it."

"I am afraid that is not possible at the moment."

"Why not?"

"One of them is already on assignment."

"Pull him off."

Smith tried to sound reasonable. "Mr. President, there is nothing as yet to direct him to. If this bombing proves to be part of a larger problem, I will bring him in. Until then, it is more important to learn precisely what we are dealing with. One of the earliest reports I read indicated that it may be no more than a ruptured gas line."

"Do you think that's what it is?"

"I am dubious," Smith admitted.

"So what are you arguing for? There's a bomber loose out there. I had TWA, Oklahoma City and Centennial Park take place on my watch. Those things dragged on forever. I want this one finished fast and neat. Is that understood?"

Smith's bloodless lips thinned. "Mr. President, do I need to repeat myself yet again?" A hint of impatience colored his lemony tone.

There was icy silence for a long moment. At last, America's Chief Executive spoke.

"It's within my power to disband your organization," the President of the United States said, hoarse voice flat.

Smith would not be baited. "Mr. President, if you wish for CURE to cease operations, you need only give the word."

There was another pause, during which Smith heard only the President's labored breathing.

"You don't like me much, do you, Smith?"

The words seemed to come from nowhere. Smith was surprised at the frankness of the question.

"It is not my place as director of this organization to either like or dislike a sitting President," he replied.

"But you'll be happy when I'm gone."

"Mr. President, I am no longer a young man. It is possible that you will outlast me."

"*Anything* is possible, Smith," said the President of the United States. "Anything at all."

The line went dead in Smith's hand.

Slowly, the CURE director replaced the receiver. He pushed the bottom desk drawer closed.

In the background, the grainy television continued to play its visions of horror. Bland announcers described the carnage in soft, measured tones. Smith was no longer listening. He turned slowly in his chair.

The one-way glass at the rear of his office overlooked the sprawling back lawn of Folcroft, which crept down a steady slope until it was swallowed up by Long Island Sound.

In his cracked leather chair, Smith watched the gently rolling water lap the shore.

The President was right. Smith didn't like him.

Since taking over the helm of the secret organization, the director of CURE had found something to like in every President. There had been only two who, in his opinion, had neither decency nor integrity, but they were at least easy to get along with on a professional level.

Every man he had served under had been from the World War II generation. Smith's generation. Whether they were saints or sinners, he flattered himself to think that he had understood them all.

But this new Chief Executive was cut from a different cloth. There were those who said this younger man represented a tidal shift in American politics. And if he was the future of America, then perhaps at no other time was it more obvious that Smith was part of its past.

There was no doubt that the President's last

words had been a cryptic threat to remove Smith from CURE. It didn't matter. Smith had known from the outset that that time would one day come. Lately, his aging body had been warning him that the time might nearly be at hand.

When his last day finally came, Smith would leave willingly, knowing that he had made a difference. To ensure that any secrets he possessed died with him, he would swallow the coffin-shaped pill hidden in the pocket of his gray vest. And with his last breath, Harold W. Smith would pray not only for America's future, but also for the men who would lead the nation there.

But all of that would come another day. Until then, he had work to do.

Tearing his eyes away from the rolling black waves, Smith spun quietly back to his computer.

8

Remo heard about the bombing in New York on his car radio while driving back to the Cabbagehead Productions offices. He pulled over at the first pay phone he saw. When he got out of the car, the air in the street was thick with the smell of freshly brewed coffee.

Beside the booth, a street performer flailed away on an electric guitar. The screeching sounds emanating from the wobbling amplifier at his feet rattled windows five blocks away. To remove the noisy distraction, Remo punted the musician's amp half a mile down the street. It splintered into blessedly silent fragments in front of a coffee shop.

The performer—who looked about nineteen—spun to Remo. Filthy blond bangs slapped against his pasty face.

"That was Nirvana, dude," he snarled as Remo scooped up the telephone receiver.

"No," Remo explained, pressing the multiple-1 code that would connect him to CURE's special line. "Nirvana is a transcendent state in Buddhism of pure peace and enlightenment, achieved by stuffing a guitar down someone's throat. Wanna help me get there?''

The look in Remo's eyes cowed the sidewalk minstrel. Gibson guitar in hand, he beat a hasty retreat down the damp street in the direction of his smashed amp.

Smith answered on the first ring.

"What is it?" the CURE director asked tensely.

"I just heard about the explosion in New York," Remo said. "You want me to fly back?"

"There is nothing concrete yet," Smith said, voice flirting on the edge of exasperation, as if he'd already been through this with Remo.

"Is something wrong, Smitty?" Remo said, brow furrowing. "You're not generally on the rag right out of the gate."

The tension drained from Smith's voice. "I'm sorry," he sighed. "It's been a trying morning." He cleared his throat. "The explosion in Manhattan is barely forty-five minutes old. No useful information has yet been learned."

"They're saying terrorists on the radio."

"That is not known yet. And speculation is pointless and potentially dangerous at this juncture," Smith cautioned. "I need not remind you of the wild accusations that followed in the wake of the federal building bombing in Oklahoma City. I will continue to monitor the situation in New York and will decide on a course of action once the facts are known. Until then, do you have anything to report there?"

"It's weirder than I thought," Remo began. "Turns out this is a profit-making scheme after all. I met some of the entrepreneurs this morning."

"Explain."

Remo provided a rapid rundown of what he had learned from Leaf Randolph, including the fact that he'd been hired over the phone and that he and his companions were responsible for only the two Florida murders.

"I will have the apartment searched," Smith said once he was through, "in addition to checking phone records."

"Start with calls from California," Remo suggested. "I know independent movies usually love being up to their ankles in corpses, but this plot's way too complicated for them. Which reminds me, you didn't tell me the Cabbagehead backers list reads like the Fortune 500."

"What do you mean?" Smith asked.

"I mean you can't fling a dead cat at their offices without it landing on a check from some slumming Hollywood moneybags. They've got millionaires up the wazoo up here."

"Remo, according to my information, the studio is owned by one Shawn Allen Morris."

"Don't believe everything you read," Remo advised.

Smith hummed thoughtfully. "Give me some of the names, please," he said, his tone betraying mild intrigue.

Remo could almost hear the CURE director's fingers poised over his keyboard. He decided to go for the bombshell first. "Try Stefan Schoenburg on for size," he suggested.

The CURE director paused. "I have heard of him."

"So's everyone else on the planet. He's been picking all our pockets for the last twenty years."

Remo then mentioned a few of the other names he could recall. Even though the rest were celebrities in their own right, Schoenburg was the only one Smith recognized. When he checked the others, he found that all were millionaires. One was actually a billionaire.

"One moment," Smith said, puzzled.

A few minutes of rapid typing ensued. When Smith returned to the line, his confusion was unmistakable.

"I believe I have found a partial list of investors," he said. "There are many more individuals than those you named. I have rarely encountered a more convoluted money trail. It is a veritable Gordian knot of finance."

"Must have hired Gary Coleman's accountants," Remo said. "So what's the deal?"

"I am looking at one producer's financial information now," Smith said. "He seems a typical Cabbagehead investor. Roughly half of the funds he invested in the Seattle film group seem to have been filtered through companies that distribute films of an, er, adult nature. The other half was routed circuitously through real-estate ventures."

"Were they just fronts?" Remo asked.

"No. The distributors and land transactions were legal. That some of the money was then siphoned to Seattle seems almost an afterthought during the normal course of business."

"Hmm. I'd heard that everybody in Hollywood was into either land or porn," Remo mused.

"Yes," Smith agreed uncomfortably. "Although knowing this does not answer the underlying question. Why would men who are successful in their own right seek to associate themselves with such a small-time film operation and then seem to act to cover up that association?"

"They'll only cover up until Oscar night," Remo explained. "After that they'll be pushing each other into the orchestra pit trying to grab the gold."

"I am being serious, Remo."

"Me, too," Remo insisted. "I'm only telling you what I heard. And given our past experiences in Hollywood, I don't think it stretches credibility. These numbnuts already have all the money in the world. Now they want recognition."

Smith mulled Remo's argument. "Perhaps," he admitted after a moment. "But what is the likelihood that Cabbagehead films could produce an award-winning movie?"

"C'mon, Smitty. Get out of the office once in a while. The sort of junk they make wins awards all the time."

The weary sigh of Harold Smith carried over the line.

On the other side of the country, alone in his Folcroft office, Smith was thinking of his conversation with the President. Perhaps he was a relic of another age, too far behind the times to be useful in this new era.

"If it is as you say, then it is possible the motivation here is egocentric," the CURE director admitted tiredly. "I will attempt to follow the money chain further. In the meantime, I would advise you to return to your source. He was helpful already— perhaps he knows something that could be of further use."

Remo balked. "Oh, come on, Smitty," he complained. "There's got to be some other way. Quintly Tortilli is a dingdong with a capital *ding*. You've got to stick him on the roof just to shut him up, and he dresses like a Latvian pimp. I got motion sickness just from looking at his shirt."

"Please, Remo," Smith pressed.

From his tone, he sounded too fatigued to argue.

At the Seattle phone booth, Remo spun to face the road.

Row after row of coffeehouses faced one another across the street as far as the eye could see. Too many, it seemed, for all of them to be sustainable. Yet people continually entered and exited shops at a pace so steady Remo was certain they had to be going out one door and into the next. He closed his eyes on the seemingly choreographed activity.

"Fine, I'll track down Tortilli," Remo relented.

"But if he isn't dead already, I just might kill him myself."

Before Smith was able to ask if he was joking, Remo dropped the phone back into its cradle.

WHEN THE SLACKER generation had first found a home in the independent-film industry, it seemed a match made in heaven. Every loafer with no job and an eight-millimeter camera could be a genius in his parents' basement without suffering through the mundaneness of everyday family, work or life responsibilities. But with the elevation of indie films beyond cult status, a new pressure was brought to bear on an industry not famous for its strong work ethic. The success of low-budget movies at Telluride, Cannes, Sundance and other film festivals had upped the ante even more. *The Blair Witch Project* only made matters worse. The urgency to be the studio to create the next Quintly-esque counterculture hit grew more intense with each season. At the moment, no one felt the pressure more than Shawn Allen Morris.

"We can't survive this," Shawn wailed to the gray, mist-filled sky. "How can we have a Quintly Tortilli film without Quintly Tortilli?"

"Everyone else does," pointed out a soundman who worked part-time bagging groceries at a local supermarket.

"They are producing knockoff shit. We had the *real* Tortilli. A Tortilli original out of Cabbagehead would have gone all the way to March."

"The studio has had a few hits lately."

Shawn waved a dismissive hand. "Flukes. Art-house hits. We could have had a box-office bonanza here."

He was sitting on a plastic milk crate on the parking-lot set of *The Butcher, the Baker and the Candlestick Maker*. The blood machines were idle. The cast and crew of locals hired for the production sat glumly on crates around the roped-off area.

The ropes were just for show. In a week of shooting, the only thing that had dropped by the set was a single stray dog. It had wandered away from a pack that stalked the woods around the nearby reservoir. At the moment it was sleeping at Shawn's feet. The filthy reservoir dog snored loudly, unconcerned for Shawn Allen Morris or his studio's plight.

As Shawn sat bemoaning his fate, an engine purred to a stop beyond the string of ropes. When he glanced up, his dispirited gaze alighted on a familiar car. The Cabbagehead executive watched glumly as Remo Williams got out.

The dog at Shawn's feet lifted its nose. After sniffing the air, it laid its head back down to the damp asphalt.

Remo's expression was sour as he crossed to Shawn.

"Where's Tortilli?" Remo asked, glancing around.

Shawn wanted to snort derisively, but the ache

Darrow/*L.A. Law* thing. Bidda-boom, bidda-bing, I'm back on the street. Christ Almighty, how I love the revolving-door prison system.''

"That's great," Shawn said, with a total lack of conviction. "See, the thing is, Quintly, it's Tuesday. A lot of our cast skipped school for this..."

"He's leaving," Remo said. Grabbing Tortilli by the arm, he began bouncing the director toward his rental car.

"I am?" Tortilli asked. "Cool!"

"He's *not*," Shawn begged, running alongside them. "Quintly, you've got a movie to finish here."

"You don't get it, Shawn," the director announced, his balled-fist face red with excitement. "This is the man. I mean, there are men. And there are men who are the man. But this is, like, *the man.*" Beside the rental car now, he turned to Remo. "You are protoman. You are like the first monkey to swim up out of the primordial ooze. I prostate myself at your feet."

"Pros*trate*," Remo corrected, opening the passenger's-side door. "Prostate is where your head's gonna be if you don't shut up." He tossed the director inside, slamming the door.

As Shawn stomped impotently on the pavement, Remo rounded to the driver's side.

Inside the car, Remo turned to Tortilli.

"A—shut up. B—your last lead was a bust. You think you can find another?"

Tortilli was torn by the conflicting commands. His worried eyes darted left and right. "I guess so," he ventured at last. He threw his hands protectively in front of his face. His ferret eyes squinted, awaiting the blow.

None came.

All he heard was the car engine turning over.

Tortilli opened one cautious eye. They were driving across the parking lot. The director's shoulders relaxed.

"There were five of them," he enthused, his voice a conspiratorial whisper. "You knocked off five at one time!"

"Think how easy one would be," Remo cautioned.

Tortilli nodded in understanding.

He still had one more question. Since Remo seemed to be in a more agreeable mood than normal, he decided to risk it.

"How long you gonna leave Shawn up there?" he asked.

He nodded to the hood. Shawn Allen Morris lay plastered to the wet surface, his legs dangling out over the grille.

"*Please,* Quintly!" Shawn's muffled voice shouted.

Remo's response was nonverbal.

At the supermarket entrance, Remo cut the wheel sharply. Shawn flew off the hood into a cluster of shopping carts.

Over the rattle of the carts, Quintly Tortilli swore he heard the sound of crunching bones. Just like in the movies.

The rented car tore off down the street.

9

"I don't think we can last much longer under these conditions," the assistant director pleaded. "He's got us all walking on eggshells. He screams at us. Bullies us. He's never happy with anything I'm doing. I've never been on a set where the tension level was this high. And I spent six months on the *Rosie O'Donnell Show*."

Arlen Duggal was in the Taurus Studios office of Bindle and Marmelstein. The studio cochairs sat behind a gleaming pair of matching stainless-steel desks.

"Are you sure this isn't just a personality conflict?" Bruce Marmelstein asked calmly.

The assistant director shook his head frantically.

"When I told him I wanted to break for the day yesterday, he threatened to eviscerate me if I didn't get back to work," Arlen said pleadingly.

"That doesn't sound so bad," Hank Bindle suggested.

"Oh, no? I looked it up. It means 'disembowel.' He's a maniac. He's completely out of control. You've got to *do* something."

Bruce Marmelstein was leaning back in his

swivel chair, salon-tanned hands steepled beneath the nose he'd ordered from his plastic surgeon's summer catalog.

"Bottom line," Marmelstein said. "This production was twenty-three days behind schedule before he got here. He's only been here forty-eight hours and we're already through twelve of those lost days. Even at this rate, *Assassin's Loves* will be finished just barely on schedule."

"Can't we change the working title?" Bindle asked, his face pinched in displeasure. "That was just to cover Lance during location shooting. I mean, *Assassin's Loves?* Pee-yew."

"It's already on the crew jackets, hats and script binders," Marmelstein said. "Belt-tightening time. Remember?"

"Have you seen what we've shot in the past two days?" the assistant director begged, steering them back to the topic at hand. "It's crap."

"Editing will punch it up," Hank Bindle assured him. "We'll fill it with digital fluff. Hell, we'll even see if we can get John Williams to score it."

"We can't afford John Williams," Marmelstein cautioned.

"Oh. How about Danny Elfman?"

"Think second-string."

Bindle was horror-struck. "Not Henry Mancini!" he gasped.

"He's dead, isn't he?" Marmelstein frowned.

"Oh, thank God," Bindle replied, clutching his chest in relief. "We'd be the laughingstock of the industry. In the first testosterone-injected block-buster of the summer, the hero doesn't blow up a helicopter or bang a broad to 'Moon River.' Course the fags might like that. Maybe for homo crossover appeal we could get Celine Dion to do a 'Moon River' cover for the banging scene.''

"Probably too much, but I'll call her people," Marmelstein said.

Nodding, Bindle leaned back in his chair.

"We still have a problem on the set," the assistant director interjected. Arlen was nearly crying now as he stood, shifting uncomfortably before their desks.

"Are you still here?" Bindle asked, frowning. "I thought we'd settled this."

"We had," Marmelstein stressed. "The picture was hopelessly behind schedule. Now it's only behind. In two days it won't even be that anymore. Problem solved."

"It wasn't my fault we were behind," the assistant director whined.

Hank Bindle tapped a finger on his desk. "Look, who's directing this picture?" he asked.

"I wasn't contracted to," the A.D. argued.

"That's not the point."

"But he put two union reps through a wall to-day," Arlen pleaded, his tone desperate. "Through a freaking *wall*."

"They were insolent louts."

The unexpected reply didn't come from either

Hank Bindle or Bruce Marmelstein. The singsongy voice came from the direction of the office doors.

Arlen jumped a foot in the air. He wheeled in time to see the big office doors swing quietly shut. The Master of Sinanju was padding silently across the carpet.

Chiun stopped next to the panicked assistant director.

"O Magnificent Oneness," the A.D. said, terror in his quavering voice. "I thought you were at the commissary."

"They did not have proper rice," Chiun said, his eyes slivers of suspicion. "Why are you not at work?"

"I...it...I—I was just reporting on our progress."

Hank Bindle smiled. "Arlen was telling us how pleased he was with your managerial skills, Mr. Chiun."

"Yes," Bruce Marmelstein agreed, an overly white grin spreading across his deeply tanned face. "He's very impressed. Says you're a real motivator."

Heavy lids parted a fraction, revealing questioning hazel orbs. "Is this true?" Chiun asked the A.D.

The man glanced desperately at Bindle and Marmelstein, then back to the old Korean. "I...that is...yes. *Yes.*" He nodded emphatically.

A sad smile cracked through the harsh leathery veneer of the Master of Sinanju. "I am deeply touched," he intoned. "But alas, your words of praise cannot be true."

"Of course they are," Arlen said, sensing an opportunity to ingratiate himself with the terrifying old man. He forced warm enthusiasm into his voice.

"No, no," Chiun said, raising a hand to ward off further undeserved approval. "For if this were the case, would you not be on the set right now?"

Chiun's thin smile vanished in an instant, replaced by a granite-cold glare. His protesting hand was still raised. Arlen's sick eyes traced the contours of the old man's daggerlike fingernails.

The assistant director gulped audibly. "I, um...better get, um... *Look!*" Pointing out the big office window, he turned and ran from the room.

As the door swung shut, a placid expression settled on the weathered creases of the Master of Sinanju's face.

"Damn, if the movie business doesn't fit you like a glove, Mr. Chiun," Marmelstein said, genuinely impressed at the way the old Korean had handled the assistant director. "Why, the look of pure terror you just put in that man's eyes? It's like Jack Warner's come back from that big projection room in the sky." His own eyes were misting.

"You've really given the production a kick in the pants," Bindle agreed enthusiastically.

"These people lacked discipline," said Chiun. "Their leader did not inspire order."

"Leader," Bindle snorted sarcastically. "Don't even get me started on that one."

Chiun raised an eyebrow. "Is something wrong?"

"Nothing," Marmelstein shook his head. "Sore subject. Anyway, your presence here is really working out great. We're tearing through script pages like a runaway train."

As usual, Chiun didn't know what the executive was saying. "This is good?" he asked.

"Good? It's great! It means we'll make our May premiere date after all, which means we get a jump on the rest of the summer competition, which means we get a bigger chunk of the summer box office, which means those gross profit points you negotiated are worth even more."

This the Master of Sinanju understood. "I love the movie business," he enthused.

"And it loves *you,* baby," Hank Bindle said warmly. He rose from his desk, coming around to the tiny Asian. Bruce Marmelstein came behind him.

Bindle put his arm around Chiun's bony shoulder. Such a move of familiarity would ordinarily cost someone at least one arm, if not his life. But Chiun felt such love in the room that he didn't object to the touch. Nor did he protest as Bindle and Marmelstein began to lead him from the office.

"You're an asset this town can really use," Bindle said. "I can see a long relationship between the three of us. You as writer and set inspiration, us as resident executive geniuses. The sky is the limit.

Anything you want, you just ask your old pal Hank Bindle.''

"Or Bruce Marmelstein," Bruce Marmelstein offered as he pushed the door open. They entered the lobby.

"Since you mention it, I had come here to suggest higher quality rice at the eating place of the commissar," Chiun said.

"Huh?" Marmelstein asked.

"Commissary," Bindle explained to his partner.

"Japonica rice. And fish," Chiun said. "Perhaps some duck. Duck is always nice."

"Whatever you say." Bindle nodded.

"We'll get right on it," Marmelstein agreed.

"If I think of anything else, I will tell you."

"We're *anxious* for your input," Marmelstein enthused.

They ushered Chiun onto the elevator. After the doors had closed on the Master of Sinanju, the two of them let out a single relieved sigh. They returned to their office, plopping down behind their huge executive desks.

"Are you thinking what I'm thinking?" Hank Bindle asked once they'd settled in. He was staring at the glass office doors.

Marmelstein nodded. "That old fart's sold us a bill of goods," he said. "This thing is a bomb waiting to go off."

"Why didn't we see it before?" Bindle wailed. "We wasted our money on the rights. I mean, come on. An honest cop fighting the system alone? Snore, snore, snore.''

"We should have seen it wasn't workable.''

"Workable? We'll be lucky if we're not sever-anced off with a big fat check and a pile of stock.''

"Golden parachute?'' Marmelstein asked.

"It's happened to all the biggies at one time or another,'' Bindle moaned. "Ovitz, Katzenberg. Re-member Tartikoff? Most of them never recovered. The worst day of my life will be the day they give me that hundred-million-dollar check.''

Marmelstein shuddered. "Don't worry. It'll probably never come to that.''

Bindle sighed. Leaning an elbow on his gleaming desk, he looked over at his partner. "So what's the story on our little mini-sneak preview?''

"No one's made the connection yet. I think it might be because of the chaos on the set. No one's seen the reports.''

"Hell, if it goes on much longer, *I'll* go down and tell them,'' Bindle said, slouching in his chair.

"That wouldn't be smart. We really shouldn't link ourselves to it. If it goes on another day, I'll leak it by e-mail to *Entertainment Tonight* from one of the dummy accounts.''

"I don't know how one little blown-up building in New York is going to pull this turkey out of the oven,'' Bindle grumbled, "let alone bring it back to life.''

"It probably won't,'' Bruce Marmelstein ex-plained. "We take it in steps. New York first, then the really big one. With the interest we'll generate, we could have a box-office hit yet.''

''Or the biggest bomb in history.''

Bruce Marmelstein laughed. ''That's what's going to *give* us the box office.''

Hank Bindle nodded, bracing his forehead against his palm. ''Movie promotion can be so demanding,'' he sighed.

10

Pink plastic lawn flamingos lined the wall behind the hideous paisley sofa. The living-room rug sported images of cavorting blue Smurfs. The thick glass sheet that was the coffee table was held aloft by a single faux elephant foot.

A substance resembling clear gelatin filled a thirty-gallon fish tank on the shelf near the kitchenette. Suspended at various points in the tank were severed doll limbs.

Posters from films such as *Surf Nazis Must Die*, *A Bucket of Blood* and *Frankenhooker* adorned the walls, held in place by cheery multicolored thumbtacks.

It was a lot to take in all at once. Remo wasn't sure if he wanted to throw up or run screaming into the hallway. Settling reluctantly on a third option, he followed Quintly Tortilli inside his Seattle apartment.

"You like it?" the famous director asked as he dropped his keys near a plastic Fred Flintstone bank on the table near the door.

"Blind whores have better taste," Remo said.

Frowning, he flicked at the grass skirt on a tiny hula dancer attached to a table lamp.

"Yeah," agreed Tortilli. "They always know, like, the best yard sales. My book's in the bedroom."

Leaving Remo, he danced down a short hallway.

Every inch of space in the living room was crammed with forced kitsch. From Felix the Cat wall clocks whose eyes moved back and forth with each tick of their tails to upright ashtrays fashioned to look like cowboy boots to a closet from which spilled clothes made of fabrics that had been to the moon. Anyone unfortunate enough to enter the apartment was pummeled by Quintly Tortilli's obnoxious personality.

On an oil-stained desk, which looked as if Tortilli had rescued it from an abandoned factory, lay a dozen scripts. When Remo opened one, he found that the margins were filled with notes. The others he checked were in the same condition: all loaded with crazy pencil marks. He was about to turn from the desk when one of the script covers caught his eye. Surprised, he picked it up. He was skimming through it when Tortilli returned.

"We're in business now," the director enthused, waving a mint-condition 1970s *Josie and the Pussycats* binder.

"What the hell is this?" Remo asked, holding up the script.

"Huh? Oh, I do script-doctor work sometimes. *Blood Water, The Lockup.* Strictly uncredited. Million bucks for a week's work. Those are the latest. I get 'em all the time.''

Remo looked at the cover of the script in his hand. "You're doing the rewrite on a TeeVee-Fatties screenplay?"

Tortilli nodded. "Yeah, man. That's a great one. Originally it was all magic clouds and happy sunshine. In mine Tipsy gets cheesed off at Poopsy-Woopsy for using his scooter, so he beats him to death with a bag of frozen TeeVeeFattie muffins.''

"Unbelievable." Remo tossed the script back on the desk.

"Yeah," Tortilli agreed. "The violence and drugs were always, like, *there* in TeeVeeFattie-Land, man. I just brought them to the surface." Notebook in hand, he went over to his Starship Enterprise telephone.

While the director looked up numbers and dialed, Remo leaned against the door, arms crossed.

"Do you have to try so hard all the time?" Remo asked.

"I have an image," Tortilli explained. "Unfortunately, I don't know where it ends and I begin anymore." He straightened. "Hi, Bug?" He said into the phone. "Quint. How ya doin'?"

After a few minutes of questioning, Tortilli gave up. The director had learned nothing. The next three calls proved fruitless, as well. He got lucky on the fifth.

"Where?" Tortilli asked excitedly. He fished a *Mork and Mindy* pencil from his polyester pocket.

Though he was poised to jot the address on his notepad, he didn't have to. "I know the place," he said. "Yeah. Yeah, I heard about it. One of them cut off his head shaving, right? Ouch. Break out the Bactine."

Covering the receiver, Tortilli snickered softly. Pulling himself together, he returned to the phone.

"I'm all set," he said, clearing his throat. "Remind me to make you a star. Later." Hanging up, he looked expectantly to Remo. "I think we've got something. The guy I called knows a guy who claims another guy was bragging he was in on the box murder. You know, the one with the torso."

"I heard," Remo said flatly.

"On the phone? You mean you can hear *both* sides of a phone conversation?"

"It's hard to hear anything over your suit," Remo said dryly. He pulled the door open. "Let's go."

Jogging to keep up, Quintly Tortilli hurried after Remo into the hallway. As he shut the door, he flicked off the lights, drowning the garish decor in blessed darkness.

SEATTLE'S DESPAIRING youth had early on established the Dregs as the city's premier grunge bar. For a time, the pervasive gloom and hopelessness of its clientele was money in the bank. But then disaster struck. Resurgent optimism suddenly began to sweep the nation. One morning, the bar's owners woke up to find hope and enthusiasm saturating the popular culture. The change seemed to come overnight.

The morose lyrics set to mournful tunes that had made Seattle the rage of the music scene only a few short years before were replaced by the upbeat sounds of the Backstreet Boys and Dixie Chicks.

With grunge fading and alternative poised to die a sudden death, the Dregs had become the last bulwark for the music that had made the city famous.

When Remo Williams walked through the front door, it was as if a pop-culture time machine had taken him back six years. He scanned the sea of plaid shirts, torn denim pants and goatees that filled the bar.

"Looks like a beatnik lumberjack convention," he grumbled.

A few of the nearest slackers looked his way, some suspicious of his T-shirt and chinos. But when a second figure popped in behind him, they instantly relaxed.

Quintly Tortilli. The Hollywood genius was a frequent visitor to the Dregs. Accompanied by the young director of *Penny Dreadful,* the stranger couldn't be all bad.

"Isn't this place great?" Tortilli yelled to Remo over the blaring sound system. Tables wobbled from the pounding bass. Ragged figures moped around the dance floor.

Remo nodded to the crowd. "Stick a two-by-four up their asses and I could get them all work scaring crows."

"Yeah," Tortilli agreed. "The ripped-jeans-and-flannel thing is still only a couple years retro. But if it holds on long enough, it'll come back into style." He sized up Remo. "Actually, if you don't mind, Remo, maybe you should think about updating your look. Don't take this as criticism—I'm saying this as a friend—but, I mean, how long have you been doing the whole T-shirt-chinos thing? Retro's one thing, but maybe you should think about keeping up with the times, man."

"Look, dingbat, it's bad enough I'm stuck with you and that Teflon jumpsuit you're wearing without listening to your cockeyed fashion tips," Remo growled. "Hurry up."

According to Tortilli's source, the man they were looking for was someone the director knew—if only vaguely. As he turned to the packed bar, his dull eyes narrowed. He looked from pasty face to pasty face.

"I don't think I see him," Tortilli said in a disappointed tone.

"Your pal seemed sure he'd be here," Remo insisted. As he spoke, he rotated his thick wrists impatiently.

Quintly was still glancing from face to face. "You really could hear him, couldn't you?" He grinned, impressed. "You know, we should really talk about me writing your life—" He stopped dead. "Got him," Tortilli announced abruptly.

With laserlike precision, Remo honed in on the director's line of sight.

The man was a burly slacker in red flannel. He sat alone at a cheap plastic table on the other side of the bar.

"I don't know, man. He's kinda big." Tortilli frowned. "You might have trouble wasting this one. Whaddaya think?"

When he turned, he found that he was talking to empty air. Quintly glanced back across the room.

It took him a minute to spot Remo's white T-shirt. When he finally found it, he was surprised that Remo was already halfway across the bar. He was gliding through the dense throng like a silent spirit. Though people crushed in all around him, he seemed no more substantial than air.

Tortilli shook his head, impressed.

"How much for your life story, man?" he said in wonder. He ordered a rum punch from a passing waitress and quickly found a seat of his own, settling in to watch the floor show.

IN THE COUNTERCULTURE environment of poseurs and criminal wanna-bes, Chester Gecko was the real deal. All 211 pounds of him.

In an age where nearly every high-school student got a diploma and a pat on the head, regardless of academic achievement or lack thereof, Chester had failed to meet even the basic, lax requirements for graduation. Twice forced to repeat his senior year at Bremerton's Coriolis High School, he was finally thrown out after his geometry teacher made the mistake of asking him to demonstrate the use of a protractor in front of the class. It was eight years later, and the woman still used makeup to mask the scars on her cheek.

Chester had been in trouble with the law nearly all his life, but thanks to a criminal-justice system that sometimes seemed even more hesitant to deal with unruly elements than the public education system, he had yet to do any major time. It was actually a shame, really, for Chester was the type of individual who would have been happier in prison than he was in civilized society.

Whenever he stopped in the Dregs, people instinctively knew to steer clear of Chester Gecko. He was easy enough to avoid; a burly, slouching figure with ratlike eyes, Chester drew more flies than friends. He generally sat alone at his table, practically daring someone to approach. And in five years, no one ever had.

Until this day.

Chester was sullenly sucking at his beer when he saw the skinny guy show up with Quintly Tortilli.

Chester didn't like Tortilli anymore. Mr. Bigshot didn't answer his mail. Besides, he'd seen the director in the Dregs before, so it was easy enough to lose interest.

He glanced away for a second. When he looked back, the stranger with Tortilli had disappeared.

Just like that. Vanished. As if the floor had opened up and swallowed him whole. Chester assumed he'd ducked back out the front door. But when he returned his bored attention to the dance floor, he saw something that made his stomach twitch. A few yards away, Tortilli's companion was melting out of the crowd.

That was the only way Chester could describe it—melting. It was as if he didn't exist one moment and in the next had congealed into human shape.

Chester blinked. And in that infinitesimally brief instant when his eyes were closed, the stranger materialized in the chair across from his.

Chester jumped, startled. He quickly recovered.

"Get lost," he grumbled, forcing a gruff edge to cover his surprise. With a flick of his neck, he shifted his dirty brown bangs from his forehead. He took a swig from the half-full beer bottle clutched in his big hand.

Across the table, Remo nodded. "After I've killed you," he promised. "Now, there's an easy—"

"What?" Chester Gecko snarled, slamming his bottle to the table.

"Hmm?" Remo asked.

"What did you just say?" Chester demanded.

Remo frowned, confused. "About what?"

"Did you just threaten me?"

"Oh, that. Yes." That settled, Remo continued. "Now, there's an easy way and a hard way to do this."

"Go pound sand," Chester growled. Stuffing his bottle back in his mouth, he took a mighty swig.

"I see we've opted for latter," Remo mused, nodding.

And as Chester pulled the bottle from between his lips, Remo's hand shot forward.

Too fast for Chester Gecko to follow, the flat of Remo's palm swatted the base of the bottle, propelling it forward.

It skipped out of Chester's hand, launching back into his stunned face. As Remo's hand withdrew, Chester suddenly felt a great tugging just below his eyes, as if something were pulling on his nose. When he reached for the source, he found his beer bottle dangling from the tip. It hung in front of his slack mouth.

He snorted in pain. Beer stung his nostrils. He gagged, spitting out the liquid.

"I'd gobba kill you," Chester choked. But when he looked up, Remo's eyes were cold. Frighteningly so.

"Bet you I can fit your whole head in there," Remo said evenly.

The confidence he displayed was casual and absolute. And in an instant of sharp realization, Chester Gecko knew that this thin stranger with the incredibly thick wrists was not joking.

Chester held up his hands. "Dno," he pleaded. The bottle on his face clacked against his front teeth. He yelped in pain, grabbing at his mouth.

"Okay, let's establish the ground rules," Remo said. Reaching over, he gave the bottle a twist.

The pain was so great, Chester couldn't even scream. His eyes watered as his bottle-encased nose took on the shape of a flesh-colored corkscrew.

"Those are the ground rules," Remo said, releasing the bottle. "Understand?"

Chester nodded desperately. The dangling bottle swatted his chin with each frantic bob of his head.

Remo's expression hardened. "Who hired you to butcher that girl?" he asked.

Chester felt his breath catch. Yet he dared not lie.

"I don gno," he admitted. "Phone caw. Don gnow who he wath." He fumbled to twist the bottle back to its starting point.

Remo frowned. Another phone call. The same method that had been used to hire Leaf Randolph.

"How'd you get paid?" he pressed.

"Potht offith boxth," Chester said. Blood streamed from his encased nostrils, dribbling into the bottom of the bottle. The golden liquid was taking on a thick black hue. This time, Remo remembered the question he had forgotten to ask at Leaf's apartment. "How much?"

"Pive hunred thouthanth."

Remo thought he had misheard. He made Chester repeat the amount. He found that he wasn't wrong. Chester Gecko had been paid five hundred thousand dollars to butcher a woman and stuff her torso into an orange crate.

It was a lot of money. An insanely *Hollywood* amount.

Remo's thoughts instantly turned to Cabbage-head's wealthy backers. That much money would have been chump change to any one of those men.

Chester had told him everything of value. He just had one question left.

"You know who killed that family in Maryland?" he asked.

Chester shook his head. "Wathn't uth," he promised.

"Who's the rest of 'us'?" Remo asked.

Even as Remo spoke, Chester's fearful eyes darted over Remo's shoulder to the front door. For an instant, a glimmer of hope sprang alive in their black depths.

Remo squashed it immediately.

"Three guys. Three guns. Just came in the front door," Remo supplied without turning. "Are they 'us'?"

Chester's shoulders slumped. He nodded.

As he did so, his dangling beer bottle banged somberly against the table's damp plastic surface.

"Okay, let's take it outside," Remo said thinly.

Rising to his feet, he grabbed Chester's bottle in one hand. He was pulling the grunting killer to his feet when he heard a familiar determined crinkling of artificial fabric hustling toward him.

"Remo," Quintly Tortilli urged, bounding up beside him. He was glancing over his shoulder to the main entrance.

"I see them," Remo said, voice level.

"They hang with him," Tortilli insisted, pointing a pinkie and index finger at Chester. "I seen the dudes in here before. Maybe we better fly?"

Tortilli was more skittish than usual—even by

Quintly Tortilli standards. Gone was all of his earlier bravado. Dropped in the middle of a real life-and-death scene, the director's natural instinct for self-preservation had kicked in.

Remo nodded tightly. Tugging Chester by the bottle, he led them to the rear exit. He waited long enough to be sure the trio of armed men had seen them before ducking outside.

The rear door of the bar spilled into a cluttered alley. A mountain of garbage bags was heaped against the grimy brick wall. Swinging Chester by the bottle, Remo tossed the thug onto the trash heap.

"I think they saw us," Quintly Tortilli whined. He bounced from foot to foot a few yards down the alley from Remo. His body language screamed "Retreat."

"They didn't..." Remo began.

Tortilli's shoulders relaxed.

"...until I waved them over."

"You what?" the director asked, fear flooding his darting eyes. "You're kidding, man, right?"

Remo held up a finger. "Hold that thought."

He hadn't even lowered his hand before the rusted door burst open. The three hoods he'd waved to from across the bar spilled into the alley.

"Guns!" Quintly Tortilli shrieked. He became a flash of purple polyester as he dived behind a cluster of trash bags.

All three weapons were drawn before the thugs had even bounded out the door. Although they twisted alertly, none of the men had expected their target to be standing a foot from the door. Before they knew it, Remo was among them.

He danced down the line, swatting guns from outstretched hands. At the same time, his flying feet sought brittle kneecaps. Guns skipped merrily away along the soggy alley floor, accompanied by the sound of popping patellas.

When the men fell, screaming, Remo was already pivoting on one leg. A single sweeping heel punished three foreheads. All three men dropped face-first to the ground. As the life sighed out of them, Remo turned to Chester Gecko.

Chester was attempting to sit up on the pile of heaped trash, blood-filled bottle still dangling from his nose.

"That was the preview," Remo said icily. "Time for the feature presentation."

Chester tried to scurry backward up the garbage mountain. Bags tore open beneath his kicking heels, spilling their rotting contents into water-filled potholes.

"Wait!" he cried. "I gnow more!"

When Remo paused, Chester sensed his opportunity. But before he could speak, they were both distracted by a shrill sound issuing from beside the garbage mound.

"Whoa, you are *heavy duty*," Quintly Tortilli whistled.

Sensing the end of the battle, the director had just come crawling into view. His eyes darted from the trio of bodies near the door back to Remo. "I am *going* to option your story," he stated with firm insistence.

"Put a sock in it, Kubrick," Remo snarled. He returned his attention to Chester Gecko. "Spill it," he demanded.

"Da one we did wath juth a little job," Chester insisted. He was panting in fear. "I gnow thome guyth who dot hired to pland a bunch ob bombth. Dey were hired to blow up a whole thtudio."

Remo glanced at Quintly Tortilli. The director's balled-fist face was drawn into a puzzled frown.

"Cabbagehead?" Remo asked Chester.

The hood shook his head. "Thmall botatos. Dith ib a Hollywood thtudio. Ith going down today. We arranged da bomb thupplieth." When he nodded to his dead friends, his expression weakened.

"Where'd you hear this?" Tortilli asked.

"Da guy who dold me already dot paid." Chester shrugged.

Remo's stomach had twisted into a cold knot the instant Hollywood was mentioned. "What studio?" he said hollowly.

Chester sniffled. He winced as he inadvertently sucked a noseful of bloody beer back into his mouth.

"Tauruth," Chester burbled.

It was the last word he ever spoke.

Quintly Tortilli didn't even see Remo move. In a mere sliver of time, the dangling beer bottle had swung up and launched forward.

Facial bones surrendered to the thick glass spear, puckering Chester's face in at the center.

As the hood collapsed to the garbage heap, beer bottle skewering his brain, Quintly Tortilli let out a low whistle. More a reaction to Chester's revelation than to the killer's abrupt death.

"Taurus," he said. "Man, they've taken their hits over the last few years but—*ka-blammo!*—this has got to be the mother of them all." He turned to Remo. "You know, I—"

Tortilli found that he was alone. Glancing around, he spotted Remo racing toward the mouth of the alley, arms and legs pumping in furious, urgent concert.

At Chester's revelation, unseen by Quintly Tortilli, a rare emotion had sprung full-bloom on the cruel face of Remo Williams. And that emotion was fear.

11

In the wake of the Oklahoma City bombing, tightened federal regulations had made it increasingly difficult to purchase massive quantities of fertilizer without proof of need. This was deemed necessary to keep terrorists from visiting explosive death on another unsuspecting domestic target. But difficult wasn't the same as impossible. Lester Craig could attest to that.

"You realize we've got enough shit back there to take out half a city block?" Lester asked proudly from the driver's seat of a large yellow Plotz rental truck.

It was as if his seatmate didn't hear him.

"Guard," William Scott Cain said in icy reply.

Lester had met William the day they'd started work on this project. Lester didn't like his partner at all. Lester was more of a good-old-boy type. His passenger was more an Ivy Leaguer whose snobbishness was never more evident than in the condescending way he gave out commands.

Guard. William Scott Cain made that simple, five-letter monosyllabic word sound like an insult.

"I see him," Lester griped, muttering under his breath, "ya smug little bastard."

They were at the north gate of Taurus Studios in Hollywood. The high white wall of the motion-picture studio ran in a virtually unbroken line all around the complex.

Lester steered up the slight incline in the road where the high walls curved around to the simple guard shack. They stopped at the plain wooden barricade.

"Passes," the guard said tersely.

The attitudes of studio guards traditionally ran hot and cold. Hot was reserved for celebrities and executives. For the likes of Lester and his companion, the attitude of all guards bordered on hostile.

"He wouldn't ask Tom Hanks for his pass," William groused even as Lester flashed each of their laminated cards at the guard.

Once the guard was satisfied, he leaned in his booth. A moment later, the gate rose high in the air.

"Thank you kindly." Lester smiled at the guard, for what he knew would be the last time.

The two-and-a-half-ton truck with its cargo of ammonium nitrate eased past the uplifted wooden arm. With an ominous rumble, it headed deep into the Taurus lot.

THE MASTER OF SINANJU stomped his sandaled feet angrily as he whirled onto the exterior set.

It was a mock-up of a New York slum. Post-production computer effects would erase the large Taurus water tower that rose proudly in the background.

"I cannot leave you for a moment!" Chiun cried, his high-pitched voice sending shock waves of fear through the gathered cast and crew. The hems of his scarlet kimono billowed about his ankles as he flounced up to the assistant director. His hazel eyes were fire. "I take but one rice break, and the instant my back is turned you lapse into indolence! Why are you not working, goldbrick?"

Arlen Duggal was clearly petrified. At Chiun's typhoonlike appearance, he broke away from the female assistant he'd been talking to, backing from the fearful wraith in red.

"It's not my fault...." he pleaded.

"It is *never* your fault, slothful one. Nor will it be *my* fault when I remove your sluggish head from your lazy neck." Chiun glared at the comely young assistant.

"Let me explain," the A.D. begged.

The old man didn't hear. "Have you halted production on my epic saga to chatter with this hussy?" he demanded, pointing at the assistant. He raised his voice to the crowd. "Hear me, one and all, for I do issue a decree. From this moment forth, there shall be no females on this set. Remember to tell this to this slugabed's successor."

"Mr. Chiun," Arlen's assistant interrupted.

"Silence, harlot!"

Tears were welling up in Arlen's eyes. "It really

isn't my fault," he begged. "The extras aren't here."

Chiun's eyes narrowed. He spun from the director and his assistant, scanning the gathered crowd.

Most of the faces he saw belonged to behind-the-scenes crew. Very few appeared to be actual performers.

"Where are my overcasts?" he asked all at once. "The scene we film today requires a multitude."

"They haven't shown up yet," Arlen informed him.

Chiun wheeled on him. "This is your doing," he said, aiming an accusing fingernail. "Your laxness infects the lower orders like a plague."

Arlen ducked behind his assistant, grabbing her by the shoulders. Positioning the woman like a human shield between himself and Chiun, he ducked and wove fearfully.

"I think they might be afraid," the A.D. squeaked.

Chiun's furious mask touched shades of confusion. "Afraid of what?" he demanded.

"Of all the tension on the set?" the A.D. offered.

Chiun's face flushed to angry horror. "Are you creating tension on my set, as well?" he accused, his voice flirting with the early edges of cold fury.

Hoping to defuse the situation, the woman behind whom Arlen was cowering spoke up.

"They *are* here," she offered, wincing at the painful grip on her shoulders. "I saw a couple of them not five minutes ago. They were over by Soundstage 1."

For an instant, Chiun seemed torn. As the old man stood stewing, Arlen saw his opportunity. Releasing his assistant, he began tiptoeing away in an awkward squat. He got no more than four teetering feet before a blur of scarlet swept before him. A daggerlike nail pressed his throat. When he looked up, he dared not gulp lest he risk piercing his Adam's apple.

Chiun's eyes were molten steel.

"Know you this, lie-abed," the Master of Sinanju hissed. "Your skills alone preserve your life." Spinning to the crew, he called, "Make ready, malingerers! I will see to the missing overcasts."

As the old Korean marched away, the gathered throng let out a collective sigh of relief. Arlen Duggal dropped to his knees. After touching his throat with his fingertips, he relaxed. No blood. The tension drained from his shoulders.

"Worst thing about this is I'd still rather put up with him than Rosie," Arlen muttered.

He watched as the wizened figure disappeared around a building mock-up. Unbeknownst to Arlen, the tiny Asian was marching straight into the blast zone of the first of six powerful truck bombs.

REMO STOOD ANXIOUSLY at the bank of phones in the bustling terminal building at Seattle-Tacoma International Airport. Beyond the huge tinted windows at his back, massive idle aircraft sulked along the tarmac. Far off, a 747 rose into the bleak sky.

Remo was on hold with Taurus Studios for five minutes before someone in the movie company's executive offices finally deigned to answer.

"Taurus Studios. This is Kelli. How may I direct your call?" The woman's voice was bland and efficient, with a faint Midwestern twang.

"Get me Bindle or Marmelstein," Remo insisted.

The woman didn't miss a beat. "Who's calling?"

"Tell them it's Remo."

"First name or last?"

"First."

"Last name, please?"

Remo stopped dead. He couldn't remember the cover name he'd been using the year before while on assignment in Hollywood.

"'Remo' will do," he said after a second's hesitation.

"Oh. Like Cher," the woman droned doubtfully. He could tell she was about to hang up.

"Wait! How about their assistant, Ian?"

"He was hired by Fox to produce the next Barbra Streisand picture," the woman said frostily.

Remo was getting desperate. He *had* to get through to warn Chiun.

"Okay," he pressed. "There's a movie being made there right now. I know the screenwriter. Just—"

But it was already too late. At the mention of the word *writer,* the line went dead.

Remo slammed the phone down into the cradle. The receiver cracked and split open at the midpoint between earpiece and mouthpiece. Strings of multi-colored wires were all that held the dangling plastic receiver together.

He stood there for a moment, frozen.

He had to warn Chiun.

Smith. He'd call Smith.

Remo hurried to the next phone. Scooping up the receiver, he quickly began to punch in the special code to CURE's Folcroft headquarters. He had only depressed the one key a few times—not enough to make the connection—when he froze.

He couldn't call Smith. Not without telling him why Chiun was at Taurus. And if Remo blabbed to Smith about the Master of Sinanju's upcoming movie, the old Korean would resolve to make Remo's every waking moment a living hell for the rest of his life. If he was lucky.

Even if he told Smith, that was no guarantee of guarding Chiun's safety. If the CURE director sent a swarm of police to Taurus, the bombers might turn skittish. Cops could spook the terrorists into setting off the bombs sooner.

"Dammit, Chiun, why do you have to complicate everything?" Remo griped. He snapped the next phone down in its cradle.

Exhaling angrily, Remo spun away from the bank of phones. The instant he did, he spied a familiar purple leisure suit bobbing and weaving toward him through the main terminal concourse.

Quintly Tortilli had caught up with him in the parking lot at the Dregs. On the way to the airport, Remo had been in too much of a hurry to throw him out of the car.

A few heads turned as Tortilli shoved through the crowd, waving a pair of airline tickets over his head.

"We're all set!" Tortilli panted, sliding up beside Remo. He slammed into the phones, out of breath. "Two tickets on the next flight to L.A. We've got about seven minutes." His famous face was slick with sweat.

Remo was trying to think. "Yeah, and the bombs could go off before that," he muttered.

"But maybe not," Tortilli stressed. "This is a business charter jet," he added, flapping the tickets at Remo. "We can be in L.A. in an hour and a half. Maybe less."

"And stacked up over LAX for two days," Remo complained. There had to be another way. Every minute in the sky worrying about the Master of Sinanju would be torture.

Tortilli shook his head. "I can get us cleared to land as soon as we get there," he insisted.

Remo's head snapped around. "How?"

"Puh-lease," Tortilli mocked, raising an eyebrow. "I'm *me*."

Remo frowned. "What kind of perks do you get when you make a *good* movie?" he asked.

Before Tortilli could mention a word about his People's Choice Award, Remo reached over and grabbed an extrawide purple lapel. Dragging the director behind him, he sprinted for the departure gate.

"YOU THERE!"

The sharp words sliced into Lester Craig's marrow. He pretended he didn't hear the voice. Averting his eyes, he continued walking briskly alongside the massive building that was Soundstage 1.

"Hold!" the singsong voice commanded.

Lester wouldn't have listened under ordinary circumstances. Never would have listened under these particular conditions. But at the moment, the fury in that voice was more frightening to him than the jury-rigged truck bomb he was fleeing.

Lester stopped dead. William Scott Cain stumbled into him.

"What do we do?" William demanded.

"Remember the extra who tried to run from him yesterday?" Lester said from the corner of his mouth. "Traction for six months, minimum."

Flies in amber, the two men remained stock-still as the Master of Sinanju bounded up behind them.

"Are you two layabouts not employed as overcasts on my magnificent film?" the tiny Asian demanded as he slipped in before Lester and William. Narrowed eyes squeezed glaring fury.

They knew better than to lie. The two men nodded dumbly.

The Master of Sinanju's tongue made an angry clicking sound. "That man's laziness is a disease," he hissed to himself.

"Actually—" Lester ventured.

The word was barely out before long-nailed hands appeared from the voluminous sleeves of Chiun's kimono.

"Silence!" he commanded. Angry swats peppered the faces and heads of both extras. "Return to work immediately or you will never breathe in this town again."

They didn't need to be told a second time.

Turning from the furious, slapping dervish, the two men ran off in the direction of the dummy New York exterior. In spite of the knowledge that, in less than two hours, a massive, earthshaking explosion would reduce the entire set and the studio on which it sat to smoking black rubble.

12

The charter jet skimmed over the border between Oregon and California with steady, confident speed.

In the cabin, Remo watched the skimpy white film of clouds dissipate beneath the sleek, gently shuddering wings. Glinting sunlight illuminated tense lines on his hard face.

Quintly Tortilli had gone to the cockpit while they were still over Washington. To Remo's relief, he didn't return for a large chunk of the flight. Only when they were flying over California's Salmon Mountains did the young director wander back down the aisle.

Tortilli plopped into the seat next to Remo.

"I'm back," he announced.

Remo continued to stare out at the wing.

"I'm thinking of doing a disaster movie on a plane," the director said enthusiastically.

"It's been done," Remo grunted.

"Not with curse words," Tortilli replied happily. "I plan on using a lot of them. Every other word will be an *F* word." He held up his hands defensively. "I apologize in advance. I know you don't like that kind of language."

beneath his new wrist cast warned him against it. Instead, he settled on a self-pitying sigh.

"In jail," Shawn said morosely from his milk-crate seat.

"Grand theft plot?" Remo frowned, unsure whether or not he should be pleased that Tortilli was even alive.

"No. Something about killing people or something." Shawn waved, uninterested. "I didn't talk to him. And who cares about that now? How am I going to finish this picture? I need a genius that rivals Quintly Tortilli."

Remo pointed to the sleeping dog. "Give him a beret and megaphone," he suggested. He bit the inside of his cheek.

It was bad enough to have to ask the director for more help; he didn't want to have to spring Tortilli from jail.

Remo was considering leaving Tortilli to take the rap for the murders of Leaf Randolph and his friends when a new engine's roar overwhelmed the parking-lot background noise.

When he turned, he saw a yellow cab speeding quickly across the lot. It hadn't even rocked to a stop behind Remo's rental car before the rear door popped open. A familiar purple leisure suit sprang into view.

"*Veni, vidi, vici!*" Quintly Tortilli announced grandly.

Whirling to the cab, he flung a fistful of crumpled bills at the driver.

Shawn clambered to his feet, face ecstatic. "Thank God!" he proclaimed. He spun to the cast and crew. "Quintly's back!" he shouted. "Places, everybody! Let's go!"

With grunts and groans, the set began to come alive.

Beaming joyfully, Shawn hurried to meet up with Tortilli as the cab headed back to the street.

"Quintly, I didn't think you—"

Tortilli marched past Shawn and straight to Remo.

"It was great!" he enthused. "What a rush! And I owe it all to you. Dead bodies. Blood, heads and brains everywhere. The whole *Starsky and Hutch* and *Baretta* jail thing. Man, what a high-flying, hightailing, highfalutin trip!"

He tried to shake Remo's hand. Somehow, it was never where it seemed to be. Tortilli kept clutching air.

"Damn, how do you do that?" the director gushed.

"Let's go, dummy," Remo replied, peeved.

Shawn had hurried up behind Tortilli. At Remo's suggestion, he shrieked. The Cabbagehead executive quickly inserted himself between them.

"I thought they said they'd booked you or something," Shawn said through clenched teeth. As he spoke, he leaned toward the set, trying through body language to guide Quintly back to work.

Tortilli didn't budge. "Booked, fingerprinted and stuck in a cell with Otis the freaking town drunk," he enthused. "My lawyers did the whole Clarence

"What?" Remo frowned, finally turning from the wing.

"You don't like swear words." Tortilli nodded. "You made that clear when you were strangling me. But when I use swear words in my movies, it's like poetry. All the critics say so."

Remo couldn't even remember what he had said to the director at their first meeting. He decided he didn't really care. He turned back to the window.

The ensuing moment of silence between them was filled by the constant hum of the engines. Soft murmurs of conversation rose from around the cabin. Somewhere close behind, a flight attendant banged items on a serving cart.

"Anyway," Tortilli continued after a short time, "the airplane movie is just one idea I'm working on. Do you realize I've got seventeen sequels in production for my werewolf movie *From Noon till Night?*"

"I'm sure whoever invented Roman numerals is committing suicide right now," Remo muttered.

Tortilli didn't hear him. "Course the first five sequels tanked, but we're bound to hit with one of them," he mused. "Say, do you remember that invasion trouble in Hollywood last year? All those tanks and troops from that Arab country? I forget the name."

In spite of himself, Remo found that he was being drawn in. It was probably good to get his mind off Chiun.

"Ebla," he supplied. "Yeah, I remember."

Tortilli grinned. "That's it. Well, something you might not have heard about was the bombs. There's a rumor that the terrorists wired all of Hollywood to explode. Boom! Everything gone, just like that." He snapped his fingers.

"No kidding," said Remo Williams, the man who had stopped those selfsame bombs from going off.

"Oh, sure. It was kept quiet afterward. I think the government was embarrassed about letting all those tanks and troops and explosives into the country. They gave them all a pass because they thought it was part of a movie."

Remo was rapidly losing interest. "Is this like one of your movies, or do you have a point?" he asked.

Tortilli nodded conspiratorially. "The first movie of the summer season is a make-or-break actioner from Taurus based on those events. *Die Down IV: Don't or Die.*"

Remo's face clouded. "They turned all that into a movie?" he said, appalled.

"It's a fictionalized account," Tortilli replied. "A lone cop is dropped into the middle of the occupation and has to fight his way out. It's gonna be a blockbuster. Opens two weeks before Memorial Day."

"Did it ever occur to whoever's responsible that it's in incredibly bad taste to capitalize on an invasion of America?" Remo asked.

Tortilli frowned at the unfamiliar term. "Bad what?"

Remo shook his head. "Does Hollywood at least get blown up?" he asked hopefully.

"Among other things." Tortilli nodded.

Remo crossed his arms. "Good," he murmured.

"The point is, in the movie, the terrorists smuggle the explosives onto the studio lots. Ring any bells?"

Remo frowned. He'd been so concerned with the Master of Sinanju that he hadn't thought about how all this might relate to his current assignment. Worse, it took Quintly Tortilli to explain it to him.

"They're copying the movie," Remo said dully.

"I guess Cabbagehead wasn't mainstream enough. They've branched out from indies to the summer blockbusters."

Remo considered the implications of what Tortilli was saying. Summer movies were notoriously big on mindless destruction. If the same people responsible for duplicating the plot points from the small Seattle film company had moved on to big-budget Hollywood films, the real-world terror could have just shifted from the equivalent of a firecracker to a nuclear bomb. Literally.

Beside Remo, Quintly Tortilli seemed unfazed by his own deadly deduction.

"*Die Down IV*. Now, that's got some action that'll knock your socks off," the director confided. "The cop is the same one from the first three movies. He has to run through Hollywood, as well as other parts of the country, fighting terrorists and defusing bombs. It's wall-to-wall action.''

"Can't you people make a single summer movie without blowing something up?'' Remo asked, annoyed.

Tortilli shook his head. "You need explosions,'' he argued. "Each big action sequence adds at least ten million to the domestic gross. And they eat the stuff up overseas. My theory is, the more bombs you have going off in a movie, the less dialogue. If no one's talking, foreigners can forget they're watching Americans.''

Again, Tortilli was making sense. It was unnerving.

"*Die Down IV* is so loaded with explosives Lance Wallace—he's the star—barely has to open his mouth,'' Quintly said, pitching his voice low. "Which is a good thing if you've ever seen him act. But don't tell him I said that. I directed him in *Penny Dreadful*. The guy's a loose cannon. If he heard what I *really* thought of him, he'd probably shoot me, then claim he thought I was one of the IRA terrorists.''

"What IRA terrorists?'' Remo asked.

"They're the villains in *Die Down*.''

"I thought you said it was based on what happened in Hollywood last year?'' Remo said, confused.

"It is.''

"Those maniacs weren't IRA. They were Eblans.''

"And Eblans are Arabs, and Arab villains are a big no-no in movies. You can only use white guys. We've replaced the Arabs with a fringe IRA group led by a fey Englishman."

"That's insane," Remo said. "An Englishman is the last person on earth a fringe faction of the IRA would listen to."

"Hey, Hollywood only reflects reality," Quintly Tortilli argued. "Therefore, anything produced in Hollywood must be reality. Therefore, the Arab terrorists must really have been IRA. Maybe they had suntans."

Remo had known it couldn't last. Tortilli was starting to sound like Tortilli again. Blinking wearily, he turned away from the director.

"Here's some Hollywood advice," Remo said, eyes firmly on the wing. "Every second of screen time doesn't have to be filled with dialogue."

Tortilli scrunched his already scrunched face. "Is that a polite way of saying shut up?"

Remo didn't answer. Face concerned, he stared unseeing out the small window.

Quintly Tortilli eventually grew bored.

Getting up from his seat, he wandered up the aisle. He found a stewardess to talk to for the rest of the trip to Los Angeles. When he asked for her number, he told the woman it was all in the name of research. He was thinking of doing a movie where the main character was a female flight attendant. Tortilli was sure it would make a ton of money.

THE RED STUDIO JEEP with its white-striped cloth canopy roof tore off Fifty-seventh Street onto Broadway. Driving crazily through the dodging crowd, it came to a screeching halt in the middle of Times Square.

The vehicle had been built with no doors. Through the wide opening behind the driver's seat flew two frightened blurs. The pair of men slid to a flesh-raking stop at the edge of the crowd. Several bruised hands reached down to help the shaking men to their feet.

The Master of Sinanju emerged from the jeep. "These are the last," Chiun announced darkly.

He had enlisted a driver to help him locate the rest of the missing extras. Luck proved to be on his side. The extras had all been located in the vicinity of six very similar trucks that were parked all around the studio lot.

There was a total of only nine men. All of them seemed afraid to move away from one another. The two new arrivals blended in with the huddled group.

Chiun scanned the line of men, turning with fresh disapproval to Arlen Duggal.

"Why are there not more?" he demanded of the assistant director. "I have been to the vile city after which this fabrication is patterned." He nodded to the mock-up of New York. "Hordes fill its fetid streets."

"This is after the first bombing," Arlen explained as he made some quick notes on his shooting script. "Panic's gripped the city. Most people are afraid to go out."

Chiun allowed a nod of bland acceptance. Padding over, he took up a sentry post behind the A.D., hands thrust deep inside his kimono sleeves. He glowered at the crowd.

Finishing a notation, Arlen looked up from his script.

"Okay, we've wasted enough time already," he called to cast and crew, "so I want this thing done fast and I want it done right."

"Or else," Chiun interjected from behind him.

Arlen flinched, then forged ahead. "We've gotten strong first takes the last couple of days, so let's try to nail it down out of the gate."

"Or the next nails you will see will be those being hammered into your coffins," Chiun said menacingly.

Arlen couldn't take this much longer. Everyone's nerves had been rubbed raw by this maniac screenwriter. The backseat driving and constant threats were already more than he could bear. It was worse than if they'd hired Kevin Costner to star.

It would help morale if they could get the old man off the set, even if it was just for an hour or two. But his vanity was such that he didn't trust Arlen alone for a min—

A thought popped into the assistant director's head.

"People," he muttered, nodding. He wheeled to

the tiny Korean. "Mr. Chiun, you're right," he said excitedly, snapping his fingers.

Chiun's face was bland.

"Of course I am," the Master of Sinanju sniffed. "What is it that I am correct about this time?"

"People. We *do* need more on the streets. A bomb scare wouldn't keep everyone inside. Not in New York. The bravest, wisest, handsomest people would still go outside."

"Perhaps," Chiun admitted, stroking his sliver of beard. "If I needed to."

"Exactly!" the A.D. enthused. "You're wasted behind the scenes. You belong in front of the camera!"

Chiun's hazel eyes sparkled. "Do you really think so?"

"*Absolutely.* Wardrobe!"

One of the wardrobe mistresses hurried forward.

"I want Mr. Chiun outfitted with an appropriate costume," Arlen insisted. "I want him to look perfect, so be sure to take your time," he stressed.

"Is there something wrong with your eye?" Chiun questioned.

Arlen stopped his frantic winking. "I was merely blinded by your dazzling charisma," he covered quickly.

On the sidewalk, the sweating extras seemed thrilled at the thought of Chiun leaving. All nine simultaneously glanced at their watches.

"I understand." The wardrobe woman nodded.

"Sir?" She directed Chiun toward the jeep he'd commandeered.

The Master of Sinanju was only too delighted to go.

"I cannot wait to tell Remo," the old man said, beaming. "I have been discovered."

As Chiun got in the back, the woman climbed in next to the driver. A moment later, they were zipping back in the direction from which Chiun had come mere minutes before.

"Thank God," Arlen exhaled as the jeep vanished down Fifty-seventh. "Next film I work on? No writer," he vowed.

Script in hand, he hurried over to his assistant.

REMO KNEW they were dangerously close to Hollywood airspace when the copilot and navigator came back to discuss the scripts they'd each written. Tortilli took their numbers and shooed them back to the cockpit.

Not only did the director arrange to have their plane land immediately upon arrival over Los Angeles International Airport, but he'd also used the phone on the jet to call ahead for transportation. A long black limousine was waiting for them on the tarmac. They were speeding away from the sleek aircraft less than thirty seconds after they'd deplaned.

"Any news about Taurus?" Tortilli asked the driver.

"Taurus?" the limo driver said. "Are they still in business?"

In the backseat, Tortilli glanced to Remo. "Guess that means it hasn't blown up yet, huh?"

Hope tripped in Remo's chest.

"Put on the radio," he commanded the driver.

"There's one back there, sir," the man offered.

Remo looked down on the row of knobs and buttons arranged on the seat panel. It looked more complicated than the cockpit of the plane he'd just left behind. He saw a TV screen set into the console. Remo opted for this over the radio.

He flipped a switch. A panel opened over an ice bucket. He hit another button. The sunroof slid open, revealing sunny, blue California sky.

"Just put on the damn radio," Remo ordered sourly.

The driver did as he was told.

There was nothing about Taurus Studios on any of the local stations. If a bomb had leveled the place, it would have merited a bulletin. He listened for only a few minutes.

"Shut it off," Remo insisted, sinking glumly back into the plush seat.

His heart thrummed an anxious chorus. As he tapped nervously on the seat, his eyes alighted on the car's phone.

He could have called Smith. Under any other circumstances, *would* have called him without hesitation. But thanks to Chiun, he couldn't. This was all his fault.

"Old egomaniac," he muttered to himself.

"What?"

The voice drew him from his trance. When he glanced at Quintly Tortilli, his gaze was immediately pulled beyond the director. There was a car parked next to them.

Remo suddenly realized they'd stopped.

"Hurry up," he ordered the driver.

"I'm sorry, sir," the limo driver apologized. "The freeway's clogged."

Craning his neck over the driver's shoulder, Remo saw that it was true. Bumper-to-bumper traffic extended as far as the eye could see. At this rate, it would take forever to get to Taurus. By the time he got there, anything could have happened.

"Dammit, Chiun," Remo barked.

Tortilli shot him a worried glance. "Did you say Chiun?" he asked, voice betraying concern.

Remo raised an eyebrow. "Yeah. Why?"

Tortilli bit his cheek. "Oh, no reason," he said with forced casualness. Tugging the creases from the knees of his purple pants, he leaned forward. He rapped his knuckles on the lip of the lowered privacy screen.

"Hurry up," he whispered urgently to the limo driver.

When he glanced back at Remo, his smile was weak.

THE WARDROBE TRAILER for Chiun's film had been

stuffed mostly with police uniforms gathered from the main wardrobe department of Taurus Studios.

Since the film wasn't a period piece, the street clothes the bit players and extras wore onto the lot were generally usable for any given scene. Even so, there were still a few costumes other than uniforms hanging on the racks. These mostly consisted of ordinary suits. The wardrobe mistress directed the Master of Sinanju to one of these.

"It'll be a little big on you, but we can fix you up," she assured him, holding out the double-breasted suit.

Chiun looked first at the suit, then at the woman.

"You are joking," he said dryly, as if she'd just asked him to crawl into the belly of a dead horse. "I will not wear that."

The wardrobe mistress was surprised by his strong reaction. "It's just a suit, sir," she stressed.

"'Just' is correct," Chiun sniffed. "The Master of Sinanju does not wear 'just' an anything. The garment defines the man. *I* am defined by more than just a 'just.'"

Spinning, he marched boldly over to the racks of police uniforms. "I would wear one of these," he proclaimed after an instant's inspection.

The woman laughed, assuming the tiny Asian was making a joke. After all, he'd make about as convincing a police officer as Wally Cox. But when she saw his withering glare, the laughter died in her throat.

"I guess that's okay," she ventured slowly as

she replaced the plain gray business suit on the rack. "But any of those would have to be taken in to fit you, as well."

"Yes, yes," Chiun dismissed. He stroked his wisp of beard as he made his way down the line of blue uniforms.

The wardrobe mistress trailed behind him.

She'd indulge the little man, even though it didn't really matter. Whatever he picked out, it would absolutely not make it into the finished film. She was only supposed to keep the old nuisance busy. This in mind, she forced a patient expression as she stood at Chiun's shoulder.

As he walked, Chiun periodically reached out to feel material. A sleeve here, a lapel there. He har-rumphed his disapproval each time.

At the far end of the rack, the Master of Sinanju stopped abruptly. "*This* is my costume," he gasped, ecstatic.

Grasping hands stuffed deep into the rack, from the knot of uniforms, he extracted an ornate outfit. Gold piping surrounded the cuffs. Matching braids hung from epaulets on each shoulder. It looked as if it hadn't seen the light of day since the silent era.

"That's a little out of date," the woman warned.

"Fashion is fleeting, but style is timeless," Chiun sang happily. He thrust the uniform at the woman. "Tailor it."

The wardrobe mistress bit her tongue. "Whatever you say, *sir*," she said tightly. She gathered the material in her arms.

"I will endeavor to find more to complement my costume," Chiun chimed. Face gleeful, he dived back into the racks.

As the wardrobe woman turned from the squealing lump of bouncing costumes, she had already made an important career decision. If this uniform actually made it into the final print, she would petition to have her name struck from the film's credits. For the survival of the uniform into the finished print would be a sign of something much larger. A box-office bomb.

Eyeing the garish uniform, she doubted her career would survive an explosion of that magnitude.

"I THINK he's gonna be gone for a while," William Scott Cain said in a hoarse whisper. Sweat dotted his upper lip.

The simple boom shot they'd just finished had taken more than forty minutes. The crew was setting up to film the same shot from a different angle.

Lester Craig nodded anxiously. Cold perspiration stained his underarms. "Now would be a good time," he hissed. "While they're busy."

"The setups aren't taking long," whispered another extra, whose truck bomb had been parked closest to the outdoor set on which they stood. Nervous red blotches had erupted all across his chiseled face and tanned neck. "They could be ready any minute."

All nine of the bombers wanted desperately to

leave, yet not one of them moved. Fear of the crazed Asian screenwriter rooted them in place.

Lester's panicked eyes scanned the New York set. There was still no sign of the psycho Korean.

"Look," he said reasonably. "We don't have a whole hell of a lot of time to get out as it is. Either we get blown to bits or he kills us as we try to escape."

"He's so damn fast, though," someone said softly.

"And he sneaks up on you like a frigging cat," another offered. "I bet he's out there right now. Watching us."

Nine pairs of worried eyes scanned the area.

Lester shook his head sharply. "This is ridiculous. We're gonna be blown up, for Christ's sake. I'm taking my chances."

Shoulders tensed, he took a single sidestep from the group. The rest of the men held their breath.

Nothing happened. The demented old Asian who had filled their lives with fear for days didn't come swooping like an angry hawk out of the shadows.

Lester took another hesitant step. Then another.

The crew failed completely to notice, they were so occupied with their own tasks.

Lester made his increasingly rapid way through the cluster of technical and service people toward the edge of the set.

He was home free. It was clear the old man wasn't hiding nearby after all. The fuse was lit for the rest.

They had almost no time left.

The remaining extras went from zero to sixty in one second. They flew—running, shoving, screaming—across the set. Scripts and wires flew everywhere. Booms toppled into cameras in their frantic rush for safety.

A cameraman was pushed into Arlen Duggal. Staggering, he looked up in time to see his handful of extras fleeing the set like the people of Pompeii before the rushing lava.

Even as he shouted after them, his first thought was that Chiun had returned to the set. But the old Korean was nowhere to be seen. And soon neither were his extras.

THE FREEWAY CONGESTION gave way near an off-ramp. It was a mad dash to the Hollywood studios of Taurus. To Remo, the time spent in the limo seemed longer than the plane ride that had preceded it.

Remo was greatly relieved to see the familiar broad white walls of the studio and the huge silver water tower rising high above the lot. He had feared they'd find nothing more than a smoking crater.

The limo squealed to a stop at the main gates.

Unimpressed by one limousine in a town of thousands, the guard on duty was taking his time walking from his shack until Quintly Tortilli shoved his frantic, knotted face out the back window.

"Get your fat ass out of the way!" the director screamed, squinting against the bright sunlight.

The guard recognized him at once. Running into the booth, he raised the wooden arm. As the limo sped onto the lot, Tortilli smiled tightly at Remo.

"Fame has its perks," he said.

"Yeah," Remo replied. He was already scanning for the Master of Sinanju. "It gets you into the belly of a bomb that much faster."

They raced deeper into the tight cluster of whitewashed buildings.

CHIUN STOOD on a squat stool in the wardrobe trailer. His pipe-stem arms were stretched out wide as the wardrobe mistress fussed around the hem of his uniform.

Three body-length mirrors—the two on either side angled slightly inward—stood across from the Master of Sinanju. He was admiring his reflection in the polished glass.

"If only Remo could see me now," Chiun lamented. His eyes were moist.

The wardrobe mistress knew by now that Remo was the old man's son. Adopted. But a good boy nonetheless. Most of the time.

"I'm sure he'd like it." She smiled through a mouthful of straight pins.

"Perhaps," Chiun said. "Perhaps not. My son wears underwear as a shirt and calls it style. However, it would be nice to have someone to show off to. Have you contacted the magicians Bindle and Marmelstein as I have instructed?"

"They're out to lunch."

"Remo has said that about them many times," Chiun nodded. "Have they left the studio?"

"That's what they said at the front office."

"Why would they not eat here?" Chiun asked, puzzled. "The dining hall of the commissar now serves adequate rice."

"That seems like all they serve here now. Maybe they don't like rice," the wardrobe woman suggested. She straightened, rubbing her lower back. "All finished."

All thoughts of the studio executives were banished. Chiun turned to examine himself in the mirrors.

The old-fashioned commissioner's dress uniform he had chosen was not enough for the Master of Sinanju. He had garnished it with his own small touches.

In addition to the gold braids, cuff stripes and shoulder boards that had originally been on the dark blue suit, he had added every police medal he could find on every other uniform and in every case in the wardrobe trailer. With all of these arranged around the chest and back of the uniform, the old Korean now looked like a Communist premier-Christmas tree hybrid.

He had decided that blue was too somber a color for him and so had collected a bright green woman's scarf from a wall peg. He had instructed the wardrobe mistress to pin the scarf under the epaulet of his right shoulder and then pull it to the left side of his shiny leather belt.

His holster was empty, for he refused to carry a handgun. In it, he had arranged a pair of fiery red gloves. They spilled out near the knot in his make-shift sash.

"It is perfect," he announced, a catch in his voice.

"Maybe I should redo that cuff," the woman ventured.

Chiun had noticed her stall tactics early on. He had encouraged her to move more quickly.

The Master of Sinanju shook his head. "It is magic time," he intoned, stepping grandly from his stool.

Chiun gathered up one last garment from the floor.

Somehow, he had managed to locate a Napoleon hat. The woman still had no idea where he'd found that item. He'd had to stuff it with a dress shirt in order to make it fit.

Chiun perched the hat on his bald head. He examined his image in the mirrors one last time before turning.

"I am ready to make history," he breathed.

Huge black boots clomped loudly as the tiny Korean marched from the trailer.

REMO SPOTTED the truck immediately. The big Plotz rental was parked near the front of Soundstage 2, its back closed tightly.

He sprang from the limo and ran to the truck.

No one in the immediate vicinity seemed interested in either him or the vehicle. If it had belonged to a film that was being shot on the Taurus lot, someone would have been yelling at him to get away from it by now.

Quintly Tortilli jogged up from the limo. "What's wrong?" he panted.

"There's the first bomb," Remo replied, jerking a thumb toward the truck.

Tortilli blanched. "Should—should we drive it out of here?" the director whispered, as if his voice alone might set it off.

"That's one way to clear freeway congestion," Remo said dryly. "We have to figure out a way to disarm it." He reached for the lock on the truck's back door.

Tortilli leaped between him and the truck.

"Wait a minute! Wait a minute!" the director snapped. "You can't even figure out how to run a radio."

"Are you volunteering?" Remo said evenly.

Tortilli considered. "Hey, I only do movie explosions," he said finally, taking a nervous step back.

As the director watched anxiously, Remo snapped the thick chain that had been wrapped around the rear handle. Tortilli held his breath as Remo threw open the door.

The bomb didn't go off.

Tortilli exhaled relief. He'd been afraid that it was somehow wired to the handle. When he inhaled, the biting stench from two and a half tons of ammonium nitrate left baking in the Californian sun burned his nostrils. Retching, he pulled the lapel of his polyester suit jacket over his mouth and nose.

Remo kept his own breathing shallow as he climbed into the fetid trailer.

Wan light filtered through the translucent plastic roof. Ominous piles of fertilizer lurked in the shadows.

"Hey, Remo?" Tortilli called from outside, his voice muffled by his suit coat.

"Stop using my name," Remo replied absently. "People will think I know you." He looked around for a detonator, not sure what he'd do when he actually found one.

"There's some guys heading this way," Tortilli pressed.

Remo was frowning deeply. "Tell them to run."

"They *are* running." Tortilli was looking away from the truck, deeper into the center of the studio complex. "I think maybe..." His darting eyes squinted. "I *know* one of them!" he announced suddenly. "From Seattle!" When Remo spun to him, the director had dropped his jacket from his face. "The Dregs!" he cried anxiously. "He must be one of the bombers!"

Remo stuck his head around the rear of the truck.

A group of nine men was racing madly in their direction. Screaming as they went, they shoved people out of the way as they ran, fear and exertion filling their sweat-streaked faces. They ran like men who had glimpsed the future.

Jumping from the truck, Remo flew to the waiting limo. He flung open the rear door.

"Quick! Inside!" Remo yelled to the running men.

Sheer panic offset good judgment. The nine men dived and scrambled into the back of the car. Remo hopped in behind them, slamming the door on the studio lot.

In the limo, the men were panting and swallowing.

"We've got to get *out* of here!" one of them cried. "This place is going to blow!"

Their guilt confirmed, Remo needed to get their attention. Fast. Reaching over, he grabbed one of the men by the throat. He jerked up.

The extra rocketed off the seat at supersonic speed, his skull impacting with a metallic thud against the roof of the car. The roof gave. The man's head gave more.

When Remo dropped him back to the seat, the extra's head was as flat as the bottom of a frying pan. He dumped the dead man into the foot well.

The panting around him stopped with a single unified gasp. Eight pairs of sick eyes were riveted on Remo.

"How many bombs, and where are they?" Remo pressed.

It was Lester Craig who answered. His expression was ill as he glanced at the lifeless form of William Scott Cain.

"Six," he admitted weakly. "All over."

"You all know how to disarm them?" he demanded.

Rapid nods all around.

"You're first," Remo said, grabbing Lester by the shirt.

When he popped the rear limo door, Quintly Tortilli had to jump from its path. Remo dragged Lester onto the road.

"What's going on?" Tortilli pressed nervously.

Remo didn't respond. Striding past the director, he flung Lester through the open back of the parked truck. The extra landed on a pile of reeking fertilizer.

Hopping onto the rear platform, Remo grabbed the door.

"Work fast," he instructed coldly.

He pulled the door closed on the panicked would-be bomber, crushing the lock to prevent escape.

Jumping down, Remo hurried over to the limousine. When he stuck his head inside, seven frightened faces darted up from the body of William Scott Cain.

"How many more of you assholes are here?"

Seven heads shook in unison. "None," seven fearful voices chirped.

A minor silver lining. No one left to set off the remaining bombs. But that wouldn't matter if time ran out on even one of them.

Remo's thoughts spun to the Master of Sinanju. Fear for Chiun's safety kept him from asking how soon the bombs were set to go off. By the looks on the faces of his captives, it had to be any minute.

He hopped into the limo, barking over his shoulder, "Get onto the stages. Warn everyone to clear the lot."

Anxiety flooded Tortilli's face, yet the director didn't argue. As Remo's limo tore off in a squeal of smoking tires, Quintly Tortilli ran toward the nearest soundstage.

13

When Chiun strode grandly onto the set, resplendent in his altered police commissioner's uniform, he was certain his magnificent raiment would cause a jealous stir. Unfortunately, at the instant he appeared, he was upstaged before both cast and crew by some unknown interloper who came racing onto the New York mock-up from the opposite direction.

"It's a bomb!" Quintly Tortilli was screaming at the top of his lungs. His eyes bugged wildly as he ran, arms flailing.

Arlen Duggal turned to the commotion.

"Quintly?" the assistant director asked, as if seeing a ghost. He seemed both surprised and relieved at once.

"It's a bomb, Arlen!" Tortilli screamed, grabbing the A.D. by the biceps.

Arlen pitched his voice low. "I've been thinking the same thing," he whispered. "But no one will listen."

He sucked in his breath when Tortilli squeezed his arms tighter, a look of mad desperation in his eyes.

"Clear the studio!" Tortilli screamed. "There

are bombs set to go off all around us! They're blowing up the studio!''

A crowd was gathering.

''What are you saying, Quintly?'' Arlen asked, confused.

''The extras! The extras planted truck bombs!'' Tortilli released the man, spinning to the others nearby. ''This whole studio is one big bomb! Run for your lives!''

His frantic mannerisms sent a charged ripple of fear through the crowd. As one, those gathered suddenly remembered the urgency with which the missing extras had been running. As if for their own lives.

There was a single frightened moment of clarity. Then hysteria.

Men yelled; women screamed. The pandemonium rippled out from Tortilli all across the set. By the time it reached the approaching Master of Sinanju, it was a tidal wave.

People ran in every direction. Whatever they'd been doing was abandoned. Whatever they'd been holding was flung aside in their desperate charge for safety.

Eyes narrowing to furious slits, Chiun clomped in his big boots through the stampeding mob.

A burly teamster tried to shove the tiny Asian out of his way. His crumpled body fell in the wake of the crowd. No one offered him a hand.

Trailing the rest came Quintly Tortilli. As he ran

past the Master of Sinanju, panic on his face, the old man snagged him by the arm.

It was as if Tortilli had been hit by a truck. He went from a full sprint to a dead stop. His arm felt as if it had been wrenched from the socket. And as he twisted, trying to pull free, Tortilli was confronted by a being who breathed menace from his every pore.

"What is the meaning of this?" Chiun charged, voice low.

"It's a bomb, Sidney Toler!" Tortilli announced.

If it was possible for Chiun's eyes to narrow any more than they already were, they did. A laser would have failed to penetrate the furious slits between his crinkled lids.

"You dare?" Chiun barked.

"What?" Tortilli asked, sensing he'd stepped over some unwritten line. For an instant, confusion vied with fear.

Most of the cast and crew were gone already. The New York lot of Taurus was virtually deserted. Distant shouts rose from beyond the facades of buildings.

"I have heard this term before. You insult my film."

"I don't know what you mean," Tortilli begged. "We've got to get out of here!"

"A boom is another way of saying that a movie is not good," the Master of Sinanju intoned. "By saying *Assassin's Loves* is a boom, you insult my talent."

"This film is *yours?*" Tortilli asked, anxious understanding ignited his face. "*You're* Chiun?"

The old man's nod was crisp. "It is your privilege to know he who will remove your insolent tongue," he menaced.

"Remo!" Tortilli shouted.

The director hadn't even seen the old Korean's fingers flashing toward him. He jumped when the bony hand with its five deadly talons locked in place before his face.

"You know my son?" Chiun asked. His frozen hand did not waver.

"He's your kid?" Tortilli asked, eyeing Chiun's fingernails with no small concern. "Wow. Must run in the family. Yeah. Remo told me— Remo!" He seemed to suddenly snap back to reality. "This studio's a bomb!" he yelled.

Chiun's fingernails retreated inside the baggy sleeves of his police costume. "Explain."

"There are truck bombs everywhere. Remo's trying to defuse them now. He wanted me to clear the studio."

Chiun's eyes widened. "Remo sent you here? Where is he?" the old man demanded.

"I don't know," Tortilli replied hurriedly. "In a limo somewhere on the lot. He's got the terrorists with him. Listen, we've got to get everybody out of here. These things could go off any second. You should get out of here as fast as possible."

When Tortilli turned urgently away, Chiun let

him go. The gangly young man raced from the deserted studio back lot.

Behind him, a frown spread across the parched leather face of the Master of Sinanju.

Chiun could scarcely believe it. His crowning moment of cinematic brilliance, ruined. By Remo, no less.

He'd thought they had put this all behind them. But here it was again, after all these months. Remo's jealousy had returned.

Well, it was high time he put a stop to his pupil's rampant, green-eyed envy once and for all.

Girding his thick leather belt around his narrow waist, the Master of Sinanju clomped angrily off the lot in search of his envious son.

"THERE'S ANOTHER ONE!"

The limo driver had been infected by Remo's sense of urgency. Fingers clenched white on the steering wheel, he spotted the next bright yellow Plotz truck the instant the big car rounded the side of Soundstage 4.

It was positioned in front of the bland walls of the studio's executive office building. The big vehicle was parked across both Hank Bindle's and Bruce Marmelstein's personal parking spaces. In the back of the limo, Remo was stunned the executives hadn't had it towed away.

On the seat across from him, the terrorists were lined up like ducks in a shooting gallery.

When the limo screeched to a stop next to the

parked truck, Remo snatched the next man in line. He popped the door and bounded for the truck. The lock surrendered to a pulverizing blow, and the trailer door rolled open.

Up and in, he flung the terrorist onto the baking fertilizer. Before even a hint of odor could escape the rear, he yanked the door back down, welding the handle in a crushing grip. With two steps and a leap, he was back inside the limo.

"Next," he snapped to the six remaining extras.

"Soundstage 5 is closest," one offered quickly.

Remo didn't even have to ask the driver if he knew the way. The man was already peeling across the lot in a cloud of smoking rubber.

The next truck proved as easy as the first two.

Remo was beginning to think they might make it after all. He had slammed the trailer door and had just dived back into the limo when he heard the first shrieks. The limo was speeding through a shadow cast by one of the soundstages.

"We've got company," the driver said worriedly, easing up on the gas.

Remo leaned over the seat. Through the front windshield, he saw the first screaming man race into view. Blind panic filled his ashen face.

"I hope that's Goldie Hawn's makeup guy," Remo said thinly.

The first man was followed by another. Yet another man and three women followed hot on his heels. The driver had to slow to avoid hitting them.

The floodgates were opened. As Remo's limo

inched forward, a multitude of screaming studio personnel came racing around the corner. The driver slammed on his brakes as the crowd swarmed the sleek black car.

"Tortilli," Remo muttered.

He wasn't sure if he should laud the director for his bravery or kill him for his timing.

The wide avenue between soundstages was clogged with people. The crowd pushed against the car, rocking it wildly on its shocks. Some men scrambled up the hood. Leaden footsteps buckled the roof as they clambered across to the trunk. The sunlight was marred by shadows as the terrified Taurus employees slid down over the small rear window.

People were trampled underfoot. One woman was shoved roughly from behind and knocked through the open door to the nearest soundstage. She didn't reemerge.

"I can't get through this!" the driver shouted. He winced as a boot cracked the windshield.

Remo spun to the last five extras. "Three bombs left?" he asked sharply.

Nods from the terrorists. After a second's rapid calculation, Remo slammed the heel of his hand into the temples of three of the men. So fast were the blows delivered, it was the burst of displaced air before Remo's flying hand that did the actual deed. The two surviving extras watched in shock as their confederates slumped forward.

Pressure from the stampeding throng held the

door in place. Unable to open it without severely injuring passersby, Remo did the next best thing. Fingers curling around the handle, he wrenched. With a shriek of protesting metal, the door collapsed in around its frame. Remo tossed the buckled door to the wide floor.

The noise from the crowd exploded around their ears.

Reaching over the seat, Remo plucked the driver from behind the wheel. "Get ready to run," he instructed the man as he pushed him out the door.

"Wait!" the driver screamed.

Holding the man by the shoulders, Remo hesitated.

"What?" he pressed.

The driver looked sheepish. "It's just that I've got this script I've been working on. If you could let someone know what I did today—"

The rest of what he said was lost. Remo fed the man into the crowd. The limo driver was carried along with the fleeing mob to the main gate.

Plucking up the two remaining terrorists, Remo jumped from the car. He was a salmon swimming upstream as he sprang to the roof of the limo, an extra tucked under each arm. He slid from the hood and met the crowd head-on, butting people from his path by twisting the men he carried right and left. The extras were bruised and bloodied by the time Remo ducked away from the thinning crowd into an adjacent avenue. Soundstages flanked the road.

A huge 5 was painted on one side of the nearest

big building. Beneath the number sat the next Plotz truck.

Remo moved so quickly the next battered extra didn't even know what was happening until he felt himself sinking into fertilizer. Outside, Remo was sealing the door.

"Where's the next one?" he asked the final terrorist.

The man seemed dazed. Blood trickled from gashes in his chin and forehead.

"In the alley between the creative-office complex and the commissary building," he offered, wobbling uncertainly.

"And the last one?"

"Soundstage 9."

Remo had already gathered the man up and was running down the wide avenue when the extra added, "I think."

The crowds were virtually gone by then. Alone on the road, Remo was at a full sprint heading for the commissary. Whitewashed buildings flashed by.

"You don't know?" he demanded.

"I didn't park it. I'm not sure."

Remo finally asked the question he dared not ask earlier. "How much time do we have?" he said, voice grave.

Even as Remo carried him along, the man looked at his watch. He was surprised at how easy it was to read the face. There was no bounce whatsoever to Remo's confident stride.

"Two minutes, ten seconds," the extra said, a freshly worried edge to his quavering voice.

Thanks to his time spent at Taurus the previous year, Remo at least knew the basic layout of the studio. But now he had just over two minutes to eliminate the last two truck bombs on the lot. And no knowledge of the Taurus lot would help him if the last two trucks and the tons of explosive force within them weren't where they were supposed to be.

Face hard, Remo's feet barely brushed the ground as he flew headlong into the ticking maw of death.

14

"How long do we have to keep circling?" Hank Bindle asked, peeved.

The Taurus cochair frowned as he looked out the car window. They were driving down the same strip of Santa Monica Boulevard for what seemed like the millionth time.

Bruce Marmelstein was sitting in the back of the limousine with his partner. He had been staring at the face of his Cartier off and on for the past half hour.

"Don't worry. Any minute now."

Bindle closed his eyes. He took a sip from the martini in his hand. They'd packed extra liquor for this hour of waiting. But it hadn't sat well. Bindle swished the liquid around his mouth before swallowing it with a loud gulp.

"This is ridiculous. We were titans in this town once."

Marmelstein didn't disagree. The fact that he was using the same watch after nearly a full year was proof enough for him that they had fallen on hard times. There was a time he wouldn't have used a simple gold Cartier to bang in a nail.

"It isn't our fault," Marmelstein pointed out somberly. "Circumstances have conspired against us."

"Whatever. At least you have a career to fall back on," Bindle lamented.

"Hairdressing isn't much of a career, Hank."

Bindle nodded. "Yes, but you were *Barbra's* hairdresser. That's something. You know how I broke into the industry? I cleaned leaves out of Liberace's pool. I was a pool boy, Bruce. The things I did for that man just to get my first lousy job as a script reader...." Hank Bindle shuddered. He downed the last of his martini in one gulp. As soon as it was gone, he returned to the stainless-steel decanter in the limo's tiny fridge.

Bruce Marmelstein furrowed his brow.

There was a time when Hank Bindle wouldn't have mentioned the Liberace story. In fact, once he'd become a player in the industry, Bindle had fired anyone who mentioned the word *pool* within a two-block radius of him. But that was then. Now Hank Bindle was sinking into a quagmire of self-pity.

"Liberace is dead. I can't go back there. I *can't* start at the beginning. Not at my age. If this plan goes south, I'll be an unemployed fifty-year-old with a hundred-million-dollar golden parachute." He moaned loudly. "What will I *do* with the rest of my life?"

Bindle swigged his glass dry.

"Get us back to the studio," Marmelstein suddenly announced to the driver over the intercom.

Bindle sniffled. "Is that it? Is it time?"

"It'll be gone by the time we get back," Marmelstein assured him.

"Wait. I think I felt a tremor." Bindle held on to the seat, bracing himself against the imaginary quake.

"It hasn't happened yet," Marmelstein stressed.

"Hmm." Bindle didn't sound convinced. He reached for the fridge once more. "Well, it *better* work. We paid good money for this."

"Don't worry. Soon, Hank. Soon."

When Bindle offered him a martini, Bruce Marmelstein didn't refuse.

BUILDINGS FLEW BY at breakneck speed.

Even as he ran, Remo was mapping a strategy.

The Soundstage 9 truck was first. It was farther away than the other, but he had plans for the last vehicle.

Fortunately, the extra had been right. The truck was where he said it would be.

Though far from an explosives expert, Remo guessed the Plotz truck had been positioned to inflict massive damage on not only Soundstage 9, but also on any structure in the immediate vicinity. Earthquake resistant or not, the flimsy Taurus buildings would have been blown from here to Fresno if all six bombs had gone off.

As he flung the final extra into the rear of the

penultimate truck, Remo prayed the man's confederates had neutralized the other four bombs.

With barely more than a minute to spare, the extra's only hope of survival was to disarm the bomb. He was scrambling over the heap of fertilizer as Remo slammed the door. In no time, Remo was flying across the lot toward the commissary.

His face was steel, his arms and legs featureless blurs as he tore down one avenue and ripped up another.

The roads on which he ran were abandoned. The match of fear had been dropped, and the panic had spread like wildfire through the studio. Everyone had fled. Remo only hoped the Master of Sinanju had gone, as well.

Hurtling around the side of the commissary, he found the last truck precisely where the extra had said it would be. He sprinted to the vehicle.

Thirty-four seconds.

Remo didn't even bother with the trailer. He knew nothing about dismantling bombs. His only hope was to minimize the damage.

As he flung open the cab door, a horrible thought sprang to mind.

"Keys!" Remo hissed.

He'd forgotten to ask for them!

Thirty seconds.

He'd hot-wired cars before, but never that fast. He doubted he could get it done in time.

No time to reconsider. There might yet be people

in the surrounding buildings. He dived beneath the dashboard.

A dangling weight brushed his short hair. Spinning to the source, he found the keys hanging from the ignition an inch from his nose.

"Thank God for amateurs," Remo grumbled, falling back in the driver's seat.

The engine started with a rumbling cough.

Twenty-eight seconds left. How far to drive back across the lot?

Even as he wondered the distance, he was stomping on the gas. The big truck lumbered forward. Slowly at first, but with greater speed with each passing second.

Remo plowed over whatever was in his way. Clothing racks and backdrops were crushed under speeding treads.

Ahead was an open hangar door. Engine building to a throaty protest, Remo jounced through the opening, straight into the soundstage.

In the semidarkness of the huge interior, lights and cameras bounced off the grille. Thick cables thrummed relentlessly below.

Another hangar door. This one closed.

Shifting, Remo accelerated more. A final burst of speed and the truck punched through it, bursting out into bright sunlight.

An instant of relief.

He had oriented himself correctly. The truck was now headed precisely where he wanted it to go.

Eighteen seconds.

All at once, a familiar figure was standing in the truck's path. Daring Remo to run him down. Parchment face furious.

Chiun. He hadn't fled with the rest.

"Get out of the way!" Remo screamed, even as the truck consumed the final distance between him and the Master of Sinanju.

Eyes slivers of angry disbelief, Chiun stood his ground until the last instant. Only when it became clear that Remo had no intention of stopping did he bound from the rushing truck's path.

The instant after the old man's eggshell pate vanished from before the windshield, the passenger's-side door burst open. The Master of Sinanju blew into the speeding truck's cab like a raging wind.

"What is the meaning of this?" Chiun demanded from the seat beside Remo.

"No time," Remo snapped through clenched teeth.

Before them appeared the outdoor New York set. Remo had seen it on one of his bored tours of the studio last year. It looked to have been abandoned for ages. Cries for realism had forced most films and television programs to relocate to the real New York. But today there was equipment everywhere.

"I thought this place was abandoned!" Remo yelled as the truck barreled onto the set.

Equipment crashed away from the cab, flying in every direction as the big vehicle lumbered forward.

Beside him, Chiun's eyes were wide in shock.

"Remo, have you gone mad!" the old man gasped.

Fifteen seconds.

"There's a bomb on board!" Remo screamed.

Hazel eyes grew to saucers of incredulity. *"What?"*

There was no time for further explanation. Only for one last warning.

"Run!" Remo shouted desperately.

And flinging open his door, Remo dropped from the cab.

Even as Remo was jumping out one way, Chiun was leaping out the other. Both men hit the ground running.

Ten seconds.

The truck careered forward, finally crashing headlong into one of the phony buildings. The very real brick wall behind it stopped the truck dead, nose crumpling back through the cab to the trailer.

The impact didn't set off the explosives.

Wordlessly, Remo and Chiun ran. Arms swinging, legs pounding in furious concert.

Neither man looked at the other as they raced side by side for the end of the lot. They hit the main concourse to the soundstages. Still they didn't slow.

In his head, Remo was counting down the time.

Seven seconds.

He remembered the cratered Murrah Federal Building in Oklahoma City and similar blasts at embassies in Africa. They might not be far enough away.

Five seconds.

Running blindly, lungs working furiously.

Not enough distance. Not enough time to get away.

Three seconds.

A concussive wave at his back. Early. The terrorist had miscounted.

He felt himself being lifted in the air; thrown forward.

Something flashed in his peripheral vision. Hands windmilling. Slicing furiously at air. Chiun.

And in that sliver of airborne time at the hellish forefront of a consuming wave of raw explosive energy, Remo finally noticed the Master of Sinanju's costume. In his altered police uniform, the old man looked like Korea's answer to the Keystone Kops.

Remo made a mental note to ask Chiun about the outfit when they reached the Void, for there was no doubt in his mind that they were both going to die.

And as this final thought flitted through the mind of Remo Williams, the wave of intense heat from the powerful blast overwhelmed them.

15

When the sound wave screamed over his prone form, exploding with deafening force in his ears, Remo realized that he had survived the explosion after all.

The ground where he'd landed shook from the intensity of the blast. Pressure waves expelled before the rushing explosive force shattered windows in all of the studio buildings around him. Glass fragments attacked the roadway like shards of finely honed ice.

Even as the sound blew away from him, rumbling furiously into the distance, the wide stretch of road where Remo had been thrown was pelted with a hail of hot gravel and dirt. Chunks of smoldering wood from the flimsy New York facades scattered like matchsticks, curls of smoke rising from their charred ends.

The explosion and its aftermath—even the fact that he had come through in one piece—meant little to Remo. He had only one overriding concern.

As he scampered to his feet, Remo's worried eyes searched for the Master of Sinanju. His tense face became a wash of relief when he spied the old

Korean scurrying out from beneath an abandoned studio jeep. Embers from the explosion had ignited a small fire on the jeep's striped-cloth canopy.

Chiun was getting to his feet when Remo approached.

"That was close," Remo exhaled. As he walked, he slapped grime from his chinos.

"Close!" the Master of Sinanju raged, parchment face flushed red. "Have you lost your mind?" Nails like daggers were clutched in furious fists of bone.

"What's with you?" Remo griped, instantly aggravated at the belligerent stance the old man had taken.

"I will tell you what!" Chiun snapped. "This—this *outrage!*" He waved an angry hand back toward where the explosion had leveled most of Times Square.

From where they stood, only a portion of the set was visible. The buildings had been blown backward, their artificial fronts collapsed onto wooden frames. An unseen spot—presumably ground zero—belched thick acrid smoke over the roof of the nearest soundstage.

Remo was astonished. Chiun was actually mad at him. He stabbed a finger in the same direction.

"That was a freaking bomb, Chiun," he snarled.

"I am not an idiot!" the Master of Sinanju retorted, stomping his big boots in angry frustration. With each stomp, his feet hit the ground a full second after his boots' soles. "I know what it was! What did you think you were doing with it?"

"I *thought* I was saving your life!"

"A likely story," Chiun snapped.

"What's that supposed to mean?"

"You know," the old man intoned coldly. "Do not pretend otherwise."

"I don't," Remo said hotly. "And I can't believe you. The whole way down from goddamn Washington, I was worried out of my mind that you'd be blown to bits when I got here."

"And when you found me still in one piece, you decided to do the job yourself," Chiun accused.

"What the hell are you talking about?" Remo said. "How was I supposed to know you'd be standing in the middle of the street decked out for the Korean touring company of HMS *Pinafore*? And while we're on the subject, what's with that outfit?" He waved a hand from the Napoleon hat that teetered on Chiun's head down to his shiny black boots.

"Do not change the subject," Chiun huffed, adjusting his bright green sash, "from the fact that you tried to kill me."

Remo took a step back, shocked. "What?" he demanded.

"Do not insult me by denying it," Chiun sniffed. As he shook his head, great sadness swelled where anger had been. "Oh, Remo, how could you? A bomb, no less. I knew you were jealous of my incipient fame, but how could you debase our art so completely? Could you not think of a less insulting way to kill me, like a blowgun or even poisoned food? A box of asps delivered to my trailer would have at least shown some inventiveness on your part. But this..." With a sweep of his arm, he took in the smoking debris.

"Look, Chiun," Remo said, attempting to inject a reasonable tone in his voice, "you know how ridiculous this sounds. You accused me of trying to kill you before and you were wrong, remember?"

"My only error was ever being foolish enough to think I was wrong," Chiun said. His hands slipped inside the sleeves of his uniform.

"C'mon, you have to know I would never in a million years try to kill you," Remo argued.

"I know nothing of the sort," Chiun retorted. His frown spread deep across his parchment face. "There is no telling how far behind your sabotage will put this production," he complained. "Had I only known the depths to which you would stoop to undermine me, I would have convinced this studio to produce a low-budget vanity project to keep your resentful mind occupied." Skeletal hands framed an invisible marquee. *"Remo the Boom-Wielding Master: the Adventure Begins."*

"That's the stupidest frigging subtitle in motion-picture history," Remo commented.

"Go on," Chiun offered, grabbing at his chest. "Insult my creativity. Your spiteful words are further proof of your blind malice. O, what a dark day this is for the House of Sinanju. I cannot even begin to think how I will record your actions in the sacred scrolls.''

Remo had been racking his brain for a way to prove his innocence. Chiun's last words offered him an opportunity that hadn't occurred to him.

''Okay, let's look at this from a different perspective,'' Remo began logically. ''In the histories of Sinanju, you want to be called Chiun the Great Teacher, right?''

Horror flooded Chiun's face. ''You have been going through my things?'' he gasped.

Remo rolled his eyes. ''You *showed* me, remember? You were afraid I'd get the Korean characters all wrong when I took over writing the histories.''

''I do not recall,'' Chiun huffed.

''You told me that I was too stupid to get it right and that without proper instruction my Korean characters could lead future generations to think you'd trained a monkey. You had me write the damn thing five thousand times.''

Chiun's nose crinkled in concentration. ''Or perhaps I do remember,'' he admitted.

''Okay,'' Remo said, dropping his bombshell. ''Would Chiun the Great Teacher ever train a pupil who would sink to using a bomb?'' He let the words hang in the air between them.

Chiun grew mute, considering for a long moment.

For the first time since he'd met him, Remo was making logical sense. Maddeningly so. Chiun would never train someone who would deign to use a bomb. Assassinate his teacher, yes—that had been acceptable a handful of times in the long history of the House. But use a bomb? No. With great reluctance, he accepted the truth of his pupil's argument.

"Very well," Chiun grumbled unhappily. "I will grudgingly accept that you did not try to kill me."

"Amen," Remo sighed.

A long nail waggled in Remo's face. "But this does not excuse your vandalism. It would almost be better to use a bomb to kill than to wreak this sort of wanton destruction. Your childish tantrum has disrupted my film."

"Chiun, this had nothing to do with your movie," Remo said. "I really *was* trying to save your life."

"I am perfectly capable of safeguarding my own life," Chiun complained.

"In that getup?"

"My costume is not the issue, Remo. We are discussing your seething resentment of my great talent." He tipped his head, in birdlike curiosity. "But while we are on the subject, do you like it?" He held his hands out wide, offering Remo an unobstructed view of his uniform.

By his tone, Remo could tell that the Master of Sinanju had softened. With at least a semblance of normalcy restored, he felt the day's tension drain from his shoulders.

"It's great, Little Father." He smiled.

"Do you really think so?" Chiun asked worriedly. He turned to offer Remo a full view of the costume's back. "You do not think it is too much?"

Remo shook his head. "It's perfect," he said.

Nodding acceptance, Chiun returned his hands to his baggy sleeves. "I was to wear it in my big scene today," he lamented. "Now I do not know what will become of my debut."

"That's the least of your worries, I'd imagine," Remo said. "That little firecracker wasn't the only one I had to douse. There were five more parked all over the place."

Chiun squinted in confusion. "What are you saying?"

"I'm saying someone was trying to give *blockbuster* a new meaning, and it wasn't me. This studio was rigged to blow sky-high. With you in it," he added.

This time there was no questioning Remo's word. Grave understanding blossomed on the Master of Sinanju's wrinkled face. The old Korean nodded craftily.

"So, the dastards have finally shown their true colors," he uttered, his voice a menacing whisper.

"You came to the same conclusion I did," Remo said tightly. He was thinking about the truck bomb that had been parked across Bindle's and Marmelstein's parking spaces. Under ordinary circumstances, the egotistical Taurus cochairs would never have tolerated an intrusion like that.

Chiun was still nodding. "It could not be more obvious," he insisted.

"I agree," Remo said.

The old man pitched his voice low. "A rival movie studio has learned of my wonderful film and seeks now to ruin it."

Remo blinked. "Um, that's not exactly who I had in mind," he said.

But Chiun wouldn't hear it. "Do you not see?" he pressed. "This is a fierce business, Remo. Full of scoundrels and cutthroats. We must guard my film against further assault from the knaves at Paramount."

"Paramount?" Remo asked warily.

"It does not necessarily have to be them," Chiun confided. "It could very well be Twentieth Century Fox or Columbia. In truth, I do not trust any of the Warner brothers. This sort of thing would not be beyond them."

"I don't think any of them are still alive," Remo suggested. "And I don't think this was a rival studio."

"You are naive, Remo—" Chiun nodded "—as was I when first I arrived on this, the Lost Coast of America. Be warned—there are enemies lurking around every corner."

"Some corners closer than you think," Remo muttered dryly. "Listen, Chiun, the only reason I even got wind of this is because I'm on an assignment." He went on to give a rapid outline of the situation, concluding, "Is there a scene in your movie where a Hollywood studio gets blown up?"

Chiun shook his head. "There was, but it was

removed,'' he admitted. "These fools made many alterations to my original *Assassin's Loves,* but that is no longer one of them.''

Remo hummed thoughtfully, glancing at the plume of smoke still rising from the blast site. It had trickled to a serpent curl of black. In the distance, the sounds of sirens rose over the soundstages.

"It's still tied in somehow," Remo said firmly. "And I bet I know who can connect the dots.''

16

From a distance, they saw a single thinning thread of black smoke curling up beyond the high walls. It appeared to be coming from the rear lots at the far, far walls of the complex. Otherwise, Taurus Studios seemed completely intact.

"Something went wrong," Hank Bindle droned as their limo drove along the outside of the plain white walls.

Beside him, an ashen-faced Bruce Marmelstein slugged down the last of his martini before numbly dropping the empty glass to the green crushed-velvet seat.

Fearful gawkers crammed every inch along the sidewalk, among them hordes of Taurus employees.

"No explosion and now we're paying them to stand around," Bindle complained. He powered down a tinted window. "Get back to work!" he shouted to a kid on a bicycle. The boy responded by giving Hank Bindle the finger. "Did you see that?" the executive snapped at his partner. He stuck his face out the window. "I'm gonna ruin you! Try delivering papers in this town after today, you little punk!"

Many of the people spilled over into the road, clogging traffic and blocking emergency vehicles. No police at the gates meant there was no one to deny them access to the studio lot.

"Hurry up and go in!" Marmelstein snapped over the speaker when their driver hesitated at the main entrance.

Leaving the crowd behind, they drove onto the lot.

The buildings were perfect, just as they'd left them. There wasn't so much as a scratch or even a single bird dropping on the white facades.

"Maybe it hasn't happened yet," Bindle ventured.

"I think it did," Marmelstein replied. His sick eyes watched the distant smoke dissipating across the pale blue California sky. "But it was a big fat dud."

"We didn't pay for a dud," Bindle whined.

Driving deeper onto the lot, they finally saw the only obvious effects of the single exploded truck bomb. Hundreds upon hundreds of cracked windowpanes. Farther along, they could see those windows closest to the blast site had shattered completely. But otherwise, everything was exactly as they'd left it.

"This is not good," Bruce Marmelstein said woodenly as the limo stopped in front of the executive office building.

"Broken windows," Hank Bindle lamented. "A

few measly broken windows. I don't think our insurance even covers broken windows.''

The Taurus cochairs waited for their driver to run around and open the back door. Climbing out, they smelled the hint of smoke on the breeze.

''Smoke,'' Marmelstein complained. He placed a pinkie ring to his surgically altered chin. ''I should be standing this deep in rubble right now.''

A horrified gasp from his partner snapped his attention away from the lack of mess.

''What the hell is this?'' Hank Bindle hissed.

When Marmelstein looked, his partner was standing near their reserved parking spaces. A large truck had been parked across both exclusive spots. The only portion of either of their names still visible was the gilded ''dle'' of ''Bindle.''

''This is great!'' Bindle raged. ''This is fucking *great!*'' He launched a Gucci toe into the side of the truck. ''Un-fucking-believable!'' As he shouted, he repeatedly kicked the side of the truck in punctuation. ''A fucking dud of a fucking bomb and on top of every fucking other fucking fuck-hole thing that has happened to-fucking-day, a fucking truck is parked in *my* fucking space.''

Each successive word brought a more violent kick from the studio executive. Sweating and red faced, he was enlarging the dent he'd already made in the truck's side when he heard a timid voice behind him.

''Um, Hank?''

Hank froze in midpunt. Turning angrily, he saw

Bruce Marmelstein's eyes and nose peeking over the trunk of their limo. A nervous finger appeared next to the nose. It pointed carefully at the gleaming yellow truck.

"You're kicking one of the bombs," Marmelstein whispered.

Confusion lasted only as long as it took Hank Bindle to turn ever so slowly to the truck. The giant Plotz letters stenciled on its side stared down ominously at him. When he looked back at his cowering partner, his eyes were wide.

Screaming for his mommy, Bindle dived over the trunk of the limo, collapsing painfully to elbows and knees next to Marmelstein. He scurried to a kneeling position. Both Taurus cochairs peeked over the roof.

The truck remained silent.

"Do up think it's kick activated?" Bindle whispered.

"It didn't do that thing bombs do," Marmelstein said. "You know, that ka-boom thing?"

Both men stared apprehensively at the truck. It persisted in not ka-booming. Bindle took this as a sign.

He pointed to the building.

"Maybe we should go inside," he mouthed.

Marmelstein only nodded. Together, they crept to the gleaming glass doors of the executive office building.

When the cracked panes swung closed between them and the truck bomb that was capable of not only leveling the building they were in, but also obliterating several other buildings in the near vicinity, the two film executives breathed a sigh of relief.

They took the elevator up to their office suite.

The interior glass doors between their inner sanctum and their secretary's office had survived the blast. They pushed inside, trudging wearily onto the plush carpet.

They hadn't gone more than three steps toward their desks when they were surprised by a frighteningly familiar voice.

"The imbeciles return to the scene of the crime."

Stunned, Bindle and Marmelstein wheeled around. Their eyes grew wide when they saw Remo leaning against the stucco wall next to the office door. Fear clutched their bellies.

The door was blocked. As one, they settled for the next best thing. In a tangle of panicked legs, they made a mad dash for the picture window.

Hank Bindle dived into the pane headfirst. Though cracked, the glass didn't give. He dropped like a stone to the carpet, clutching his bloodied forehead.

Bruce Marmelstein did a karate-like flying kick. He missed the window completely, slamming instead into the mahogany wet bar. He bounced from bar, to desk, to floor. His landing was surprisingly soft, if a little lumpy.

"Get off me," the lump that was Hank Bindle gasped.

Using knees and fists, Bindle knocked Marmelstein off. Both men collapsed, panting, onto their backs. They found themselves staring up into Remo's hard face.

"Now that we've got the floor show out of the way," Remo said.

They had met Mr. Chiun's friend during the Hollywood terrorist crisis. At the time, Taurus had been purchased by the leader of a Mideast nation as a front for his invasion. Bindle and Marmelstein didn't know this. Even as tanks rolled down the streets of Hollywood, they were only interested in making the biggest movie ever.

Only afterward did they really learn that they had participated in the most infamous case of terrorism to ever kiss American soil. Even so, neither Bindle nor Marmelstein ever fully realized what had actually happened back then. The one thing that they did know, however—the thing that they had carried with them ever since that time—was a fear of those dark, deep-set eyes. They had never wanted to look into those eyes again. But here they were. Back once more. And more frightening than either man remembered.

"So, Mr. Remo," Hank Bindle said, smiling weakly into Remo's upside-down face, "what brings you back here?" Still flat on his back, he attempted to cross his legs casually.

"Knock it off, you ninnies," Remo growled. Reaching down, he dragged the two men into seated positions on the rug. "Who'd you hire to blow up the studio?" he demanded.

"The studio?" Marmelstein bluffed. "Oh, did that blow up?"

Fear compelled Hank Bindle into trying another tack. "Bruce hired him," Bindle blurted, pointing at his partner.

Bruce Marmelstein's eyebrows nearly launched off the top of his head. "We both did," he countered angrily.

"But he came to you first."

"He came to both of us."

"On *your* speakerphone," Bindle proclaimed. "*Your* ears were closest."

"I'll show you close ears!" Marmelstein screeched.

He was scrambling across the floor, hands snatching for his partner's bobbed ears, when he felt something grab on to his ankle. All of a sudden, he was off the floor and his desk was flying toward him very fast. When they met, his head made the desk's steel surface go *clang!* The desk, in turn, made Marmelstein's head ring. It was still ringing when Remo dumped the executive back to the floor.

"From a strictly technical standpoint, I might have been involved in the actual hiring, too," Hank Bindle admitted, eyeing his partner worriedly.

"Who'd you hire?" Remo pressed.

"He called anonymously." Marmelstein winced, rubbing the growing bump on his forehead.

"And he got through?" Remo asked, dubious,

remembering the hard time he'd had calling from Seattle.

"He said he was Hank's masseur," Marmelstein offered. "Priority stuff like that gets right through."

Bindle nodded. "I've been feeling very tight in my shoulder. I was shot last year, you know."

"Too bad he didn't have better aim," Remo said, deadpan. "What did the guy on the phone say?"

"That he had a surefire way of boosting a movie's gross. I think he might have just been putting out feelers at the time. You know, calling all the studios. Pitching the idea. This was before the Cabbagehead thing," Marmelstein said.

"You know about that?" Remo said flatly.

"Everyone in town knows about it," Bindle insisted. "What a marketing coup. *Suburban Decay* wouldn't have been a blip if it wasn't for that family getting whacked."

Remo's eyes went cold. "People died, Bindle," he said evenly.

"People never die," Bindle insisted. "Look at Freddy Krueger. He's been dead a bunch of times. How many times has Jason been zapped by lightning and brought back? Hell, Spock wasn't even gone a whole movie." He smiled brightly.

Remo wanted to be amazed. Appalled, even. But this was typical Hollywood. Hank Bindle wasn't capable of separating real life from the fiction of film.

"Of course, we know that people actually technically do die," Marmelstein offered when he saw

Remo's hard expression. "But they were going to eventually anyway. And if their deaths can spark something at the box office, why not give their lives some meaning?" He smiled and nodded, the very soul of reasonableness.

At that moment, Chiun and his movie were the only things preventing Remo from giving meaning to the lives of Bindle and Marmelstein. By Herculean effort, he kept his more violent urges in check.

"How much?" he asked, jaw clenched tightly.

"To do the lot?" Bindle asked. "Eight million."

"Which we hid in the production costs of your friend's movie," Marmelstein added. By the look Bindle shot him, he realized he had made some verbal misstep.

"It wouldn't have been too critical to the production," Bindle cut in. "After all, we've still got the Burbank lot."

"None of the principal actors were here," Marmelstein offered brightly. Again, he got the same look from his partner.

"Plus Taurus would get some ink for a change," Bindle interjected hurriedly.

"The publicity would have been worth it alone."

"And the insurance would cover the cost of everything afterward."

"Nothing but wins." Marmelstein smiled.

"Mmm-hmm," Remo said. "And how many people were on the lot when the bombs were supposed to go off?"

"Gee, I don't know," Bindle said, eyes flirting with the periphery of worry. "Bruce?"

"I'd have to check with personnel. A thousand, two thousand? We've got tons of people here all day."

"Including Chiun," Remo said, tone flat.

Marmelstein suddenly realized why his partner had been shooting him such dirty looks.

"Oh, was he here?" Marmelstein asked, all innocence.

Remo didn't press it.

"Okay, were you supposed to talk to the guy who arranged the bombing afterward?" he asked.

"For other matters," Marmelstein admitted vaguely.

"More box-office boosting?" Remo said, disgust in his face.

"That might have been an item on the agenda," Bindle said uncertainly.

"That stops now." He was thinking of Smith. If the anonymous caller phoned back, the CURE director could probably trace the call to its source.

Remo glanced down at the two Taurus executives.

Bindle's forehead still bled from his unsuccessful assault on the second-story office window. Marmelstein nursed the swelling purple lump on his own head. Sitting on the floor, they watched Remo expectantly. Dogs fearful of an unpredictable master.

Remo's thin lips were stretched tight.

"You two dolts are lucky," he menaced. "If

anything had happened to Chiun. Anything at all..."

In a whistling blur, Remo brought his hand up and around, slapping it against Hank Bindle's massive stainless-steel desk. The desk made an ugly crackling sound like that of ice dropped in warm water. A black, razor-slice fault line shot across the desk's surface. When it reached the far side, the huge steel slab dropped open.

As the two sections thundered onto the carpeted floor, Remo was already turning away. The room-rattling boom was reverberating in Bindle's and Marmelstein's ears when he slipped from the room.

It was several seconds later—as the last aftershocks were dissipating in the building's foundation—when Bruce Marmelstein finally got up the nerve to speak.

"I don't know what they've got against our desks," he whispered. Hand clapped on his forehead, he climbed uncertainly to his feet.

Bindle followed suit.

"Think we should we have told him about that other little thing?" Bindle asked as he examined the huge desk sections.

"New York? Are you crazy? Absolutely not," Marmelstein insisted. "If he was upset by almost deaths...well..." his voice trailed off.

"I suppose," Bindle agreed reluctantly. "At least we could tell him about—"

"*No!* We're not telling him anything," Marmelstein snapped before his partner had a chance to finish. "Hank, we have got to save this turkey one way or another. God knows it's not going to do any box office on its own. We need a boost."

Eyes worried, Bindle slowly nodded. But even as he agreed with his Taurus cochairman, he couldn't pull his eyes from the shattered remnants of his desk.

It was nearly half an hour since the sole truck bomb had exploded. Police and fire officials had cordoned off the Taurus lot. Remo had Soundstage 9 to himself as he called Smith from an old rotary phone he found on a desk near the big hangar's small side door.

"Report," the CURE director said without preamble.

"I'm in Hollywood," Remo replied, displeasure at his location evident in his voice. "Someone just tried to relocate Taurus Studios to Neptune."

"Yes," Smith said. "My computers just alerted me to the explosion. A truck bomb, according to reports."

"Try *bombs*," Remo stressed. "I stopped five. You're hearing about the one that got away."

"Given your presence there, presumably this is connected to the Seattle situation?"

"Yeah," Remo said. "The box-murder punks led me here."

"They were responsible for the studio bombing, as well?"

"No, I iced them back in Washington. Different

psychos, same agenda. You remember Bindle and Marmelstein?''

''I was surprised to see that they are still cochairs of Taurus,'' Smith answered. ''After the financial fiasco of last year, I would have thought they would be gone with the new regime.''

''Gotta love Hollywood,'' Remo said. ''The bigger the disaster on your résumé, the higher up you go. Anyway, they're the ones who hired someone to blow up Taurus.''

Smith was stunned. ''Their own studio?'' he asked, incredulous.

''A bomb out of Taurus,'' Remo offered. ''You have to admit, what they lack in smarts they make up for in irony.''

''Remo, what possible reason did they have?'' Smith pressed.

''Insurance, career move, a high-colonic Rorschach told them to do it? Who knows with those clowns? I don't think the studio is long for this world, Smitty. Nishitsu bought the place after the Ebla debacle, then turned and sold it to some buggy Vegas billionaire casino owner. Rumor is he's planning on selling everything off. From the studio's film archives down to the last can of Who Hash. If it's true, Bindle and Marmelstein are out on their lifted asses.''

''And as revenge they wanted to blow up the studio?'' Smith asked, amazement fading. He had met the two men once. Hard as it might be to believe, there seemed little they'd be incapable of.

"I doubt it was revenge," Remo said. "More like desperation. You've got to understand these guys, Smitty. They're not like real human people. They don't really think things through. I think they probably just want to get through their next picture."

"Explain," Smith said crisply.

"The movie's costing a bundle to make. They figured they'd trash the Hollywood studio, relocate completely to Burbank and use the notoriety of the explosion to give them a bump at the box office. If this one movie is a hit, they might be able to put the studio back on track. Either that or at the very least they could parlay that hit into a job with another studio. Course, there'd be a lot of dead bodies to clean up, but they could always put the key grips and gaffers on corpse patrol. Pending approval of SAG, the AFL-CIO and the local medical examiner's union, of course."

"Amazing," Smith said. "Were they able to shed light on who is responsible for all of these occurrences?"

"No," Remo said. "It's the same as Seattle. An anonymous phone caller arranges everything for cash. But Bindle and Marmelstein seemed pretty sure everyone in town knows about the box-office boosting that's been going on. If they're right, any of those guys on the Cabbagehead backers' list is likely to know about it, too."

"Hmm," Smith mused. "I had no luck with the phone records at the Randolph apartment in Seattle.

But if we know that the individual behind this has been in contact with the larger Hollywood studios, there might be a way to winnow out the field on that end, assuming the same phone was used.''

"That sounds like a big *if*," Remo said.

"It is all we have at the moment. I will instruct the mainframes to begin a search of phone-company records. They will sort through all of the calls to the major studios and match those that are identical.''

"How long will that take?''

"Perhaps several hours,'' Smith said, "but given the incestuous nature of the entertainment industry, it could well be several days.''

Neither Remo nor Smith was pleased with waiting that long. Particularly for a lead that might not even pan out.

"Okay,'' Remo sighed. "At least bug Bindle and Marmelstein's phones. They said the guy was supposed to call in after he blew up the studio.''

"Perhaps given his failure, the engineer will not even call,'' Smith speculated. "I will tap into their phone line just in case.'' The sound of the CURE director's efficient drumming fingers issued over the line. He spoke as he typed. "There were agents on the scene, presumably.'' Given the fact that there were six bombs in all, it was a statement of fact, not a question.

"I just talked to a couple of them before I called,'' Remo said. "They were hired like the others. A voice on the phone. If it's any help, only one of them was from Seattle. The rest were hired out of some crummy local acting class.''

"They were actors?" Smith said, surprised.

"Not real *actor* actors," Remo explained. "They were just extras on a movie that's being filmed here. That's what got them access to the studio in the first place. They got their ten bucks in the mail.''

Smith hesitated. "Remo, are you saying they were hired to blow up a Hollywood studio and kill countless numbers of innocent people for a mere ten dollars?''

"Apiece," Remo said. "And if you're shocked by that, then you've never been a struggling L.A. actor.''

Smith let it pass. "I will see what can be dredged up as far as the phone records are concerned.''

He was about to terminate the call when Remo broke in.

"While I'm cooling my heels, I could rattle a few cages around here. Stefan Schoenburg and the other Cabbagehead backers are just a derivative screenplay away.''

There was a moment of consideration during which Remo heard only Smith's nasal breathing. When he finally spoke, the older man sounded infinitely tired.

"No," Smith sighed wearily.

"C'mon, Smitty. It's either that or I hang around here watching Bruce Marmelstein apply wrinkle cream every twenty minutes. And you don't want to know where he puts it.''

"No, Remo," Smith insisted. "The situation for us is more delicate than it might normally be." The next words he spoke sounded like a guilty admission. "Schoenburg and the rest have all been generous supporters of the President."

Remo was taken aback. "We never worried about that junk before, Smitty. We're not political, remember?"

"We are not," Smith agreed. "But the President has been making things exceedingly—" he hesitated, trying to put the most tactful spin on things "—difficult of late."

"Since when?" Remo pressed. "This is the first I'm hearing about it."

"It did not concern you," Smith said. "Nor does it now. I am only informing you of this so that you do not do anything rash. Remo, I will not hesitate to send you after Schoenburg if he is implicated in this affair. Until such time, however, it is in this agency's best interest to avoid unnecessary complications."

Smith had to struggle to get out every word. They obviously did not sit well with the older man's rock-ribbed New England soul.

For a long time, Remo had told himself that he didn't like Smith. His employer was cheap, coldhearted and had the personality of a moldy cod. But for more years than he sometimes cared to remember, Smith had been a major part of his life. The CURE director had even *saved* Remo's life on a number of occasions. Like it or not, Remo had come to a reluctant conclusion a long time ago: Smith mattered to him.

And now, thanks to the time in which they now lived, the man whose conduct as head of CURE had always been above reproach was being pressured into disregarding one of the basic founding tenets of the agency he had built.

Remo wasn't particularly fond of any President, but he'd decided early on that the current occupant of the White House was a political bottom feeder. He hadn't thought he could like the man any less. Until now.

Remo decided not to press the issue.

"Let me know if you find anything," he said after an awkward moment of silence.

"I will," Smith said, a hint of relief evident in his lemony tone, as if he'd expected Remo to argue the point. "If I learn anything from the phone records, I will call you at Bindle and Marmelstein's office."

Wordlessly, Remo dropped the phone back in its cradle.

The soundstage seemed big and drafty. Like another world. In spite of the soundproofing, Remo could hear the occasional lone siren beyond the nearby wall. Most had already found their way to the New York set.

Remo heard without hearing. His thoughts were on Smith.

The President was a man who had slid to the top on a track greased with lies and false smiles. He couldn't begin to understand the sacrifices someone like Smith had made.

Although the possibility for friction had been there from the start, Smith's love of country had always superseded any personal distaste. He had worked with the nation's Chief Executive for one and a half terms. And now, with the light of day visible at the end of the dark tunnel, the President had finally turned his destructive sights on CURE.

"Just hunker down, Smitty," Remo muttered to the empty hangar. "One more year and he's history."

Unknown to Remo, forces were conspiring at that moment to reduce the President's second term by a quarter.

18

Reginald Hardwin was a brilliant actor who, for one reason or another, had never quite made it.

That he was an acting genius was without doubt. All anyone had to do was ask him. He was on a level so far above the rest of the noisome rabble, as he called his peers, that he would need a telescope to properly look down on them. If they were stars twinkling in the heavens of celebrity, his talent as a thespian was the midday sun.

But fate had conspired against poor Reginald Hardwin.

He had just missed being Richard Burton.

Too young.

He was almost Anthony Hopkins.

Too sober.

He should have been Jeremy Irons.

Too old.

For twenty years, he watched the stars of others rise higher and higher in the heavens while he toiled anonymously in repertory theaters around America. He was Prospero in Connecticut, Mercutio in San Francisco and Falstaff in Miami. His Lear was the finest ever seen in Des Moines.

Even with an impressive list of credits "on the boards," Hardwin had never snatched that elusive gold ring of acting: movie stardom.

Of course, early in his career he had pooh-poohed the entire concept of film acting. That sort of thing might be fine for the likes of Olivier and Gielgud, but he was a real actor. His first love was the stage. Anything else smacked of cheap commercialism.

Hardwin held this conceit for as long as it took him to realize that Hollywood not only was not beating down his door, it didn't even know where his door was.

He quickly changed his game plan.

Hollywood might not have sought him out, but that only meant they hadn't taken the time to pull their noses out of their plebeian scripts long enough to see what a real actor was. He decided that he would go on casting calls just for the fun of it, rejecting on principle any and all offers that came his way.

Reginald was certain that there would be offers. He was certain of this fact during the months after demeaning months he spent traipsing from one studio to another meeting with agents, directors and producers.

The realization that he'd been wrong to believe so wholeheartedly in the certainty of his eventual offers finally sank in one cool California evening when he returned home from yet another round of casting calls.

His mailbox was empty. Again.

Okay, technically it wasn't empty. Actually, it was only clear of film offers. It was full of other things. Like bills from the telephone company, the gas company, the electric company, his Strasberg Method class—what was he thinking?—and about a dozen other invoices.

That night, sitting on the stoop of his Rosecrans Avenue apartment in the Compton section of L.A., the sounds of revving car engines and the gunshots of gang warfare rising softly to his ears, Reginald Hardwin had a revelation.

He had been wrong. Desperately so.

Not about his basic thesis, mind you. He was still possibly the greatest actor who had ever lived— certainly the greatest living actor—but something else occurred to him that night. The well had been poisoned by bad actors.

He was missing out on acting jobs because all of the famous actors working in the business were so inferior to him that no one knew any longer what a good actor was.

By that time, three years had come and gone since Reginald had first started going on auditions. In that time, the happy lark that had marked the beginning of his search for film work had evolved into a much more serious quest for employment. But that night the seriousness of Hardwin's search reached epic proportions.

He started going on more auditions. Every single

one he heard of. Morning, noon or night. It didn't matter. He was like a man obsessed.

There was nothing beneath his dignity. Once, he even donned a dress and wig, hoping that it would get him a job in a panty hose commercial. After offering certain "favors" to the man casting the ad in question, the only thing his zeal got him was an appearance before a local judge.

Even with such setbacks, his new blitzkrieg did net him a few jobs over the years. He got work doing voice-overs for radio spots. He was an apple in a men's underwear ad. He even worked with Lord Larry himself in *Clash of the Titans*, but was later cut out of the final print. Hardwin suspected that it was fear on Olivier's part. The old fraud didn't want to be upstaged by a much more talented younger actor.

But the thing Reginald Hardwin truly wanted— huge success in the motion-picture industry with the accompanying chance to thumb his nose at that success—always eluded him.

Until the call.

It came late in his career. Reginald Hardwin was in his midforties—although his birth certificate back in Norwich, England, would have disputed that claim by more than a decade.

The caller had stated the obvious. That Hardwin was a genius whose talents had been squandered over the years.

"I don't even know who you are, yet you are the

most perceptive individual I have ever met,'' Reginald Hardwin told the anonymous caller.

"It must be awful to be so great and have no one recognize that greatness,'' the caller said.

"You have no idea,'' Hardwin replied.

"How would you like recognition? How would you like everyone everywhere to know your name? To never forget who you are?''

"I would rather have cash,'' Hardwin replied.

To his surprise, he had gotten it. Five million dollars arrived by courier that afternoon. Cash.

Since he was between agents at the time, Reginald didn't have to parcel out an automatic fifteen percent. And since it was in cash, he didn't have to bother with the pesky bloodsuckers of the Internal Revenue Service. Happily, he didn't have to part with one red cent.

"You got the money,'' the voice of the stranger stated in his subsequent phone call.

"I did,'' Hardwin had replied. He was trying to remain blasé. As if five million dollars were nothing to him.

"All five million?''

It was an odd question to ask. "Yes,'' Hardwin admitted.

The caller's voice seemed to soften. "I need you to do a little something for me.''

It was the way he said it. Reginald Hardwin stiffened. "I won't do anything illegal,'' he sniffed.

"In that case, give me my money back.''

The thought horrified Reginald Hardwin. "I will

not," he said. Thinking quickly, he added in a scheming tone, "Besides, I never have to admit you sent me one nickel. It was not a check, remember. There is no record. I'm afraid you're out of luck, poor boy."

"You signed for the money, Reggie," the caller said. "That alone is proof enough to the IRS. You lose half right off the top to them. Then the Feds will probably want to know where the money came from. With that much at once and no work to show for it, their first thought will be drugs. On top of all that, I have you on tape just now admitting that you accepted it. That might not be admissible evidence, but a judge could take it into consideration. Now, knowing all this, I think that you'll want to return the money to me if I ask for it. If only to keep yourself out of trouble."

Hardwin had grown more fearful as the caller went through his obviously prepared speech. It almost sounded as if he was reading. Hardwin was practically in tears by the time the man finished.

"But I want to keep my money," he cried.

"You can, Reggie. Don't worry. I have no interest in taking it back from you. Not if you do as I say. You will do as I say, won't you, Reggie?"

Hardwin had reluctantly agreed. The caller—whom he now knew only as Captain Kill—had convinced him that it was easier to do things as long as he stayed "in character." He was right.

Hardwin was in character when he had taken over the reins of GlassCo in New Jersey, the dummy company set up by his phantom employer. Many of the men working under him there were actors in character, as well. The rest were just thugs hired by the voice on the phone.

In the gig set up by his mysterious employer, Hardwin stayed in character for the duration of their planting the explosives in the Regency Building in Manhattan. He had remained in character even after he had detonated the explosives and watched the thirty-second floor of the office building blast outward in a spray of fine crystalline glass.

It was rather liberating. And most importantly, it was *acting*. A big, meaty, over-the-top role. The kind of acting he had never been able to do in his professional career.

His employer had sent Reginald Hardwin the bio of his character, who also happened to be named Reginald Hardwin.

He was a member of the British aristocracy, according to the back-story. A former member of Her Majesty's Strategic Air Services, he had had a falling-out with his government. Stumbling into the underworld, he had gotten hooked up with the Irish Republican Army. One thing had led to another after that. The British wanted him. The Americans wanted him. It was all frightfully exciting. And very, very real. For fiction, that is.

The really wonderful thing was the way he had gotten lost in the part of Reginald Hardwin. For the first time ever, he felt that he had really found himself as an actor.

Of course, the fictitious Reginald Hardwin was responsible for some truly terrible things. But the real Reginald couldn't be blamed for anything that had gone on so far. He was an actor, hired to play a part.

A part he played brilliantly.

For both Reginald Hardwin the fictional character and Reginald Hardwin the actor, the explosion at the Regency Building was far behind. It was another day, another scene.

"Exterior, street, day," Hardwin muttered to himself as he strode confidently up the broad sidewalk. The metal fence rose high to his left.

It was overcast. Swollen gray clouds painted the bleak inverted bowl that was the sky. Here and there, patches of much deeper black threatened the thunderstorms local weathermen had predicted for later that afternoon.

As Reginald walked, he heard the first distant rumblings coming from the heavens. He wondered if it might not be a portent. After all, the weather always meant much to Shakespeare.

Around him, tourists began to eye the clouds with increasing concern. Some packed away expensive cameras, ready to dash for the cover of their parked cars or tour buses if it became necessary.

It would have to go quickly. The plan demanded that he and his men be mistaken for ordinary tourists.

As he strolled along, Reginald's wristwatch timer

beeped abruptly. The moment it did, he stopped at the fence.

There were no guards here. The only ones he'd seen were at the entrance he had passed a dozen yards away.

There was a stone wall about two feet high just before the eight-foot-tall fence.

Reginald popped the latches on the briefcase he was carrying and reached quickly inside. He removed a light parcel that consisted of four small plastique charges, connected by wires. Adhesive was attached to each charge.

Efficiently, still in character, Hardwin stuck the charges to the two slender posts in the wrought-iron fence—two high, two low.

Already motion detectors and surveillance cameras would have picked him up. Inside they were already reacting. It didn't matter. There were too many of them out there. A veritable army all acting in unison.

All around the perimeter fence, dozens of men were repeating the same movements at precisely the same moment. They reached into raincoats and jackets, bags and knapsacks.

As Hardwin positioned the last charge, he felt a tug on his arm.

"What the hell are doing?" An accusation.

He turned.

Fat face. Beet red. Angry.

So typically American; leaping blindly into the fray.

Reginald Hardwin smiled at the man. "Are you a cowboy?" he asked smoothly.

The tourist seemed baffled by the non sequitur. And in that brief moment of hesitation, Reginald pulled his Heckler & Koch pistol from its shoulder holster, aimed it at the man's surprised face and pulled the trigger.

The man's brains hadn't even splattered across the neatly swept sidewalk before Hardwin was flinging himself in the opposite direction.

Poom!

The charges detonated just as he was rolling up against the protective squat wall.

He bounded up in the next instant.

The plastic explosives had ripped through the pair of metal bars. Gathering his briefcase, Hardwin quickly kicked what was left of the twisted metal out of the way. Turning sideways, he slipped inside the fence.

Others had been loitering on the sidewalk farther away. Guns drawn, they raced up now, sliding efficiently through the opening Hardwin had made.

It was the same all around the grounds. Armed men flooded in through the twisted bars at dozens of smoking openings.

The Marines charged from the residence, followed by Secret Service agents. Gunfire erupted all around the mansion. In minutes, the lush green lawns were awash in red.

It should never have happened. Most swore that it could never happen. But it did.

Reginald Hardwin and his men had the element of surprise working for them. Complacency on the part of their opponents proved to be the deciding factor.

The men protecting the President of the United States were overwhelmed in less than ten minutes.

Thanks to the leadership of a failed motion-picture actor, for the first time since the War of 1812, the White House had fallen before a hostile force.

19

While the American flag continued to flutter high above the heads of the captives cowering within the most famous residence in the world, Remo Williams was wandering, despondent, through the grounds of Taurus Studios.

The L.A. bomb squad had dismantled the timers on the Plotz truck bombs before hauling the vehicles off the lot. Beneath the tons of fertilizer in the back of one, they would eventually discover the bodies of the actors who had planted the trucks at Taurus.

Except for saving Chiun's life, this trip was a bust. Not only was Remo still no closer to learning who was behind the scheme, but also he was now stuck in Hollywood.

Hands stuffed into the pockets of his chinos, he walked back to the set where he'd driven the one live bomb.

Remo ignored the yellow police tape. Ducking underneath the fluttering plastic strip, he wandered onto the lot.

There were still many police and fire officials on hand. When one uniformed officer came running angrily over to him, Remo waved one of his many IDs at the man. He hoped it wasn't the one that said he was from the Motion Picture Association of America.

Apparently it wasn't. The cop left him alone.

Remo meandered over to ground zero. He stopped at the very edge of the newly formed crater.

The explosion had blasted a huge hole that looked like the excavation site for an Olympic-size pool. Several layers of asphalt had been ripped away in a jagged circle. The blast had dug down as far as the bedrock. Dirt was scattered everywhere. Black stains of charred ash stretched unevenly around the vast pit.

The set was demolished beyond repair. Phony building facades had been flung away like broken dominoes.

A few unused studio buildings not visible before could now be seen beyond the rubble of the New York skyline. Their fronts had been blown backward into abandoned offices. Only one had any remnants of a roof left at all.

Beyond the shattered buildings, a vacant tract of dusty land spotted with dry scraggly brush extended to the distant studio wall. The high white rear wall of Taurus had survived the blast with no visible damage.

After a few bored minutes, Remo headed away from the shattered set. With nothing to go on at the moment, he decided to kill whatever time he had to spend at Taurus with Chiun. He went back the way he had come, into the more populated center of the studio complex.

Taurus employees had only been allowed back on the lot an hour ago. Given the excitement, however, very little work was getting done.

Remo found a group of three chattering secretaries standing outside the infirmary.

"The movie that was shooting on the New York set," he interrupted the trio of women as he walked past, "anyone know where it is now?"

"Soundstage 4," one woman supplied helpfully. Her hungry smile as she appraised Remo's lean frame was mirrored by the lascivious looks of her overly made-up friends.

As he walked off, one of the woman called, "Hey, gimme your script and I can make sure it gets read." Her lilt screamed "casting couch."

"Read?" scoffed the one who had first spoken. *"Produced,"* she called to Remo. "I can get you a three-picture deal off your first script."

"I can make sure you *star,"* the third woman said, trumping her friends. "Just give your script to me. You can bring it to my apartment. Say, around eight o'clock?"

When Remo turned around, all three women were smiling eager capped teeth.

"I don't have a script," he said simply.

It was a phrase they had obviously never before encountered. Three looks of hope collapsed into expressions of utter incomprehension. Leaving the women to wrap their smoking brains around such

an unimaginable concept, Remo headed to Soundstage 4.

The red light outside the door indicated shooting
was in progress. Remo ignored it. Tugging the door
open a crack, he slipped silently inside.

An older man in a cotton print shirt sat at a plain
wooden desk inside the door. He had been scanning
a bored eye over the latest *Variety,* but when Remo
entered he dropped the paper and jumped to his
feet, shaking his gray head.

"This is a closed set," the guard whispered.

"MPAA," Remo whispered back, flashing the
appropriate identification. "This is a naughty-word
raid."

The man studied the ID for a moment, beefy face
scrunched in suspicion.

"Is this something new?"

Remo nodded. "Patricia Ireland says molesting
interns is A-okay, but swear words lead to sexual
harassment." He shrugged. "All I know is it's giving me more work to do."

Taking his eyes from the ID, the man settled in
his worn seat. He seemed satisfied with Remo's
claim.

"Yeah? Well, good luck," he whispered. He indicated the interior of the soundstage with an un-
happy thrust of his chin. "The MPAA's gonna run
out of calculators trying to add up all the swearing
this guy puts in his movies."

He returned to his newspaper.

Remo wandered from the desk into the shadowy depths of the massive soundstage.

The guard's comment was strange. The Master of Sinanju didn't appreciate the use of foul language so common in America. To him it was the height of incivility.

Of course, Remo had heard Chiun use plenty of Korean curses during their earliest training sessions. But that use of language had ended long ago. Remo couldn't believe Chiun would write a film laced with profanity.

No one interrupted him when he stopped at the edge of the packed crowd of crew members.

There was some kind of staged fight in progress. As the cameras rolled, the actors were screaming at each other at the tops of their lungs.

"You shit-heel-asshole-fuck!"

"Fuck you, you fuck!"

The last dollops of carefully scripted ambrosia dripped from the velvet tongue of a young actress standing in a mock-up of a cluttered apartment. Beyond the windows of the set, a backdrop of tenements stood in for the real New York.

The language devolved from there. The fight intensified into a romantic scene bordering on the pornographic.

Remo couldn't believe his eyes. Everything he was seeing and hearing was entirely unlike Chiun. As his disbelief grew, a familiar voice suddenly shouted from the rafters high above the set.

"And...cut! Perfect. Damn, I am *good*."

Remo quickly found the source of the self-congratulations. Quintly Tortilli sat in a squat chair behind the long arm of one of the boom microphones.

With an electronic hum, the young director was lowered from his perch. A few assistants were waiting for him when he reached floor level.

Remo slipped easily through the crowd, coming through the crush of people immediately around Tortilli. They were only aware he was there when he spoke.

"What the hell is this?" Remo demanded.

Still seated, Tortilli turned in surprise. "Remo! Hi!" he enthused. He pushed his baseball cap back on his head. "Just taking back the reins from ol' Arlen here." He nodded to one of the men in his entourage. Relief was painted large on Arlen Duggal's exhausted face.

Remo was stunned. "Don't tell me *you're* directing this mess?"

"Sure as shootin'," Tortilli said with a broad smile.

"What about that parking-lot *Battleship Potemkin* you were presiding over in Seattle?"

"That little thing?" Tortilli dismissed. "A lark. I like to indulge my artistic whims. At the height of my *Penny Dreadful* fame I directed an episode of *OR* and guest-starred on an episode of *China Girl*. I like to drive my agent nuts with stuff like that."

"Your agent and everyone else who's ever seen you act," Remo commented dryly.

Tortilli's eyes darted nervously to the others. "Hey, everybody," he called, leaping out of his seat, "get lost." The men and women scattered like billiard balls after a break. "Didn't want them to get the wrong impression viz your little verbal jests re me," Tortilli confided after they were gone.

"Tortilli, human beings don't talk like that, no matter what Kevin Williamson says. And if you're worried about everyone thinking you're an asshole, you probably shouldn't have hosted *Saturday Night Live.* Why didn't you say this movie was yours?"

"I didn't know," Tortilli insisted. "I mean, I knew I was director, but I didn't know I was, like, *the* director. Of your friend's movie, that is. At least, not until you mentioned him in the car."

"So why didn't you tell me then?" Remo asked. He remembered Tortilli's twitchy reaction to Chiun's name. At the time he'd been so concerned for the old Asian's safety that he'd chalked it up to Tortilli's general twitchiness.

"I was going to. But people have an amazing knack of winding up dead around you, man. I figured you'd be ticked at me somehow." He quickly changed the subject. "But, hey, that was some ride today, right? I mean, real bombs. That whole 'blown to bits' thing looming over our heads. Armageddon City. I mean, far out!" Jumping up and down, the director gave Remo an idiot's grin.

"You must put sugar on your Cap'n Crunch," Remo commented absently as Tortilli hopped excitedly before him. He had just spotted Chiun across the set. Leaving the director to his frantic calisthenics, he walked over to the Master of Sinanju.

The old Korean had doffed his uniform. As he turned to Remo, he was dressed in a simple marigold kimono.

"Do I need to flee?" the Master of Sinanju asked dryly.

Remo held his hands out wide. "No bomb this time." He smiled. "Promise."

Chiun nodded. He didn't seem very interested in Remo. He was looking past his pupil.

Remo glanced back over his shoulder. All he saw was Quintly Tortilli and Arlen Duggal. When he turned back to Chiun, there was a look of anticipation on the old man's face.

"You might be a little happier to see me, Little Father," Remo groused, annoyed that his teacher seemed more interested in the director than in him. "We've hardly spoken twice in the past two months."

"And yet you still take the time to try to blow me up."

He persisted in ignoring Remo. All at once, a dejected expression settled on his parchment face. When Remo looked, he saw that Tortilli and Duggal were walking away. Only when they vanished around a distant corner did Chiun look at Remo.

"Oh, you're back," Remo deadpanned.

"Do not be childish," Chiun sniffed.

Remo didn't want a repeat of the scene back at

the New York lot. The truth was, it felt good to be with Chiun again. Even if the old Korean was distracted.

"They've given you a costume change, I see," Remo said more lightly, nodding to Chiun's kimono.

"The genius Tortilli told me that my uniform did not look authentic," Chiun replied.

Remo's eyes went flat. "The *what* Tortilli?"

"The genius director of my film." Just talking about Quintly Tortilli seemed to relax the Master of Sinanju. A smile kissed his vellum lips. "You do not know what I have been through with the buffoon who had been overseeing this project. Another day and he would have had my hero dangling from the Statue of Liberty or straddling a tree trunk. But now that is all over." He pitched his voice low. "The genius Tortilli has told me that the camera loves me. He insists the eye is drawn to me even without exotic apparel."

"Okay, let's put that whopper aside for one minute," Remo said. "What's with all this genius crapola?"

"That is how he is referred to by his peers," the Master of Sinanju said, nodding sagely. "They do not speak his name without uttering his honorific."

"Little Father, according to Hollywood people, everyone in town is a genius."

"Ah, but it is the way they intone the word when they apply it to my director," Chiun explained. "They speak the word with conviction."

"Unless you count Robert Downey Jr., there *are* no convictions in Hollywood, Little Father," Remo insisted. "Tortilli made a movie five or six years ago that all the critics loved but was a piece of crap, and since then he's been coasting on his name."

The Master of Sinanju snapped alert. "Listen, Remo!" he announced, suddenly intensely worried. Bony fingers gripped his pupil's forearm.

Remo was instantly alarmed. "What?" he asked, anxious.

Worried about another bombing attempt, he broadened his normal auditory range, expanding beyond the immediate vicinity. The soundproofing of the building limited his scope, but as far as he could hear there was nothing unusual out on the farther lot.

"I don't hear anything," he whispered after a moment.

Chiun brought a slender finger to his lips. "It is there," he hissed. "The Leviathan awakes. Hark! It is a fearsome green beast, Remo. The Dragon of Jealousy."

Smiling placidly, he released Remo's arm.

"That's not very damn funny," Remo complained.

"I agree," Chiun said, smile unwavering. "Your enviousness of the genius Tortilli is a very serious matter. Almost as serious as your jealousy of my writing talent."

Remo exhaled an angry burst of air. "Fine," he said, shaking his head. "I'm not getting into this with you. If you think a moron's brilliant, that's your business."

"Fine," said Chiun happily.

"Fine," repeated Remo angrily. "So what does your resident genius have you doing anyway?"

Chiun raised a forewarning eyebrow. "I will tell you if you promise not to get jealous."

"That's it. I'm outta here."

As he spun to go, Remo felt a restraining hand grab on to his wrist. Chiun held him firmly in place.

"I have been given a wondrous place in this film," the Master of Sinanju said without missing a beat. "Tortilli, who is a genius, has told me that it is a crucial location for any actor making his motion-picture debut." His singsong became a conspiratorial whisper. "I am to be installed on the cutting-room floor." His awesome revelation unveiled, he released his grip on Remo's arm.

Remo didn't know whether or not he was making a joke. When he saw the look of blissful enthusiasm on the old man's face, he realized that Chiun wasn't kidding.

"Who told you that?" he asked slowly. "Tortilli?"

Chiun's bald head bobbed eagerly. "He said that my scenes will be the first to go there," he said proudly.

For a moment, Remo considered telling Chiun the truth. But the Master of Sinanju seemed so elated. In the end, he decided to let Chiun enjoy his moment in the sun.

"I'm happy for you, Little Father," he said.

There was a warmth to his pupil's tone that caught the Master of Sinanju off guard. A smile of appreciation curled the edges of the aged Korean's thin lips.

"Perhaps I can convince the genius Tortilli to put you on this floor of cuts, as well. Of course, you would have to take second billing to me," he added quickly.

"Pass," Remo said. "One star in the family is enough."

"You are probably right," Chiun admitted. "One brilliant actor-writer is sufficient."

"Speaking of writing, I heard an awful lot of swearing going on," Remo said. "Your handiwork?"

Chiun shook his head. "Changes were made prior to production. Tortilli says that the language is now more realistic."

"What about the premise? It looks like some kind of cop movie. After you ditched the dinosaurs and aliens, I thought it was supposed to be about assassins."

The old Asian's tone grew vague. "A script physician was enlisted to clarify certain aspects of my glorious tale."

"Out went the assassins, in came the cops," Remo said.

"Yes," Chiun replied. "But I retain screen credit."

"Smitty'll love that," Remo commented.

Chiun's eyes narrowed. "You did not tell Emperor Smith?" he asked levelly.

"Not me," Remo said. "This is your show."

Chiun nodded. "That is good. He will be honored when it is released, of course. For any increase in my flame will only shine more light on him."

"As the head of an ultrasecret agency working outside the confines of the Constitution, I'm sure he'll appreciate that," Remo agreed.

Chiun stroked his thread of beard. "I had something about that in the original story but, sadly, it was lost in subsequent drafts," he lamented.

"To the eternal gratitude of Smith's pacemaker," Remo responded. "Speaking of Smitty, I should check in. He was trying to track down whoever was behind the bombing here."

"I am curious about that, as well," Chiun said thinly. "At first, I thought our production was ruined, but then the genius Tortilli arrived on the scene. He has said that he can salvage much from that which has already been filmed and will be able to shoot around the rest."

"Chiun, you've taken a pretty big leap of faith with a guy you never met before," Remo complained.

"Have I not mentioned that he is a genius?" Chiun asked. "I must hie to him now, lest that pretender fill his brilliant head with dross." The Master of Sinanju took off in the direction Tortilli and Arlen Duggal had gone.

"I'm glad I'm not gonna be in Tortilli's shoes when this bill comes due," Remo muttered.

He turned to go. As he was leaving, he spied a script lying on a stool. On the hard leather jacket was a label reading *Assassin's Loves*: Taurus Project # K128. Oddly, they had changed everything yet retained Chiun's title.

Pausing, Remo glanced around. There was no one in the immediate vicinity.

He had been curious for quite some time. Chiun had been so damn secretive about the details.

"What the hell," Remo said to himself.

He quickly gathered up the script, tearing it from its heavy binder. Rolling the paper into a tight tube, he stuffed the script into his back pocket.

Jamming his hands in his pockets, he began whistling tunelessly. Forcing a look of nonchalance, Remo strolled off the set toward the soundstage door.

20

Alone in his darkened Folcroft office, Harold Smith was scanning the latest list of motion-picture studio phone numbers flagged by the CURE mainframes when the dedicated White House line jangled to life. He attempted to find correlations between numbers and names even as he pulled the phone from his desk drawer.

"Yes, Mr. President," he said crisply.

The hoarse voice on the other end of the line was panicked. "They're *here*, Smith," the President whispered urgently.

Smith's chair squeaked as he sat straighter. Save the almost inaudible hum of his desk computer, it was the only sound in the tomb-silent office.

"I beg your pardon, sir?" he asked, puzzled.

"They're here!" the President repeated. "At the White House!"

"Forgive me, but who is there?" The frightened tone of America's Chief Executive had already sent the first sparks of concern through Smith's fluttering heart.

"I don't know!" the President pleaded. "It could be anyone. The Indonesians, the environmentalists, the gays, the Chinese, the RNC, the DNC, the Democratic Leadership Council. They're all mad at me for one reason or another. Nobody likes me,'' he wailed.

"Mr. President, please,'' Smith said, trying to inject a rational note into a most irrational call. "Why don't you begin at the—''

"My wife!'' the President burst out. "That's who's behind this! She's wanted to rule this roost from day one. She's always threatened a coup, but I figured she'd at least have the decency to do it while I was out of town.''

In the far distance, Smith heard the sound of muted pops.

"What was that?'' he asked, instantly wary.

"Gunshots!'' the President cried. "What do I *do,* Smith? My God, I see them. They're coming across the lawn.''

America's Chief Executive sounded as if he was about to burst into tears.

"*Who* is coming across the lawn?'' Smith pressed.

Too late. The line had already gone dead.

Quickly, Smith tried to reestablish contact. The phone, which was located in the Lincoln Bedroom, rang the instant the connection was restored. But the call went unanswered.

Smith hung up, swiveling hurriedly to his computer. His hands hadn't even brushed the buried keyboard before the computer alerted him to a new crisis.

Fearing that he already knew what his main-frames had discovered, Smith opened the pop-up window.

The CURE mainframes had intercepted dozens upon dozens of messages and memos flying across the endless streams of the Internet. Computer lines from the CIA to the NSC, from the Pentagon to the Secret Service, from the FBI to the NSA, from the Capitol to the Defense Intelligence Agency, were clogged with activity.

Smith didn't need to read far in order to understand the point of all of those desperate, flashing messages.

The White House was under siege.

For a few frenzied minutes, Smith tried to make some sense out of precisely what was happening. But there were no clear accounts yet. The crisis was so fresh that not even the news outlets had logged on with stories.

The best he could glean was that some unnamed force had found its way onto the White House grounds. A Secret Service e-mail sent to the Treasury Department minutes after the President's call indicated that there had been heavy casualties taken by those guarding the chief executive's home.

That might mean something. The Secret Service was still able to log onto its internal system.

Smith's hand had already dropped on the blue contact phone when it buzzed beneath his palm. He jumped, startled, even as he wrenched the receiver to his ear.

"What's the good news, Smitty?" Remo's voice asked.

"Remo, I do not yet know the details, but the White House is under attack."

Remo's tone instantly hardened. "You're kidding, right?"

Smith shook his head impatiently. "I know nothing as yet." He typed rapidly as he spoke. "I am arranging for transportation out of Edwards Air Force Base. Get there as quickly as possible."

It was the shortest conversation they'd had since Remo was first drafted into the organization. Remo's last words were sharp as he slammed down the phone.

"I'm on my way."

21

At first, the problem for the Marines and Secret Service was containment.

The First Daughter was not at home, thank God. That was one less headache. But the President and the First Lady were in the residence. The highest priority was to keep the situation as far away from the First Family as possible.

That idea crumbled two minutes into the crisis when the assailants overwhelmed perimeter positions and swept into the mansion itself.

Option two was reached at once: remove the First Family from harm's way.

That alternative fell by the wayside when the invaders cut off all known escape routes. Even the emergency elevator, which ran from the family quarters down to the subbasement, was captured. It was as if this unknown army knew every strategic retreat the President might take.

In a running gun battle, the surviving members of the President's security force retreated upstairs to the family quarters in order to reestablish a closer defense perimeter around the Chief Executive.

They were greeted by something more horrifying

than an army of terrorists brandishing assault weapons.

"What the hell is going on here!" the First Lady screeched as the armed men swarmed into the hallway from the First Family's main elevator.

Her face was caked in some kind of dried green goop. Furious piglike eyes shot daggers from the middle of her weirdly tinted face.

"The White House is under attack!" a Secret Service agent shouted, weapon aimed down the elevator shaft.

The other agents were disabling the elevator so that no one could use it to follow them. The doors had been pried open and a mirror angled into the opening to alert them of anyone attempting to climb the shaft. Several automatics were aimed down into the darkness.

"Oh, my God!" the First Lady cried as she watched them work. Her eyes grew larger in her beauty cream mask. "They know about the duplicate billing records!"

"Ma'am, I think this is mor—" a Marine began sharply.

But the First Lady didn't hear him. She was already running down the hall, her latest pageboy hairdo bobbing crazily around her cream-caked face.

"I expect you to cover my ass if you have to get yours shot off in the process!" she shouted over her shoulder.

The First Lady disappeared inside the library. An

instant later, the whirring sound of a paper shredder echoed down the corridor. It was a familiar noise to anyone working in this White House.

The men had every intention of following the First Lady's final shouted order. They would die before they let anyone get past their fortified line. However, they soon found that it was a moot point.

The advance had halted. For some reason, unfathomable to those holed up in the family quarters, the invading force stopped on the ground-floor level of the White House.

And as the blood of the dead burbled crimson on the green spring lawn far below, the strangest standoff in America's history began.

REGINALD HARDWIN WAS seated at the desk of the President of the United States. As he carefully crossed his legs, he noticed a slight tear in the knee of his impeccably tailored trousers—the result of his awkward dive to the sidewalk.

Hardwin tsked as he examined the hole with slender, delicate fingers.

He had bought the trousers with money from his first five-million-dollar windfall. Even though he was now quite rich as a result of his current employment, he couldn't help but examine the tear with a poor man's mentality. After all, he had been poor for a long, long time.

"Five hundred dollars," he complained.

"What?"

The voice came from the lightweight cell phone

in his hand. It was crisp, efficient. Authoritative in a noncommittal way. The FBI negotiator.

"Nothing," Hardwin said. His fingers fled the hole. He became once more Reginald Hardwin, world terrorist.

"I have your President and his wife captive above me. All escape routes, including those to the old Executive Office Building, have been secured."

"What do you want?" the negotiator asked evenly.

Hardwin the terrorist smiled. He played the part with great panache. Worthy of an Oscar.

"There is time for that later." He checked his watch. "My men are about to release all of the White House employees captured during our raid. You should see them at your end right about now."

There was a pause. "I do."

Hardwin smiled, placing the palm of his watch hand delicately back on the President's desk. "If you would be kind enough not to shoot at them, that would be splendid for all concerned, I should think."

"Hold your fire! Hold your fire!"

There was a long wait while the hundreds of White House staffers and government employees trapped inside the building at the start of the siege were trundled down the long drive to the Fifteenth Street entrance.

Hardwin was inspecting his fingernails when the FBI negotiator resumed the conversation.

"What about the wounded? We'll need to come get them."

"They will be brought out to you."

"They shouldn't be moved, except by professionals."

"Agent Plover, do you really think I would allow your men to sneak onto these grounds dressed like emergency medical technicians? Perhaps I sound stupid to you."

"Unfortunately, you don't," the negotiator said.

Hardwin smiled. "It's kind of you to lie. But we both know that you do think I am stupid. After all, I am in the most famous building in the world, surrounded by FBI, Marines and Secret Service. What could I possibly want? How could I *possibly* hope to achieve my ends? Clearly, I must know that this will end in my death. I am stupid in your opinion, am I not, Agent Plover? Please, be honest. You will find that honesty is very important to me."

The FBI agent was reluctant to admit that this was indeed the case. "You could have been smarter," Agent Plover said finally.

"There. That wasn't so difficult," Hardwin said encouragingly. "I appreciate your honesty. You will find that I am not a brutal man. As with the other hostages, the wounded will be brought out to you. That is, if I have your word that my men will come to no harm."

No hesitation. "You do."

"Excellent. We have established a trust between us. Important for any working relationship."

The histrionics were unbelievable. There was no panic. No frantically screamed ultimatum. No gradual erosion of demands until the compromise of surrender was reached. There was an utter calm about Reginald Hardwin, terrorist. An icy assuredness. Hardwin's confidence radiated to Agent Plover.

"Who are you?" the FBI negotiator asked.

"I am the man who brought terror to your New York City. You would be advised to listen to me. Remember the Regency. I will be in touch."

Hardwin calmly depressed End.

He dropped his hand to the president's desk.

"And Act Two commences." He smiled. It was the phrase Captain Kill had used to describe this phase of the drama.

Thinking of his mysterious employer, Hardwin allowed his eyes to scan the rounded contours of the famous room.

It was bigger than it appeared in the movies. A few of his men patrolled beyond the French windows on the patio that led to the Rose Garden.

The drapes and furniture were ghastly. Exactly what one would expect from a hippie hillbilly, Hardwin thought.

After a few long moments of consideration, Hardwin lifted his cellular phone once more. Quickly, he stabbed out a familiar eleven-number code. When the connection was made, he pressed three more numbers for the proper extension.

"Solomon, Raithbone and Schwartz," a perky female voice exclaimed. "Mr. Leffer's office."

"Let me talk to Bernie," Reginald Hardwin the actor said. Maybe he could spin this into something bigger than underwear ads.

22

Both Washington National and Dulles International Airports had been closed indefinitely. During the crisis in the nation's capital, Baltimore-Washington was also shut down, along with all of the smaller municipal airports scattered within the entire area of Maryland. The no-fly zone extended far into northern Virginia.

The only things airborne within a hundred-mile radius of Washington were military aircraft. Jets and helicopters crisscrossed the ominous, rain-streaked night sky.

So many planes were up at one point early on, there were nearly a dozen midair collisions. The number had been pruned down now, but the dead spaces between roars of thunder were still filled with the persistent hum of unseen aircraft.

The flight from Edwards in California had taken Remo directly to Bolling Air Force Base across the Potomac from Washington National. An Air Force helicopter was waiting for him there.

The chopper flight was a short hop up the Washington Channel to the tourist section of the city. Rotors slicing tension from the very air of the nation's capital, the helicopter deposited him near the Ellipse at Constitution Avenue and Fifteenth Street Northwest.

Behind him, the darkened Washington Monument held aloft the sallow sky. The spotlights that ordinarily lighted the great obelisk had been doused. Without illumination, the ring of American flags that encircled the monument should have been taken down. But etiquette of the flag, as well as all other social and civil mores, had been abandoned at the start of the crisis.

In darkness, the wet flags flapped crazily in the wind kicked up by the departing helicopter.

As the chopper tilted south into the rain, Remo raced in the opposite direction.

The Ellipse was choked with government officials. Waterproof maps were spread on car hoods. Questions were shouted back and forth, some heated. There seemed to be a turf war going on among different branches of law enforcement.

Rather than worry about having to fish in his pockets for proper ID, Remo merely plucked a laminated tag from the lapel of an unsuspecting FBI agent. As he walked, he affixed the silver clip to the collar of his own black T-shirt.

Weaving through the crowd, he found what appeared to be the nucleus of official activity.

''I'm telling you, FBI is in charge here,'' a bulky man in a tan raincoat was insisting when Remo arrived. A drenched tourist map of the city wilted in his wet hands.

"Not in there," snapped another. He wore a sopping wet black suit. A thin white cord ran from jacket to ear. "That's Secret Service's domain."

"Take it up with the Attorney General," the FBI assistant director challenged.

"No, *you* take it up with the Secretary of the Treasury," the Secret Service agent countered.

A gray-haired Marine colonel in full dress uniform was about to interject when Remo interrupted.

"What's the situation?" Remo asked, voice taut.

All three men spun on him. The FBI man noted Remo's stolen identification with harried irritation.

"If you're FBI, you work for me, which means you shut up," the assistant director growled.

"In that case, I'm not FBI," Remo said.

There was a flash of movement, faster even than the streaks of lightning that split the sky above the darkened capital. The FBI man abruptly felt something flat and square slip between his lips.

At the same moment his tongue was tasting the ID tag's metal clip, his eyes noted that the laminated tag had vanished from the T-shirt of the man before him. Before he could spit out the name tag, the agent—who had to be an impostor—gave the ID a light tap with the tip of one finger. The assistant director's eyes shot open as the tag rocketed down his esophagus. He gagged and gulped and grabbed his throat.

As the FBI man danced in place, Remo spun to the shocked Marine colonel and Secret Service agent.

"Before anyone gets any bright ideas, I'm on your side and I can do the same thing with chevrons and sunglasses." His dark eyes were chipped from the ice-dead heart of a glacial rock. "What's the situation?"

The two men looked at the choking FBI assistant director.

The tag had gone down sideways, so his breathing was not impeded. The outline of the ID was clearly visible in the stretched skin of his neck. He coughed like a cat with a fur ball even as he jammed his fingers into his own desperately open mouth.

The man was staggering off when the Colonel and the Secret Service agent turned back to Remo.

"An enemy force of unknown origin has taken the White House," the Secret Service man said without hesitation. "Our side suffered heavy casualties. Big Creep and Shrieker are inside."

Remo assumed these were the new code names for the President and First Lady. "Are they alive?"

"So far," the colonel answered. "The terrorists are holed up mostly on the ground level. The First Family is up in their living quarters. We're still in contact with the agents who are with them."

"Why don't you come up from below?" Remo asked, knowing that the offices of the White House extended well below street level.

"They seem to know the layout even better than we do," the Secret Service agent explained angrily. "All routes of ingress have been blocked. You heard about the bombing in Manhattan the other day?''

Remo frowned. ''What's that got to do with this?''

''The head terrorist mentioned it to the FBI negotiator. 'Remember the Regency' or something like that.''

Remo's frown deepened. ''I've been in Oz the last few days,'' he said. ''What's that mean?''

''It's the name of the office building they blew up,'' the agent explained. ''When he said that, we got the preliminary report of the FBI investigation in New York faxed here on the double. They used plastic explosives to destroy an entire floor of that building.''

''Which means the White House could already be set to go up like a Roman candle,'' the Marine colonel finished.

''Stalemate,'' the Secret Service agent grudgingly admitted. Rainwater dripped down the sour lines of his face.

E Street was crawling with government agents. Remo looked across the road to the South Executive Place fence of the White House. He could see the many missing bars in the wrought iron through which the terrorists had slipped.

And as the reality of this violation sank in, a cold fury welled up from the pit of Remo Williams's stomach.

The White House taken captive by terrorists. The

single most aggressive assault ever on all that was symbolically American.

Remo might not approve of the current President or his treatment of Smith but—like the present occupant or not—the White House was the seat of world democracy. A symbol of hope for oppressed people around the world. And if Remo had anything to say about it, it would remain such.

"How many men?" he asked, voice coldly uninflected.

"Unknown at present," the Marine colonel offered. "At least two hundred."

Remo looked at the Secret Service man. His eyes were dead. "Get on the phone with the D.C. morgue," he instructed. "Order up two hundred body bags."

And with that, he was gone.

They saw him blend into the crowd of agents. But even as their eyes tried to track the stranger, he melted from their vision. He was like a ghost who had faded into the shadows.

"Who the hell was that?" the Secret Service agent asked once Remo was gone.

"I don't know," the Marine colonel admitted, his eyes flint. The chill that ran down his spine had nothing to do with the rain. "But I think you better make that call."

23

Bruce Marmelstein was on his way back to Taurus from his day's tanning appointment when the call came through.

"Put on the news, Bruce." Hank Bindle's voice was anxious on the limo's speakerphone.

Marmelstein put down his drink and reached for the control panel. "News?" he complained. "That's like *Entertainment Tonight* for losers. What do I want to see that for?"

"Just do it," Bindle pressed.

Marmelstein rolled his eyes even as the small color monitor winked on. "Okay, where do I find it?" he sighed.

"Right now, anywhere will do," Bindle said. "It's on every damn channel."

Marmelstein frowned as he watched the action on-screen.

"I don't know, Hank," he said, sipping his scotch and soda. "I usually don't question you in creative matters, but remember I just optioned *Petticoat Junction* and we've got the *Wonder Twins* with Nick Cage and Uma Thurman opening this fall. Do you really think we should give Yogi Bear the big-screen treatment?''

"Not Fox!" Bindle snapped. "One of the Big Three!"

Marmelstein reluctantly switched from the cartoon to the local CBS affiliate.

Immediately, images of a familiar residence appeared on the screen. Even Bruce Marmelstein recognized the White House. He had been there several times in the past few years. In fact, he and his partner had been on the past two inaugural committees. The building was bathed in darkness.

"Did they forget to pay the electric bill?" Marmelstein asked.

"The *terrorists* wanted it that way," Bindle supplied.

"Oh." Marmelstein nodded. He took another sip of scotch.

"The *terrorists* who took over the White House," Hank Bindle elaborated.

"I don't get this, Hank," Bruce Marmelstein finally admitted. "Frankly, I like your Yogi Bear idea better. I mean, how do you option the news?"

"We don't have to option it. We already own it."

"We do?" Marmelstein said. He didn't remember buying the rights. "Well if it's ours already, how about *Huntley-Brinkley: the Early Years?* I'm thinking DiCaprio and Van Der Beek. We could glue fake Brinkley ears on Leo—''

"The White House has been taken over by a

group of armed terrorists, Bruce!'' Bindle yelled.
''They blew through the fence and swarmed the
grounds. The President and his family are trapped
upstairs. Doesn't that scenario sound just a *little*
familiar to you?''

It didn't really click for Bruce Marmelstein until
his Taurus cochair mentioned the First Family were
hostages. In one horror-filled instant, he realized
what was going on.

''Die Down IV!'' Marmelstein gagged. Mind
reeling, he focused his attention back on the TV
screen.

''It's awful!'' Bindle cried. ''The head terrorist
is a Brit and everything. Just like in our blockbuster.''

Marmelstein clutched his gut. ''I'm going to be
sick.''

''It gets worse. The news people intercepted a
call he made with the FBI. Bruce, he mentioned
New York.''

Scotch came out Marmelstein's nose. ''The Regency?'' he gasped, wiping the brown dribble off
his chin. His nostrils burned.

''I couldn't believe it,'' Bindle moaned.

''That's copyright infringement!'' Marmelstein
sputtered. ''We'll *sue!* I'm calling the lawyers!''

''It's worse than that,'' Bindle insisted. He began
to cry. ''I think we could even go to prison, Bruce.
And that's a bad thing. Not like in *Stir Crazy* at all.
It's full of black people. And not funny ones like
Richard Pryor. Angry ones, Bruce. They could hit

you in the face and hurt you. Maybe even break a tooth.''

"But we only hired out for New York," Marmelstein insisted. "We didn't pay for this. We pulled the plug on it. If he's doing this, he's doing it on his own."

"It doesn't matter," Bindle sobbed. "It's going on whether we paid for it or not."

"Free?" Marmelstein asked, hoping he'd pronounced the alien word correctly.

"You're the money guy. Did you sign the check?"

"I don't know," Marmelstein whined. "I just use the autopen—I don't pay attention to what it's doing. But it doesn't matter. We nixed the White House idea. It was too high profile. New York was good enough. It tied in with the movie without insulting everyone's... What's that stuff called? That country-loving stuff we looked up?"

"Patriotism?"

"Yeah, that. New York is what we agreed to."

"He must have thought we needed an extra push."

Marmelstein was getting angry. "What we needed was for the goddamn studio to blow up like we paid for and we didn't get that." He looked once more at the action on the TV, then closed his eyes.

"I'm going to set up a meeting," Bindle sniffed.

"We can't," Marmelstein said. "We've got

what's-his-name to deal with. The desk-smashie guy."

"No," Bindle insisted. "He left here like a bat out of hell. No one's seen him for a couple of hours."

"You think he's gone?"

"We'd better hope so. For all our sakes."

The line went dead. Marmelstein opened his eyes. He stared at the TV screen for an instant.

"Oh, God," he muttered.

Lunging for the wet bar, Bruce Marmelstein filled his tumbler with scotch. This time, he didn't add soda.

24

The spotlights that ordinarily bathed the White House grounds in brightness remained doused. The only light to spill across the soggy lawn came from distant amber streetlights and from the many TV cameras huddled back at the police cordon. Though the shadows were long and deep, Remo's highly developed eyes drew in enough available light to make the area seem as bright as midday.

He had slipped through one of the openings made by the terrorists across from the Zero Milestone at the Ellipse. Although the grass was drenched, the soles of his loafers left not a single impression. No one saw him as he moved unmolested through the shadows toward the mansion.

The south lawn fountain sent gurgling spurts into the damp air. Remo skirted the pool, slipping from the edge of the long tulip bed around the fountain. The loamy smell of overturned earth was thick in his nostrils as he moved stealthily over to a tangle of purple magnolias.

From the shrubs, he slid across shadowy open lawn to the drive. Remo spotted the first terrorists as he approached the neatly trimmed hedge.

There were two of them. They stood beside the thick trunk of a spreading white ash beyond the hedge.

They didn't seem interested in the assault rifles in their own hands. Bored, one of the men banged his against the tree trunk, apparently unmindful that the barrel was aimed at his own stomach.

The men spoke in hushed tones. Their whispered words traveled to Remo's hypersensitive ears even as he moved—unseen—toward them.

"What are we doing here?" the first said with a sigh.

"Gotta pay the bills." The second shrugged. He tapped the tree with his gun butt.

"Yes, but what's my motivation? You know, I don't need this. I've done summer stock for the past three years. I was even in a play in New York."

"Broadway?"

"Off-off Broadway. Dinner theater mostly. But I got noticed. My agent's sister knows Neil Simon's mechanic's brother-in-law. His wife saw me and *loved* me."

Listening to the two men jabber, Remo had begun to get a troubled feeling. He hopped the hedge, landing on silent soles in the wide driveway. As the men continued to talk, he slipped around the fat angled tree trunk.

"I was up for the lead in *The Gypsy Lover,*" one terrorist was boasting.

"No kidding?" asked the other, bored. He was

staring out at the amber lights of E Street. "What happened?"

He would never know the answer.

The terrorist heard a grunt, then a *thwuck*. When he spun toward the commotion, he found to his shock and horror that the white ash tree had swallowed his partner. Or at least some of him.

The man was doubled over at the waist, his head jammed deep into a puckered knothole where once there had been a limb. His arms dangled limply to the ground. It seemed impossible for so much head to fit in so little space.

The surviving terrorist gasped, horrified. In his sheer panic, there was only one thing racing through his fear-paralyzed mind.

"If you're dead, can I still borrow your leather jacket on Monday? I've got that *One Life to Live* audition."

A face appeared before him. Hard.

"Show's over," Remo said.

The man suddenly realized what had happened to his partner. And in those dark eyes was promise of a similar fate for him. He abruptly dropped his gun and covered his male-model-perfect face with both hands.

"Not in the face!" he begged.

Remo obliged.

A two-fingered tap to the chest shocked the heart between beats. When the dead man's hands fell away, there seemed almost to be a look of relief that his handsome face had come through his death intact. He collapsed to the asphalt.

His concern deepening, Remo left the first two bodies.

Another five men waited at the top of the staircase beneath the south portico's entablature. They were using the colonnade of thick support columns for cover.

Keeping the farthest column on the left between him and the terrorist behind it, Remo moved swiftly up the left staircase. A few short bounds put him only a few feet away from the last man in line.

"I can't believe we signed on for three of these," one of the men on the long portico was complaining.

"It's pretty standard," another said. "The original with an option for two more. I guess they thought New York went well enough to warrant a sequel."

The last word finished it. *Sequel.* They were talking about the bombing in New York and the terrorist takeover of the White House in movie terms. Remo couldn't believe what he was hearing.

"What's that?" one terrorist asked suddenly.

Another helicopter was sweeping in over the Ellipse. All eyes on the portico turned to the noise. And behind the final column, Remo used the distraction to his advantage.

When the others were looking off toward the sound, Remo reached around the column. Grabbing hold of a shirt collar, he yanked. The terrorist's boots shot off the portico. He disappeared without a sound. Remo muffled the snap of cracking vertebrae with cupped hands.

While the rest of the men were still fixated on the landing helicopter, Remo skipped to the next column.

Only when he finished off the second man and was propping the body against the wrought-iron rail that ran between pillars did he realize that stealth was probably not necessary. The remaining three men seemed oblivious to everything.

"Helicopters are pretty," one said, staring wistfully at the hulking shape of the distant chopper.

"I thought they were gonna feed us," the second whined. "I've been eating nothing but margarine sandwiches for a month."

"If you guys aren't doing anything after the siege, maybe we could, I don't know, hang out," the third suggested with a leer.

Actors. No doubt about it.

Remo walked out from behind the column.

Their guns were lying wherever they'd dropped them. The men were all far too good-looking, with highlighted hair, bulging biceps and jaws that looked as if they'd been welded on.

"Oh, hello." One smiled as Remo took hold of the other pair and stuffed their heads beneath the dirt of a nearby potted cherry tree. The actor frowned as his two companions wiggled in place. "Is this in the script?" he asked, getting reluctantly to his knees. "'Cause if it's not, I want another five bucks."

The other two had stopped squirming. Remo released the inert bundles. When he looked down at the third, the man offered him the back of his neck.

"You actors drain the fun out of everything," Remo grumbled.

Taking the man by the shirt collar, he steered him headfirst into the nearest column. The head went splat. The column didn't.

Leaving the five dead thespians to shine in their new role as corpses, Remo moved swiftly to the glass south doors of the White House.

"IF YOU WANT to fire me, fire me. But listen, I'm the one who booked you this gig."

"My *talent* got me New York," Reginald Hardwin insisted. He was sitting at the President's desk in the Oval Office.

"Reg, baby, sweetheart. Listen to me. With talent and thirty-three cents you can buy a stamp. New York was penny-ante. A nickel-and-dime waste of all our time."

Hardwin didn't bother to tell his agent how much he'd made for presiding over the Regency Building bombing. It was only two days since he'd hired Bernie Leffer. Like all Hollywood agents, if he learned of the amount, he'd somehow find a way to tap into the five million Reginald had been paid to do the Regency.

"It was a first step," Hardwin argued into the phone.

"*First step* being the operative words. Like *baby* step. Washington's the big one. Do you have any idea how much coverage this stunt is getting?"

"Not really, no. A lot?"

"What, they don't have TV in the White House?"

"I don't watch television," Reginald Hardwin sniffed in his most superior British tone. "Except the occasional episode of *Masterpiece Theatre.*"

"Well, I watch it. Just like every other red-blooded American. You're wall-to-wall, Reg. Everywhere. They're not just breaking into the shows—you *are* the shows. Every network. Gavel to gavel. Front to back. Cover to cover. Beginning to end. You are *it.*"

"Yes," Hardwin replied slowly. "Doesn't that make you a little nervous? After all, there is hardly a neat way out of this situation." He had risen to his feet and was peeking around the drapes. The activity around the White House hadn't lessened. If anything, it had only gotten worse.

"There is a way out," Bernie insisted. "A way out that'll make you a multimillionaire. We discussed this, remember? You agreed."

"Yes, I remember," Hardwin admitted.

He was finding it difficult to stay focused. Reginald Hardwin the man had begun to eclipse Reginald Hardwin the terrorist character. His hours of waiting idly in the White House were beginning to jangle his nerves.

"Ours is a celebrity-driven culture, Reg," the agent reminded him. "It doesn't matter how you get famous, as long as you are famous. Maybe being British you don't understand it, but that's the American way. Now, I can spin this off a million different ways. Even if it doesn't go the way I know it's going to go—and I'm 110 percent certain it will—but *if* it doesn't I can still spin it to your advantage. If everyone goes all ga-ga patriotic on us, we can license I Hate Reginald Hardwin T-shirts and bumper stickers. Hell—and this is off the top of my head, could be completely off base here— but think Reginald Hardwin toilet paper! People'd *kill* to wipe their asses on your face!"

Hardwin was aghast. "Bernie, we never discussed—"

"Got a call on my other line, babe. Gotta run."

Closing his eyes on the mocking buzz of the dial tone, Reginald Hardwin replaced the President's phone.

This was the tenth call he'd made to his agent since the start of the White House siege and the ninth for which he had used the phone of the President of the United States. Let the Colonials pick up the tab.

Bernie had avoided him the first nine times. Hardwin was beginning to think that things weren't going as well as his agent claimed.

Wishing he'd gone with CAA, he left the phone

and the President's desk. Hands behind his back, he strolled past the glass doors to the Rose Garden, walking grimly into the secretary's office to the right of the Oval.

His men weren't there.

They were all struggling American actors he'd hired either in New York or Los Angeles. And since they were actors, whenever they weren't sneaking off to have sex with one another in the study, they were off stealing towels and soap from the bathrooms. In between those times, there was only one other thing that kept the men busy.

"Not *another* bloody union break," Hardwin complained.

He marched into the hall. It was empty.

This was unforgivable.

"If you do not show yourselves immediately, I'm canceling the deli platter!" Hardwin shouted to the corridor.

The bellowed threat should have brought a stampede of actors, all flapping towels and zipping flies. When none materialized, Reginald Hardwin felt the first twinge of concern.

He had studied the White House blueprints carefully before taking this job—especially the special sketches given him by his employer. The voice on the phone had told him the optimum points where his men should be stationed. He went to each of them in turn.

Checkpoint after checkpoint was left unguarded. By the time he reached the north portico without encountering even one of his men, his anxiety had grown wings of full fluttering fear.

Hardwin peeked out the door.

Cars jammed the street between the battered White House fence and Lafayette Park. Helicopters sat like angry insects on the grass, rotor blades whirring in perpetual readiness.

It seemed that the enraged eyes of an entire nation were focused squarely on him. Reginald Hardwin panicked.

Fumbling in his pocket, he pulled out his cellular phone. He was ready to accept anything—even another demeaning underwear ad—if only Bernie could get him out of this.

"Solomon, Raithbone and Schwartz."

"Get me Bernie Leffer!" Hardwin begged.

The woman's voice took on a frosty tone that indicated his call wasn't unexpected.

"Mr. Leffer is with a client and can't be bothered for the rest of the day," she said.

"Week," Bernie's voice wailed from the background.

"The rest of the week," the woman parroted.

"What?" Hardwin demanded. *"What?"* he repeated when his phone floated out of his hand. He jumped back.

It was true. His cellular phone had taken on a life of its own. For a surreal moment, it seemed to hover in place.

Hardwin's first thought was that the White House was haunted. But then an even stranger thing happened. A body seemed to materialize from the shadows around the floating telephone. The apparition—possessed of the cruelest face Reginald Hardwin had ever seen—spoke into the phone.

"He'll call you back," Remo said coldly.

He squeezed his hand shut. The cell phone cracked into brittle plastic fragments. Remo dusted them off his palms.

Hardwin gulped, backing slowly away from the intruder. "Will I?" he asked, voice tremulous.

"No," Remo said, eyes dead.

"That's what I thought." Hardwin nodded.

Turning, he ran screaming out the door. He got only as far as the middle of the portico before he found he wasn't making anymore progress. Even when he realized that the terrifying specter was holding him aloft, preventing him from fleeing, Hardwin's spindly legs continued to pump madly in the air.

To escape unscathed, he would have to inspire fear in this fear-inspiring demon. A lifetime's worth of acting skills burst forth in one brilliant thespianic flash. For an instant, Reginald Hardwin the man was replaced once more with Reginald Hardwin the fiendish character.

"Release me," he commanded, in his best diabolical-villain sneer, "or I swear to you Lucifer himself could not imagine a more terrible fate for you."

"Okeydoke."

Remo set Hardwin down. Legs still pumping, Reginald promptly ran at a full gallop across the north portico and straight into one of the white Ionic columns.

The crunching impact smashed his nose, one cheekbone and an eye socket. Hardwin was pulling himself off the portico when Remo approached.

"Stop!" Hardwin commanded, desperately trying to stay in character. "Or you consign your President to death. This building has been wired to explode in one minute. Only *I* can stop the countdown." He spit out a few bloodied incisors.

"Give it a rest, Dr. Evil," Remo said, annoyed. "Bombs have an odor and I didn't smell any. You're just some dingwhistle actor who was hired to pull off this cockamamy plan. Now, what the hell is going on here?"

As Remo spoke, Reginald Hardwin felt more and more of his character slip away until in the end there was nothing left but the actor beneath the role.

"I want a lawyer," Hardwin squeaked. Tears welled up, stinging his injured eye.

"We're beyond lawyer. Think undertaker," Remo said. "Who hired you? And if you tell me it was a voice on the phone who you never met in person and who paid you through the mail, you're going over that railing, ass, accent and all."

Since this was precisely what had happened, Hardwin weighed the risk of lying and being thrown off the balcony or, apparently, telling the truth and being thrown off the balcony, as well. His eyes darted left and right in search of a third alternative that wouldn't result in his winding up airborne. He chirped in cornered fear.

"Dammit, not again," Remo snarled. "What did he say?"

Hardwin offered a hopeful, snaggletoothed smile. "Well, after we blew up the Regency—" he shrank from Remo's glare "—he called about this," he continued timidly. "He knew his way around the White House. He gave me blueprints and sketches. Things not known to the public. He was the one who arranged for the explosives in New York and the guns and the charges for the fence here. He seemed very connected with the underworld."

"If you factor in whores and drugs, so's pretty much everyone in Hollywood."

Remo was thinking of Stefan Schoenburg and his contributions to the President. His donations could have bought him an insiders' look at the White House layout. Face stern, Remo reached for Hardwin.

"Die Down IV!" the actor gasped, jumping from Remo's hand.

The name caught Remo off guard. "What?" he asked.

"This," Hardwin insisted, waving both arms grandly to encompass both White House and grounds. "All this is part of *Die Down IV*. An extended action sequence takes place here."

Remo's brow furrowed. "Someone told me *Die Down IV* is based on the Hollywood invasion last year," he said.

"It is," Hardwin explained. "This is an interpretation of those events. An extrapolation, if you will. My contact didn't tell me this. I learned it through the actors' grapevine. I don't know if it's helpful, but if it's information you desire, I give you this freely in exchange for my life." His eyes were pleading.

Remo was thinking about Bindle and Marmelstein. Quintly Tortilli had said *Die Down IV* was a Taurus production, set to kick off the summer movie season in just a couple of weeks. If this had anything to do with that, then—Chiun or not—the two Taurus cochairs were going to have more than just a little explaining to do.

Before him, Reginald Hardwin took Remo's silence for agreement to his terms. The actor smiled. His eye behind his broken socket winced.

"Sorry about all this, dear boy," he apologized. "Bit of a mess we've made for you, I suspect." He spotted a couple of his teeth on the portico and put them in his pocket. "Can't really blame me, though. Remember our credo—an actor *lives* to act."

Remo looked up absently. He was biting his cheek in thought. "You're the exception that proves the rule," he said.

Reginald Hardwin almost saw the hand that ended his life. He definitely saw stars. Unfortunately, none of them were him. And then the stars fell, the universe collapsed and the curtain came down on the most brilliant acting career that never was.

25

When Remo swung up from the darkened elevator shaft into the hallway of the First Family's residence, the first instinct of the Secret Service agents was to open fire. They found their fingers clutching air instead of triggers.

To their astonishment, they saw that their guns were lying in a neat pile on the carpeted floor a few feet from the open elevator door.

"Remo Barkman, assistant treasury director," Remo said, waving an ID at the startled agents. "Downstairs should be secure, but you better check. Until you know for sure, I don't want anyone announcing anything over the radio."

The men quickly obeyed. A contingent remained to safeguard the First Family while the rest collected their guns and raced downstairs.

Remo's sensitive nose detected a thin wisp of smoke in the air. He followed it to the library.

Inside, the First Lady was in full shred mode. In her haste, she was destroying every scrap of paper she could lay her hands on. It looked like a ticker-tape parade had passed through the room. She stood ankle deep in strips of paper, a demonic look on her beauty-cream-caked face.

"What the hell do you want?" the First Lady demanded when Remo stuck his head around the corner.

She was stuffing the D.C. Yellow Pages into the smoking shredder. Yellow confetti flew out of the overstuffed bin.

"Just checking to see if you're okay, ma'am," Remo said.

"Do I look okay?" the First Lady snarled. She had finished with the phone book. An angry hand grabbed up a book of Walt Whitman's poetry. With the hilt of an antique sword that had belonged to Ulysses S. Grant, she began stuffing the volume into the shredder. The machine clunked and whirred in pain.

"Who's that? Is it safe?" a familiar muffled voice whined timidly from the closet. Beyond the closed door, a dog barked.

"Shut that damn dog up," the First Lady snapped. She was having trouble with the cover of the poetry book. She pounded it down with the sword hilt. "I swear, if that mongrel was female we'd be combing your DNA out of its mangy fur," she muttered.

As the smoke detector began to sound, Remo ducked back out of the room. The poor overused shredder continued to clonk in pain as he headed to the Lincoln Bedroom.

THE CRISIS in Washington had crawled into the silent postmidnight hours, and still Harold W. Smith had not left his desk. Eyes burning with fatigue, he was sitting in his battered leather chair scanning the latest information from out of the nation's capital when the red White House phone buzzed to life.

He jumped in his chair. Fingers fleeing his keyboard, he quickly picked up the receiver.

"Yes?" he said, voice tentative. As if unsure who might be on the other end of the line.

"Break out your checkbooks—the White House is safe once more for Chinese arms dealers and South American drug lords," Remo's familiar voice proclaimed.

"Remo," Smith exhaled. "Is the crisis over?"

"I wouldn't want my daughter interning here," Remo replied dryly, "but if you mean the terrorists, they're history. You can start sending in the cavalry in a couple of minutes. Just give me a sec to sneak out of here."

"The President?" Smith asked.

"He's okay, Smitty," Remo said. "Although he did about as well as his ROTC commander would expect. He's hiding in the closet with the First Mutt while Lady Macbeth shreds the life out of every scrap of paper in a three-state area."

Smith let out a protracted sigh. "That is a relief."

"If your definition of relief is having these two in the pink, I don't want to know what you think anxiety is."

The CURE director refused to get caught up in discussing the personalities of the First Family.

"Who was behind the siege?" he pressed.

"Hold on to your socks, Smitty," Remo said. "It's the same crew we're already after."

Smith's voice was sharp. "How can you be certain?"

"Because I'm up to my armpits in SAG membership cards," Remo said. "According to the nitwit in charge here, this was all staged to help the new *Die Down* movie. Oh, and the bombing in New York is tied in with all this, too."

Smith could scarcely believe what he was hearing. "I will see which studio is producing that film," he said, swiveling to his computer.

"Don't bother," Remo said. He took a deep breath and prayed Chiun wouldn't hold this against him. "It's Taurus, Smitty," he informed the CURE director.

"Bindle and Marmelstein," Smith breathed.

"I'll talk to them when I get back to Lalaland."

"Be sure you do," Smith insisted. "It appears they are more deeply involved than you had earlier determined."

"Yeah, but this wasn't on the agenda, Smitty. At least not when I talked to them."

"There have not been any suspicious calls to either their homes or office," Smith explained. "If the telephone is the means by which the mastermind of these events contacts his employees, then this must have been planned prior to your visit with them.''

"Maybe," Remo said. "It's amazing that even a couple of dopes as big as Bindle and Marmelstein would go to these lengths to make sure some stupid movie is a hit."

Alone in his drab office, Smith shook his head. "Not really," he said. "I have been doing some research. The market is very competitive. A big-budget Hollywood film can cost anywhere from 50 to 150 million dollars to produce. Some have gone even higher. Given the lucrative overseas and home-video markets, some would apparently do anything for a hit." Smith drew their conversation to a close. "Remo, if this is all, you should leave there. I do not like the idea of you staying in the White House any longer than is necessary."

"There's something else that could be important, Smitty," Remo said gravely, before Smith could hang up. "The Twit of the Year in charge here said he had blueprints and diagrams of the White House layout. Stuff the public wouldn't have. I'm thinking big Hollywood contributors buying access."

Smith pursed his lips. "Is it possible the President would jeopardize his personal security for a contribution?"

"Where have you been, Smitty? For a thousand-buck legal-defense-fund contribution, you could probably buy the nuclear football. Anyway, I don't know what director or producers are behind *Die Down IV,* but there's hardly a summer that passes without Stefan Schoenburg or those other guys having a blockbuster.''

"I will look into that angle," Smith promised.

"Okay, that's it. I'm outta here."

The line went dead in Smith's ear. The instant it did, the CURE director turned to his keyboard. He began entering the commands that would send agents swarming into the White House. He wasn't concerned that Remo would be caught. Smith knew better. He had seen Remo in action too many times.

After he was through, Smith paused at his keyboard.

His thoughts turned to Stefan Schoenburg and to the anger the President would doubtless display if his Hollywood friend were disgraced by CURE. Or worse.

In that moment, Smith decided that it didn't matter. Presidents came and Presidents went, but America and CURE had always survived them. He would use any and all means to learn who was behind this plot. The President's personal considerations be damned.

At that moment of decision, it was as if a weight had been lifted from the CURE director's frail shoulders.

Dropping his arthritic hands to his keyboard, Smith threw himself into his work with renewed vigor.

26

The blinds were drawn tightly. The light dimmer was set just a hair above pitch-black. Bindle and Marmelstein were dark shadows in the claustrophobic gray of their sprawling Taurus office. They had built a barricade from the broken halves of Hank Bindle's desk. They hunkered behind their personal Maginot Line, bottles and tumblers arranged around them on the floor.

The only sound for a long time was the tinkle of glass on glass followed by grateful slurping. As the shadows around them lengthened, Hank Bindle finally peeked nervously over the desk.

"Are you crazy?" Bruce Marmelstein charged, dragging him back to the floor.

"I have to pee, Bruce," Bindle complained.

Marmelstein shoved an empty Waterford decanter into his partner's hands. "Here," he whispered.

Bindle took the crystal container reluctantly.

"Maybe we shouldn't stay here," he suggested as he filled the decanter with the contents of his nervous bladder. "He knows this is our office."

"Which is exactly why we should stay here,"

Bruce Marmelstein argued. "If he connects the White House thing to us, then he'll come looking for us."

Bindle put the now full decanter down. He was careful to separate it from the rest. "But won't he come straight here?" he asked, zipping up.

"Yes," Marmelstein agreed. "But since he knows we'll know he's coming here, then he'll think we wouldn't be stupid enough to stay here."

"But we *are* here," Bindle stressed.

"Which proves we're innocent," Marmelstein concluded.

"Stop it, Bruce," Bindle moaned. "You're making my boo-boo hurt." He held the cool crystal of his empty glass to his forehead. The bruise he'd gotten from bashing his head off the window pane was masked with makeup.

"America has a short attention span," Marmelstein argued. "Think MTV generation. No one'll remember the White House thing tomorrow. Not even Mr. Desk Hater."

But Bindle wasn't convinced. "I don't know," the Taurus cochair whispered. "The White House is, like, famous or something. What if they don't forget?"

"Hey, it was not our fault," Bruce Marmelstein hissed angrily. "Sure, we blew up one measly floor in some nothing New York building and tried to blow up our own—stress *our own*—studio complex. But that's it."

"But they might be mad about New York."

"Naw." Marmelstein waved dismissively. Bourbon splashed out of his tumbler. "That was just promotion. Everyone'd understand that."

Quietly, Hank Bindle hoped that Remo was part of the "everyone" to whom his partner referred. He was reaching for a fresh bottle when a soft bell sounded in the outer office. Their private elevator.

Bindle froze, hand locked around the neck of the bottle.

"It's him," he hissed.

Fear propelled them to their knees. As they watched from behind the shattered desk, a dark shape appeared in the glass office doors. Bindle and Marmelstein's eyes were sick as they waited for Remo to enter.

The figure cupped hands over eyes, peering into the darkness of the office interior. Slowly, the door pushed open. The dark shape slipped inside the room.

"Jeez, it's like the mummy's tomb in here," a nasal voice complained. "You guys ever see *The Mummy?* Boris Karloff acting, Karl Freund directing. I swiped enough from that to pad three movies. And mine had swearing."

A balled fist jabbed out in the darkness, punching the dimmer control on the wall near the door. The office was suddenly awash in glaring light.

Bindle and Marmelstein blinked away the stabbing pain in their eyes as they tried to focus on Quintly Tortilli.

"Turn that off," Bindle said.

"Why? So the big Oogidy-Boogidy can't find you?" Tortilli asked, fluttering his fingers. The director wore a neon-yellow leisure suit and a clashing green ruffled shirt.

"We wouldn't have to hide if you didn't do what you promised you wouldn't," Marmelstein pouted as Quintly strutted over to them. "Why did you take over the White House?"

As he perched on the side of the overturned desk, a grin split the knotted fist that was Quintly Tortilli's face. "What's it always about, fellas? Box office," he proclaimed.

"That doesn't help us," Bindle whined up at him. "This studio is going down the tubes, Quintly. Ten blockbusters won't pull us out of the hole we're in."

"*One* blockbuster *and* blowing up the studio might have helped," Marmelstein interjected. "If we'd collected the insurance money."

"Might have," Bindle agreed. "But you didn't blow it up, Quintly. And you promised."

Marmelstein sniffled morosely. "At best, we've got one piddling blockbuster, a failed studio, two golden parachutes and the entire industry laughing at us when *E.T.* shows us in line at the Tinseltown unemployment office."

Both Bindle and Marmelstein ducked behind the shattered desk. They reappeared a moment later, fat tumblers filled to the brims with scotch. They downed their drinks in simultaneous gulps.

"Turn those frowns upside down," Tortilli said.

"You're thinking, like, yesterday. I'm thinking to-morrow."

"You can afford to think that way," Marmelstein said, his voice taking on an angry edge. "We might not even have a tomorrow. There's some desk-smashing psycho out there who's already been snooping around. You could have told us before yesterday you were the guy calling us for the past month, Quintly. But, no, you had to wait until you got back from Seattle—after you cashed all our checks. Now you've tied us in to the White House thing—which, as a promotional tool, was discussed, considered and ultimately rejected. By the by, if the cash for that was from a Taurus account, I want it back."

"Sorry, man, no can do." Quintly shrugged. "It's already gone."

"Well, you didn't blow up the studio," Bindle sniffed. "We want *that* money back."

"Listen, guys, your fiduciary concerns viz the studio-nonblowing-up event are grounded, but are, you know, totally rejectable. Just because the place didn't blow up, it doesn't mean the money wasn't spent. Remember, guns and explosives don't come cheap."

"It was doody," Bindle whined.

"Shit costs," Tortilli said simply. "Plus the ac-tors weren't free."

"Extras are a dime a dozen," Bindle said. "It's that Hardwin ham you paid too much to. He's a freaking underpants pitchman, for God's sake.

Couldn't you have gotten someone like an F. Murray Abraham or a Stacy Keach type?''

Tortilli put on a reasonable tone. ''If the utterly inconceivable happens and the shit hits the fan and this is traced back to you, do *you* want F. Murray Abraham associated in any way with a Taurus film?''

They considered for half a heartbeat. ''Okay, the Hardwin cash was worth it.'' Marmelstein nodded. ''But do you really think this White House stunt of yours will help?''

''It'll get us partway there.'' Tortilli nodded.

''What does it matter?'' Bindle asked morosely. ''Even if this is the biggest blockbuster of the summer, we're going to be stuck. Taurus is over. Our careers are shot.''

Tortilli smiled. ''Don't worry,'' the director said. ''With the final act I've got planned, we won't just have the biggest blockbuster of the summer, but the biggest moneymaker of all time. I'm gonna sink *Titanic* and *Phantom Menace*. You'll be able to spin your way into the top spots at any studio in town. We'll all be sitting pretty.''

''There's more?'' Bindle asked, eyes worried.

''We've only had Acts One and Two. Don't forget Act Three.'' Tortilli smiled.

Bindle and Marmelstein exchanged a single worried glance. Their shoulders slumped.

''We're gonna trust you on this one, Quintly,'' Marmelstein sighed. ''Since you're a genius and all.''

To celebrate their partnership, Bindle poured them all a drink from the decanter at his knees. The three men drank greedily. For some reason the liquor was warm and watery.

"Tastes salty," Hank Bindle observed as he polished off the last of the strange yellow liquid.

27

Lee Matson had wanted to be a Green Beret ever since he had seen the John Wayne movie of the same name.

"They're all over this killing stuff," he had assured his Berwick, Pennsylvania, high-school guidance counselor, who was trying to convince Lee to give college a try.

"Yes," Mrs. Patterson had said uncomfortably.

Since striding into her office in his fatigues and boots, Matson, Lee W., had seemed a little too preoccupied with blood and bludgeoning and eviscerating small woodland creatures. He also never blinked. Not once. Her flesh crawled underneath her sensible cotton blouse.

"That's maybe something we can see as a goal a little farther down the road," the middle-aged woman offered, clearing her throat. "But have we considered the sound foundation college can give us?"

"Speaking of sounds," Lee enthused, unblinking eyes wide with enthusiasm, "did you know I've recorded eleven separate and distinct sounds a chipmunk makes when you hammer a nail into its head?''

As he went on to mimic each individual mortal squeak, Mrs. Patterson was already on the phone to the local recruiting office.

Just like that, he was in the Army.

And just like that, he was out two weeks later.

''I swear I didn't know the bayonet was loaded, Sergeant,'' Lee begged as the boot-camp gate was locked behind him. ''And that landmine was like that when I got there!''

The sergeant used a bandaged hand to push his hat back on his head. His eyes—one of them black-ened—were pools of roiling menace. ''In ten sec-onds, I open fire.''

''But I want to proudly wear a green beret,'' Lee whined.

''Join the Girl Scouts.''

To Lee, it was the most devastating thing that could possibly have happened. He had only one dream in life: to kill with the Green Berets. Now that dream had been dashed.

After washing out at boot camp, Lee began to take stock of his life and his future prospects.

Things hadn't turned out the way he had ex-pected. Okay. The same could be said for a lot of people. Lee decided to grab the bull by the horns. He might not be able to enjoy the legal protection of killing in the name of the American government but, by all that was holy, he would kill.

Of course, Lee didn't just run out and kill the

first person he met. He wasn't crazy, after all. In spite of what his parents, teachers, Mrs. Patterson, his mailman or the United States Army thought.

Instead, Lee decided to hire himself out as a commando. A soldier of fortune with a don't-mess-with-me attitude and a high-tech, kick-ass arsenal for hire. Unfortunately, there just wasn't that much call for mercenaries in junta-free Berwick, Pennsylvania. Lee moved to New York.

It would have been great there for him if he hadn't come to the city during law-and-order Mayor Randolph Gillotti's ironfisted reign. The one time he tried to distribute his assassin-for-hire pamphlets in Midtown, he'd been arrested.

There was a long kill-free dry spell. Things got so bad that Lee was about to go the serial-killer route. He was on his way out the door of his apartment one evening to pick up his first tunnel-bunny hooker victim when the phone rang.

Lee had placed classified ads in all the major commando niche magazines. It turned out that the one in *Guns and Blammo* had caught someone's eye.

"Is this Captain Kill?" the giddy, rapid-fire voice asked. The caller sounded like a record recorded at 33 rpm and played back at 45.

Visions of murdered prostitutes dancing in his head, it took Lee a second to remember his top-secret commando code name, known only to a few thousand magazine readers.

"Yeah, that's me," he admitted gruffly. "Whaddaya got?"

Lee tried to sound like a cool professional. But when the voice on the phone began to outline the specifics of the job for which Lee was being hired, the novice soldier of fortune balked.

"You want me to kill a family?" Lee asked uncertainly.

"Not just any family. Their name's gotta be Anderson. Has to be a mom, dad, son, daughter. The whole Donna Reed thing."

"I don't know," Lee said. "My specialty generally is overthrowing neo-Communist regimes. Maybe you have a South American dictator you want iced?"

The caller was adamant. Name had to be Anderson. Family of four. And there were other specifics.

"Why a tunnel?" Lee frowned.

"Do you want me to call someone else?"

"No, no," Lee said hastily. "Tunnels are good. We dug lots of them in Nam."

Lee, who was born two years after the fall of Saigon and whose only knowledge of Vietnam came from his favorite John Wayne film, listened intently to the plan the caller outlined for him.

It sounded almost like a plot synopsis. So detailed—even down to the methods that were to be used for killing the two Anderson females—that Lee felt an involuntary chill.

His only question came at the end, after his

would-be employer mentioned once more how important it was that the family be named Anderson.

"Where do I find them?" Lee asked.

"Anywhere. Try a Maryland phone book."

"Why Maryland?"

The caller was so happily casual it was almost unnerving. "Why not?" he suggested.

After two weeks of legwork, Lee found what he was looking for in his third randomly selected phone book.

It had taken a while to dig the tunnel, but once he was through, the rest worked like clockwork. The murders, stealing his precious Girl Scout beret and sash as trophies, his escape. It was like poetry.

"Congratulations," his employer had said delightedly the day after news of the slaying broke in the papers.

"Just doing my job," Lee bragged. He was back in his New York apartment.

"And you're good at it, man. There's a bonus already on its way. Enjoy it. Catch ya soon."

True to his word, the bonus had come by special Taurus studio courier that afternoon. The bag was even adorned with the famous constellation insignia of Taurus.

Lee found it all very strange. Strange enough to think something bigger than a simple multiple murder was going on.

When the film *Suburban Decay* opened a few days after the events at the Anderson household, Lee Matson began to put two and two together.

The other two similarly strange cases were listed in some of the Anderson articles. The box murder and the coed slayings were said by some to be part of a larger conspiracy. But the three movies that mirrored the real-life events were from a place called Cabbagehead Productions in Seattle. Lee's money had come from Taurus, in Hollywood.

What was the connection? He found the answer in, of all places, a copy of *Entertainment Weekly*.

Taurus was gearing up for the new *Die Down* film. In the article Lee read, studio cochair Bruce Marmelstein was crowing about the fact that they had snagged hotshot Quintly Tortilli to direct the latest entry in the film franchise.

For Lee, it all clicked in that moment. That voice on the phone was the same one he'd heard on the Jay Leno, Charlie Rose shows and in a bunch of bit parts in a handful of really bad movies. Quintly Tortilli had hired him to murder an innocent family.

He was even more certain when the caller phoned back.

"Hey, Lee, baby. How the fuck are you with explosives?" the man Lee now knew to be Quintly Tortilli asked.

Lee became the front man for Hollywood's hottest young director.

Tortilli called Lee, and Lee called everybody else. Thanks to the Internet and the friendly folks at Radio Shack, Lee was able to construct a rabbit repeater box. With this, he managed to manipulate his phone line's ID just in case anyone got smart and tried to trace all this back to him. As far as he knew, it was unnecessary. It had been smooth sailing straight through hiring Reginald Hardwin—at Tortilli's urging, of course—to assembling the explosives and weapons necessary for the Regency and the White House operations. He had even had a hand in some of the grunt work in Operation Final Cut, the failed attempt to wipe out Taurus Studios.

It was all pretty simple stuff. Tortilli would call Lee with instructions, sometimes send him orders, and Lee would regurgitate the pertinent information to the men in the field. Lee was the go-between that would allow Tortilli deniability if the shit ever hit the fan.

To Lee Matson, it was all a great deal of fun. Plus if the time ever came that he grew bored with their arrangement, he could blackmail Tortilli. With what he had on the director, Lee could clean him out so completely the young *Penny Dreadful* genius would have to go back to his original job of ushering in a movie theater.

The day of the assault on the White House, Lee was sitting at his old Smith-Corona in his crummy Queens apartment. On the nineteen-inch TV, reporters talked in serious tones about the ongoing crisis in the nation's capital. Lee wasn't really listening to them. As the nation watched with rapt attention, he was hunting and pecking at the old manual typewriter, tongue jutting between his lips in concentration.

Lee was reaching for the Wite-Out when the phone rang.

"Captain Kill," he said, swabbing at the *S* that should have been a *D*.

"Hiya, Lee. Me again."

Tortilli. Lee capped the Wite-Out.

"What can I do for you?" he asked, bored. He sucked a bit of the steak he'd had for lunch from his bicuspids.

"Another little job, man. Good press. Bigger than what's going on right now. Should get banner headlines."

"What's the deal?"

"I don't want to talk about it like this," Tortilli said. "I'll fly you to L.A. We'll talk then."

Once the arrangements had been made and Tortilli had hung up, Lee quickly gathered up the pages of the screenplay he'd been working on. He was on the next flight to California.

A Taurus jeep brought him from LAX to a fancy Beverly Hills hotel. The phone was ringing before he'd even given a fifty-cent tip to the bellboy.

"Cap Kill here," Lee announced blandly, lying back on the soft bed.

"How do you feel about assassination, Lee?" the voice of Quintly Tortilli asked.

"In my business, that's just a fancy word for killing," Lee said confidently. "What do you got?"

"I'm going to make you the most famous killer of the new century." Tortilli giggled. "You'll be right up there with J. Harry Osmond and what's-his-name. The guy who killed Reagan.'' The director was beside himself with joy. Murder talk always sparked giddiness in the young auteur.

"How much?" Lee Matson asked.

"A million up front and a back-end million."

Lee sat up, dropping his feet delicately to the floor. He had only gotten a hundred thousand for the Andersons.

"Okay," he agreed slowly. "I'll accept the job on one condition."

"What's that?" Tortilli asked suspiciously.

"Well, I don't know exactly who you are," Lee lied, "but the Taurus jeep, the studio envelopes, the fact I'm here in L.A. I kinda gotta think you're in the movie business somehow."

"And?" Tortilli asked, annoyance creeping into his tone.

Lee cleared his throat. "Well," he began, "it's just that I've got this script I've been working on...."

HOURS LATER, with the promise from Quintly Tortilli of a production deal and screenwriting credit plus executive-producer status, Lee Matson found himself at the loading dock behind the Burbank Bowl. Standing in his fatigues, he watched as the stagehands removed the heavy crates from the back of the Taurus Studios truck. They grunted under the weight.

Tortilli had made all the arrangements on this

one. All Lee had to do was flip the switch and watch the world dance.

He'd learned upon his arrival that the day at the bowl had been a frantic one. Management wasn't certain if the unfortunate circumstances back east might keep their most famous guest away. But the crisis had ended abruptly. According to the advance people, he was on his way after all.

Under pressure from the front office, the stage crew was being pushed to get everything perfect. Cursing management all the way, two stagehands struggled to get the first of Lee Matson's two equipment crates to the loading dock.

Lee strolled alongside them, hands in his pockets. He chewed languidly at a thick wad of gum.

"You really a musician?" one of them queried, straining to carry the crate. He was looking at Lee's hat.

"At least till I get my screenplay produced," Lee replied. With one hand, he adjusted his green Girl Scout's beret. The sash he'd taken from the Anderson house had been folded lengthwise and slipped through his belt loops.

"Yeah?" the man panted. "I got a script in turnaround. Hey, this thing weighs a ton. What's in this?"

"You familiar with Tchaikovsky's *1812* Overture?" Lee Matson asked as they mounted the stairs. His wide eyes didn't blink.

"That's the one that ends with the cannons, right?"

Lee smiled. "Tonight we finish it, but good."

Hauling the first of Lee Matson's cannons, the men ducked in the stage door of the Burbank Bowl. They moved quickly, for there was still much to do before the arrival that night of the President of the United States.

28

The airports around Washington remained closed until late morning the day after the White House drama. Remo had forgotten all about Chiun's script until he sank into his first-class seat on the flight from Washington to L.A.

Pulling the tightly rolled tube of paper from his back pocket, he laid it across his service tray. With a simple sweep of his hand, he returned the coil of papers to a flattened state. He had just begun reading the script when another passenger dropped into the seat next to his.

"Can you believe this?" the man drawled. "I'm supposed to be flying *my* plane back to L.A. Here I fly to Washington to discuss religious persecution with the President, and not only can't he see me because of some stupid terrorist thing he's scheduled for the same day, but they won't even let any private jets take off until they've searched them."

Remo glanced over at the man. He found that he was staring into the vacant eyes of Jann Revolta.

The actor had been a star in the 1970s only to become a has-been in the 1980s. If Quintly Tortilli hadn't resurrected him from box-office death by casting him in *Penny Dreadful,* the actor would have been relegated to B-movie sequels featuring talking babies for the rest of his inauspicious career. Thanks to Tortilli's retro mentality, Revolta was now in virtually every movie Hollywood produced.

"What are you doing?" Revolta asked, curious.

Half standing, Remo was craning his neck, trying to see if there were any vacant seats. Unfortunately, the cabin was full. Exhaling annoyance, he sat back down.

"I'm *trying* to read," Remo muttered.

"Oh." Revolta nodded. "I don't do much of that. I'm too busy making movies to read even half the scripts I do. Hey, is that a script?" he asked excitedly, leaning toward Remo's tray. His ample paunch made it a struggle. "Gimme twenty million and I'm in." As soon as he saw the main character's name, the actor's face grew deeply disappointed. "Ohhh, I can't be in that movie," he groaned. "It's a Lance Wallace vehicle."

Remo had heard of the actor. But he couldn't be in Chiun's movie. Remo hadn't seen Wallace during any of his time on the Taurus lot. Revolta supplied the answer to a question Remo didn't have time to ask.

"Lance is back as the hotshot cop, but I heard he finished his work a month ago," the actor said. "Of course, Quintly wanted *me* to star at first. Back then, it was this weird little story about assassins working for the government or something, but then the studio changed the focus and moved it the franchise route. Did I mention I have an airplane?"

Remo had quickly lost interest in anything the actor had to say. He was focused back on the script.

Hoping to shut Revolta up without having to deal with the questions a paralyzed voice box might bring, he went the Machiavellian route.

"Horshack carried you," Remo said blandly. He didn't even glance at the actor.

Revolta frowned. "I'm sensing coldness here," he said.

"Think how much colder it'll be when I stick you out on the wing at thirty thousand feet."

"Is this a test? If it is, you can't upset me with your hostility," Revolta insisted. "*I'm* a 40.0."

"If that's your IQ, it's about twice what I expected."

"Just what I'd expect from a 1.1," Revolta said firmly. "I'm talking about the Timbre Scale. It plots the descending spiral of life from full vitality all the way down to death. You're a 1.1. Someone who exhibits covert hostility."

Remo was a little disappointed in himself. He thought he was being as overt in his hostility as possible.

"*I* am a 40.0," the actor continued proudly. "Someone who experiences complete serenity." He fumbled in his carry-on bag, producing a thick paperback book. "If you want to change your life for the better..."

With a lunatic's grin, he offered the book to

Remo. On the cover, an ominous black tornado ravaged a desolate plain. The word *Diarrhetics* was printed at the top. "By Rubin Dolomo" was printed in smaller type at the bottom.

Remo remembered hearing about this on TV. Revolta was one of the many celebrity members of the Poweressence cult. A few years before, he had even gotten the president to chastise Germany for its treatment of cult members in that country. In exchange, Revolta agreed to dull the sharper edges of his performance as the President in a film based on the Chief Executive's 1992 campaign.

Remo accepted the Poweressence bible from the actor.

"Here's a little trick the First Lady taught me," he said, smiling.

His hands became chopping blurs. By the time he was finished four seconds later, Revolta's book had been transformed into a heap of confetti on the actor's lap. Revolta's eyes were wide as he stared, slack-jawed at the mound of shredded paper.

"Thanks," Remo said. "I feel better already."

He returned to Chiun's script.

Snapping his fingers, Revolta summoned a stewardess to remove the remnants of his bible.

"You're mean," he proclaimed once the woman was gone. "I wouldn't be in your movie for all the twenty million dollars in the world." He tipped his head, considering. "Unless the back-end deal was sweet enough. Twenty million plus enough points to cover your meanness and maybe buy me a new airplane. Of course, I'm playing Poopsy-Woopsy in the TeeVeeFatties movie that's coming up. Time is tight, but I could do your movie after that. I've got about a week. Okay, it's a deal,'' he exclaimed grandly. When he found that Remo was still engrossed in Chiun's script, he bit his lip. ''Are they still calling that thing *Assassin's Loves?* I can't believe they didn't come up with a better working title after they rewrote it into *Die Down IV.*''

Remo had been doing his best to ignore Revolta. But at the mention of the movie title, a twinge of concern knotted small in his stomach.

''What do you mean, *Die Down IV?*'' he asked.

''That's the latest *Die Down* movie,'' the actor said, pointing at Remo's script. ''They do that with movies sometimes—retitle them during production. Especially franchise ones like this. Throws people off the scent. I don't know how good it works, though. Everybody in the industry knows Taurus got the rights to the series and that Tortilli is directing it.''

Remo looked down at the script with disturbed eyes. His thoughts turned to Reginald Hardwin and the White House siege. If what Revolta was saying was true...

''But I know the guy who wrote this,'' Remo said. ''I don't think he's ever even seen one of those movies.''

''I told you. Things change in development. Like when I was making *I'm Talking to You, Too.* Originally, there was only supposed to be one craft-services truck. But my leading lady had gotten so fat by the sequel they were bringing pizzas in by the..."

Remo was no longer listening. Hands flashing, he skipped rapidly ahead in the script.

He found what he was looking for on page forty-two. In a detailed action scene, a group of armed terrorists invaded the White House and took the First Family hostage. Skipping back, he located another long section where the same terrorists blew up a floor in a Manhattan office building.

"Damn," he muttered.

"...the Jaws of Life to get her out the door," Revolta finished. Glancing over, he noted the look on Remo's face. "Oh," he said, looking down at the script. "Does it still end with the big gun battle at LAX? When Quintly mentioned that to me, I told him it reminded me too much of *Die Down II.*"

Remo hadn't even thought to see how the screenplay ended. He was still trying to digest the fact that for much of the day he had been holding a virtual blueprint of the White House siege in his back pocket.

Remo had been ready to blame Bindle and Marmelstein. But now he realized Quintly Tortilli was a better actor than he'd thought. The director had been faking it back in Seattle. And in Hollywood, he'd neglected to mention that the movie that would benefit most from the recent news events—*Die Down IV*—was his.

In an instant, it was all clear. Tortilli was the mastermind.

Remo skipped to the end of the script. He could see nothing of a battle at Los Angeles International Airport.

"It looks like it's on a boat," he said aloud.

"Must have rewritten it again." Revolta nodded.

"Definitely a boat," Remo said, talking more to himself than to the actor. He was riffling through the script. "Terrorists steal a mothballed battleship from Long Beach."

"Isn't that closed?" Revolta said. "Anyway, I don't like it. Too much like *Under Siege*. Although that was a *Die Down I* rip-off." He glanced around, annoyed. "Are they going to feed us or what? I haven't eaten since the airport."

Only now were they taxiing for takeoff.

Remo wasn't paying attention to the actor. He was thinking about how Chiun's screenplay ended.

It seemed anticlimactic after invading the White House. The theft of a retired battleship was mild compared with what had already gone on. But here it was in Remo's hands.

The Master of Sinanju already suspected that Remo was jealous of his great movie deal. Remo didn't know how Chiun would react when he told him about Quintly Tortilli. And for the first time in a long time, Remo didn't give a damn how all this would affect Chiun's movie. After so many months of lies and secrecy and having to deal with the old

Korean's ballooning ego, he wished he could savor the sensation.

His face was grim as he settled back in his seat for the long flight to California.

29

Alone in his trailer on the Taurus lot, Quintly Tortilli studied himself in the long door mirror. His garish purple polyester tuxedo with its brazen green ruffled shirt, sequined maroon cummerbund and giant floppy yellow felt bow tie would have embarrassed a circus clown.

To the rose-colored eyes of Quintly Tortilli, the reflection staring back at him could have just stepped off the cover of *GQ*. It had been a long time since he'd had so much *fun* dressing up.

Die Down IV was nearly finished.

He'd finished the bulk of the film weeks before, wrapping up work with the principal actors just before flying to Seattle. In Washington, he used the Cabbagehead facilities to edit the Arlen Duggal-directed footage that was flown to him on a daily basis.

There was no doubt about it. In spite of what Bindle and Marmelstein and Duggal thought, although he seemed to take an unconcerned attitude with this film, it was his baby. Quintly Tortilli was in charge of the project from start to finish. And the finish line was in sight.

The special-effects house hired to complete the various miniature, matte and pyrotechnic shots would have their work back in less than a week. *Die Down IV* would make its pre-Memorial Day release date. And Tortilli would have a hit. Finally.

He'd had a hit before. But *Penny Dreadful* was more like an indie film that had somehow crossed over. Quintly Tortilli—the genius, the maverick, Hollywood's hottest young director since Stefan Schoenburg—had never been able to duplicate that early success.

In the mid-1990s, he was ubiquitous. He made all the talk-show rounds. He tried his hand at acting and producing. On a whim he'd even directed that episode of the highly rated television hospital drama, *OR*.

That was when Quintly Tortilli was at the top of his game. But the fire that he thought would never go out soon threatened to be extinguished. And with it, his career.

Without something to promote, the talk-show circuit eventually dried up. His acting was universally panned. The films he produced were all box-office bombs.

Actors could coast for years on just a little box-office success. The young genius of *Penny Dreadful* found that forgiveness didn't extend to directors.

The truth was Quintly Tortilli needed a hit. Badly. But few respectable offers came in.

As his bank account dwindled, Tortilli found that he needed something even more basic than a hit.

He needed a job. Of course, he always had his script-doctor income, but lately even the paychecks for that were shrinking. A high-profile directing job could pump his asking price back up into the stratosphere. When word came from Taurus Studios that Tortilli was wanted to direct the next *Die Down* sequel, he had accepted without hesitation.

There were troubles from the start.

First, Lance Wallace didn't want to do it. He claimed he had said everything he wanted to say with his lone-cop character in the first three films. A twenty-two-million-dollar paycheck and gross points changed the actor's tune, but his salary cut seriously into the film's budget.

The script offered Tortilli another challenge. The original *Die Down* formula had been copied so many times that the new chapter threatened to cover the same ground all over again. Quintly's harshest critics had always claimed he didn't have an original thought in his ego-swelled head. He *had* to do something different with his comeback film.

To this end, somewhere during their earliest script discussions, Hank Bindle and Bruce Marmelstein had brought Quintly a script by an unknown writer. The Taurus cochairs had insisted that their discovery was absolutely super-talented and that Quintly absolutely had to use his script even if he had to change everything in it to do so. As they sang the praises of their new screenwriter, the two men were sweating visibly.

When Quintly resisted, Bindle and Marmelstein

had insisted. Since this was long before the Regency or the failed attempt to destroy Taurus Studios, and the blackmail opportunities they presented, Quintly, unable financially to walk away from the project, had accepted the novice screenwriter's story.

Over the course of the next few months, Tortilli changed so much in the original script that it was unrecognizable.

When the script changes were mentioned to the Taurus cochairs, both Bindle and Marmelstein were afraid that their screenwriter might object.

"You're worried about a *writer?*" Tortilli had asked.

"We're worried about *this* writer," Bindle replied.

"But he's a writer," Tortilli argued. "They're just...well...writers. No one in this town worries about writers."

"You've never met him," Marmelstein said uneasily.

"And I'm gonna keep it that way," Tortilli said.

And he had. All through the rewrites, he avoided the crazy old man. In fact—much to Bindle's and Marmelstein's relief—the writer stayed away straight through the final change in which the stolen-ship ending was jettisoned. When Lance Wallace finished up his work on the film, Tortilli had booked it to Seattle, just in time to avoid meeting Mr. Chiun. He let Arlen Duggal take the heat from the famously ill-tempered screenwriter.

Once in Seattle, Tortilli not only began work on the independent film he was doing for Cabbagehead Productions, but he completed the behind-the-scenes arrangements that would ensure financial solvency for the rest of his life.

Tortilli was just one of the many well-known Hollywood backers of Cabbagehead. He had bought his interest in the studio back in his post-*Penny Dreadful* heyday, when it seemed the money would never run out.

No one else worried about the success of the studio. Indeed, most of the backers had probably forgotten all about it. It was only something that their accountants fretted over when tallying up their strategic losses at tax time. If Cabbagehead had a hit, great. If not, big deal. Tortilli was the only one who had genuine financial concerns. And he turned those concerns into action.

It was surprisingly easy for the director to segue from fictional murder to the real thing.

At first, his fan mail had pointed the way. Those who skulked beyond society's fringes seemed drawn to him. The mailbag had dropped Leaf Randolph and Chester Gecko into his lap. Lee Matson had been a godsend. The first classified ad Quintly had answered in a mercenary mag and he'd bagged a top-drawer psycho.

Everything came together once he'd assembled his cast. With his skills as a writer-director-producer, he was able to outline and orchestrate each scheme down to the slightest detail. And so far, everything had gone nothing but right.

After the Anderson case, he had netted a nice profit as a stealth producer of *Suburban Decay*. The same had been true for the other two Cabbagehead films.

Oh, there was the little matter of the Taurus bombing failure. But that only affected Bindle and Marmelstein.

He even had *Die Down IV* to look forward to. Now, that was the work of a genius. Formulaic crap, the movie that should have been a disaster at the box office was certain to be a hit thanks to his distinct but thorough ministrations.

The New York bombing, the White House siege and now this night. This night would feature the event that would put him over the top. A cool 125 million by Memorial Day weekend alone. The gravy train would chug straight through to the Fourth of July and on to Oscar night in March.

He would be brilliant.

He would be prescient.

He would be *rich*.

In the privacy of his trailer, Tortilli smiled at the thought. He cast a final critical eye over his outfit. He didn't really like the tie. It was a little too yellow. Orange would be better.

Pulling off the bow tie, he searched through his wardrobe for the proper tie. After knotting it around his neck, he went back to the mirror. And frowned.

Still didn't look right.

"What should one wear to a presidential assassination?" he mused aloud as he tipped his head to one side.

He finally decided to go tieless. Pulling off the bow tie, he unbuttoned his shirt down to his cummerbund.

"Perfect," he proclaimed.

Tossing the orange tie onto a chair, Quintly Tortilli marched from his trailer. He closed the door with such violence, his rack of polyester suits swayed in the breeze.

The orange bow tie slipped silently to the floor.

30

The phone on Remo's plane didn't start working until they were about to land at LAX.

"It's about damn time," Remo said angrily when Harold Smith finally picked up. "Jann Revolta's signed to do three more movies since we left freaking Washington."

"Remo? What is wrong?"

"I've been trying to call you all the way from D.C.," he complained. "I'm about two seconds away from landing in California and the bloody phone just started working."

Smith didn't seem surprised. "That was a security precaution for the President."

"What does he have to do with this?" Remo said sourly.

"He is attending a scheduled fund-raising event at the Burbank Bowl tonight. After the events in Washington, he was only too eager to get out of the city. However, due to concerns for his safety, Air Force planes doused radio signals in a wide corridor for the duration of his trip. You must have been following in his wake."

"When does this guy ever find time to run the

country between fund-raisers?'' Remo grumbled.
"Anyway, I've got news.''

"As have I,'' Smith said excitedly.

"Me first. Quintly Tortilli's our guy. He's the
one making the movie all this bullshit has been
based on.''

"As I suspected,'' the CURE director said.
"Since we last spoke, I returned to the tangled fi-
nances of the studio in Seattle. Tortilli was a producer on the three independent films made successful by the original murders.''

"How come you didn't find that out before?''

"As I said, the financial records are complex.
One of the producers was an Allen Smithee. Further
digging revealed that this was a corporation name
owned by none other than Quintly Tortilli. It is in
this name that he is also a Cabbagehead Productions backer.''

"Well he's definitely branched out from the
indies, Smitty,'' Remo said. His hand rested on
Chiun's screenplay. "I've got his blockbuster
shooting script right here. It's got the New York
bombing and the White House takeover. Barely
mentions the trouble in Hollywood that it's sup-
posedly based on.''

"You actually have his script?'' Smith pressed.
"I was not able to find it in the Taurus computer
system.''

"Yeah, well, they left it lying around somewhere,'' Remo said vaguely. "Anyway, I've got his
grand finale. He plans on swiping a Navy boat from

the Long Beach shipyard. If he sticks to the script, we should be able to head it off.''

Smith paused. ''Remo, the Long Beach naval facility was closed several years ago. I believe it has been turned over to commercial development. If the Navy has left any vessels there, they are no doubt worthless scrap.''

''All I know is what I read, Smitty,'' Remo insisted. ''According to this, that's where he's going next.''

''I will arrange to have authorities converge on the area,'' Smith said reluctantly. The sound of rapid typing filtered through the phone.

''I'll take care of Tortilli,'' Remo said. ''And, Smitty?''

''Yes?''

''If they've built a mall at Long Beach like they've done on every other strip of land that used to be a military base in this country, you might want to evacuate the Gap,'' Remo suggested, hanging up the phone.

WHEN REMO ARRIVED at Taurus Studios, he found the Master of Sinanju striding purposefully up the sidewalk. The old Korean's weathered face was pinched into furious lines.

''Need a lift?'' Remo called out the car window.

Chiun's eggshell head lifted, shaken from his burdensome thoughts. He hurried over to Remo's rental car.

''I am cursed with too trusting a soul,'' the Master of Sinanju intoned as he slipped into the front seat. His squeaky voice toyed with the fringes of indignant rage.

"This ain't the town for one," Remo agreed. "What happened?"

"I have just learned the meaning of 'cutting room floor,'" Chiun snapped as they drove up the main Taurus avenue. Dusk was falling. "It is an evil practice wherein the innocent are duped into believing their angelic countenances will appear on movie screens around the world, only to have those precious inches of film snipped and discarded by the ugly and duplicitous."

Beneath the anger was injury. Chiun had been hurt by the lie. Remo's sympathetic smile was genuine.

"I'm sorry, Little Father."

Chiun pressed the back of one bony hand to his parchment forehead. "How will I ever overcome this embarrassment?" he lamented. "I have already told all my friends."

"What friends?" Remo asked.

"I told *you*," Chiun challenged.

Remo's face warmed.

"Oh, do not get maudlin," the Master of Sinanju snapped, noting the pleased expression on his pupil's face. "I merely mean that you will not miss an opportunity to lord this shame over me, jealous as you are."

"For the last time, I am not jealous," Remo said, exasperated. "And you should look on the bright side. At least you got the chance to think you were going to be in a movie. A lot of people don't get that.''

"A starving man is not sated by the mere promise of food," Chiun replied. "The thirst of a man dying in the desert is not slaked by the mere mention of water.''

"You're being a little melodramatic, don't you think?'' Remo said. "Besides, maybe it's all for the best. Smith would have stroked out the minute he heard you were in a movie.''

"Pah. Smith,'' Chiun sniffed. "He has hidden my light under his demented bushel basket far too long.''

"Smitty's okay," Remo disagreed. He was thinking of the past few days. Smith had become human to Remo in a way he did not like. "It's not his fault they cut you out. That sort of thing happens all the time.'' He regretted saying it the instant it passed his lips. "I think— I mean, I assume. I *guess*. Probably.'' He abruptly changed the subject. "Hey, you wouldn't happen to know where Tortilli is?''

Chiun didn't reply right away. He was staring at his pupil's guilty silhouette.

"No,'' he said, after an infinitely long pause.

"I'll check with Bindle and Marmelstein,'' Remo said. He kept his eyes dead ahead as he drove to the main offices.

"Did you know already of this 'cutting room

floor?'" the Master of Sinanju demanded bluntly, eyes slits of suspicion.

"You're the movie expert in the family," Remo said, dodging the question. "I'm just Frank to your Sly Stallone."

Chiun's hazel eyes bored through to Remo's soul. Remo didn't flinch. At long last, the old man dropped back in his seat. "This is the worst day of my life," he lamented, stuffing his hands morosely into the sleeves of his kimono.

"I thought the worst day was when you met me."

"It was. You have been supplanted."

"And it only took thirty years. If you live to be two hundred, maybe I'll get pushed back to three."

"You should live that long," Chiun said.

BINDLE AND MARMELSTEIN were still hiding out behind Bindle's fractured desk when Remo and Chiun burst through the glass doors.

"If that's the limo, bring it around back," Hank Bindle's disembodied voice whispered.

"The only place you're going is out that window."

At the sound of Remo's voice, two pairs of fearful eyes sprang up above the upended desk half. When Bindle and Marmelstein saw Remo and Chiun striding toward them, two heavy tumblers thudded to the thick carpet. The executives scampered to their feet, backing to the wall.

"Mr. Remo, Mr. Chiun. What a pleasant surprise," Marmelstein said nervously.

Each man wore an ugly silk tuxedo. The suits were deep blue with black felt cuffs and cummerbunds. High white collars hugged their necks, a single black button where a bow tie should have been.

"It was Quintly Tortilli," Bindle blurted.

Marmelstein wheeled on his partner. Not to be out-stool pigeoned, Bruce added, "We didn't *know* it was him until yesterday. He did the White House thing entirely on his own. We just hired him to blow up that building in New York."

Bindle kicked his partner viciously in the ankle.

"Ow! I mean *oh*," Marmelstein stammered, hopping in place. "Shouldn't have said that. Edit that last bit out."

Before Remo could open his mouth, the Master of Sinanju bullied his way in front of his pupil.

"You have much explaining to do," Chiun challenged.

Bindle's and Marmelstein's eyes grew wide.

"We didn't know you were going to be here," Marmelstein whined rapidly. "I swear on my mother's eyes."

"We thought you were gone," Bindle agreed, pleading. "We never would have done it if we knew you were on the lot. We want to make more great movies with you, baby."

Chiun glanced at Remo, his expression one of sour confusion. "What are these imbeciles babbling about?"

"They're the ones who hired Tortilli to blow up the studio," Remo supplied. "With you in it."

Chiun spun to the Taurus cochairs, eyes blazing fire. "Is this true?" he demanded.

"It was his idea," Bindle and Marmelstein both exclaimed in unison. Each was pointing to the other. Their faces grew shocked at the betrayal. *"Liar!"* they both accused at the same time.

Bindle shoved Marmelstein into the broken desk. Bottles on the floor clanked loudly as the Taurus cochair stumbled through them.

Marmelstein flung a handful of ice from a bucket at his partner. One piece struck Bindle in the face.

"I'm blind!" Bindle shrieked. Squinting, he tried to kick Marmelstein. Missing completely, he punted the desk. A toe cracked audibly.

"Ahhh!" Bindle yowled in pain.

Thrilled to have the upper hand, Bruce Marmelstein was about to finish his partner off with a hurled bottle of martini olives when he felt a powerful hand grab him by the throat. The olive jar slipped from his hand as he felt himself being thrown through the air. He landed on the surface of his own, intact desk. With a grunt, Hank Bindle dropped roughly beside him.

When they looked up, they found Remo a few inches away. The Master of Sinanju stood at his elbow. Neither man seemed pleased.

"Tortilli," Remo growled. "Where is he?"

"Finishing location shooting," Bindle offered

weakly, his left eye squeezed tightly shut. His broken toe ached.

"I thought location stuff was done weeks ago."

"This is an add-on scene. Quintly didn't like the last boat sequence. We scrapped it for something more exciting."

Remo felt his heart quicken. "The boat sequence was cut?"

"Quintly had a flash of inspiration," Marmelstein offered. "He wrote something new that dovetails with the whole terrorist-White House angle."

"Where is he shooting?" Remo pressed.

"The Burbank Bowl," Bindle replied.

"That's where we were going," Marmelstein supplied. "It's a concert to celebrate soundtrack music."

"Only we were going to show up late, 'cause that stuff gives us both headaches," Bindle ventured.

"The President's at the Burbank Bowl, Little Father," Remo said worriedly to Chiun.

The old Korean had his own problems.

"They have edited me," Chiun moaned. "*Me*. And to add insult to injury, my own producers attempt to kill me with a boom. Oh, why did I ever think an assassin would be safe in this town?"

Remo returned his attention to Bindle and Marmelstein.

"How does the movie end?" he demanded.

"The President dies." Bindle nodded, trying to sell Remo on the concept. "Great dramatic scene.

Lance Wallace gets sworn in on the spot as the next Commander in Chief. Perfect setup for the sequel.''

Remo wheeled to Chiun. ''We've got to get to the Burbank Bowl,'' he insisted sharply.

''Gladly,'' Chiun responded bitterly. ''My only wish before I shake the dust of this heathen village from my sandals forever is to mete out justice to the mendacious Quintly Tortilli.''

Scrambling, Bindle knelt on the desk. ''By justice, you don't mean, by any chance, *killing* Quintly?''

''I will feed him his own lying heart.''

''Heart feeding is bad, Bruce,'' Bindle said out of the corner of his mouth.

''You *can't* kill him just yet,'' Bruce Marmelstein said quickly. ''Not till he's finished tonight's filming. As it is, it's already gonna be a bitch getting this puppy in theaters in two weeks.''

''But if he *does* finish tonight, he's guaranteed us 125 million by Memorial Day,'' Hank Bindle argued hastily. ''Even if it tanks afterward, that'll carry us through another hundred million, domestic.''

''And even halfway decent word of mouth could push us over three hundred million before foreign, pay cable or video,'' Marmelstein supplied rapidly. ''And a real dead President bumps foreign box office out of the solar system.''

''Bottom line, Chiun, baby,'' Bindle concluded hurriedly. ''Presidents come and Presidents go, but you keep turning out dynamite scripts like *Die*

Down IV, and you and Taurus'll be counting Oscar gold for years to come.''

Sweating anxiously, the two Taurus cochairs studied the Master of Sinanju's reaction, Bindle with one bloodshot eye closed.

The wizened Asian turned a narrowed eye to his pupil. ''Is it possible for a film to survive the deaths of the executives in charge of the project?'' he asked.

Remo was already edging toward the door. ''Little Father, every time a Hollywood honcho dies, an angel gets his wings,'' he answered quickly.

Both executives still squatted on Bruce Marmelstein's desk, looks of anxious fear on their tan faces. They seemed oblivious to Remo's words, focused as they were on the Master of Sinanju.

Chiun stood silent before them, a figure of solemn contemplation.

In a move so swift it did not have time to startle, the old Korean's hands suddenly shot up.

Bindle and Marmelstein held their collective breath. Fearful, fascinated eyes stared with rapt attention at two extended index fingernails.

Chiun paused an instant—an orchestra conductor holding a note a beat too long.

A flash. Nails dropping, thrusting forward. Puncturing soft abdominal tissue. A jerking blur. Chiun's bloodless nails retreated to his gold kimono sleeves.

With twin gasps, Bindle and Marmelstein looked down in time to see their bellies yawn open in side-way smiles. Slick red organs slopped out onto the cold metal desk. Frantic faces looked to Chiun in desperation.

"We'll give you points," Bindle gasped. With one hand, he was trying to hold in the last of his trailing internal organs. The other palm was braced helplessly on the desk.

Chiun spun away, gliding swiftly across the office. Remo was already pushing the door open.

Marmelstein toppled to the floor. "No writer gets points," he panted weakly. "We'll give you ten off the top."

"We already told him ten," Bindle wheezed faintly.

"Twenty."

Remo and Chiun were already gone.

From the top of the desk, Hank Bindle looked down with glazed eyes at his dying partner. "Net?" he panted.

"Gross."

It wasn't clear if Marmelstein was talking about film profits or the fact that they had each just collapsed into the slimy sacks of their own internal organs.

And in another moment, nothing mattered to them at all.

31

Cameras clicked like a hundred crazed crickets as Quintly Tortilli exited the main door of the Burbank Bowl. His pointy cheekbones and chin seemed more prominent in the presence of the tight rictal smile he gave the paparazzi.

The press was kept back farther than usual by a contingent of dark-suited Secret Service agents.

The armor-reinforced presidential limousine with its tiny twin flapping American flags stopped at the end of the long red carpet just as Tortilli made it to the curb. Before and behind the limo, motorcycles and official vehicles of the presidential motorcade stopped, as well.

The President climbed from the back seat with a beaming smile beneath his familiar bulbous nose and baggy eyes.

"Quintly, good to see you!" the President exclaimed hoarsely. He pumped the young director's hand for the cameras.

"Glad you could make it, Mr. President," Tortilli said, his own smile never wavering. "Thought that wacky Washington scene mighta kept you east of the mighty Mississip."

A hint of discomfort flitted across the Chief Executive's face.

"Oh, I'm fine," he dismissed. "The First Lady was pretty shaken up, but she's keeping her mind off things by staying busy. Last I saw her she was knee-deep in paperwork."

The President was only too happy to change the subject. Only in California and New York did he receive such enthusiastic crowds these days. Waving to reporters and cheering bystanders, the President began walking to the Burbank Bowl entrance, Quintly Tortilli at his side.

"How soon'll you be shooting?" the chief executive asked when they were nearly at the door.

Tortilli's smile broadened just a hair. For a flickering moment, it almost seemed sincere.

"Any minute now, Mr. President," he promised.

As the cameras flashed, the two men disappeared inside.

THE ROUTE to the Burbank Bowl was jammed with cars. Through the trees at the side of the freeway, Remo could see the parking lot was also packed.

"No time to wait for the off-ramp," he said tightly.

"The faster we finish this business, the sooner I may depart this province of broken dreams," the Master of Sinanju replied irritably.

Remo nodded. "We bail."

They ditched the rental car in the middle of the freeway. Horns honked angrily as the two Masters of Sinanju ran between cars and hopped the jersey barrier. Side by side, they skidded down the dusty embankment. At the bottom, they raced across the short stretch of woods to the fringe of the parking lot.

"Care to tell me how this picture ends?" Remo asked as they flew between rows of parked cars.

"The good version, or theirs?" Chiun retorted.

"The shooting script," Remo pressed.

"I believe there was some sort of boom device on the stage," Chiun sniffed as he ran. "Who knows if that has been changed since last week."

Remo's face was grim as they swept between cars.

"Let's hope Tortilli hasn't seen another movie since then," he grumbled. "The way he rips everybody off, he's probably got a mechanical shark swimming around the orchestra pit."

Careful to avoid Secret Service and police foot patrols, the two men raced on toward the great beveled dome of the Burbank Bowl.

THE AUDIENCE had endured the theme from *Star Wars* and *Raiders of the Lost Ark* before the orchestra finally segued into the *1812* overture.

Far away from the stage, Quintly Tortilli's purple tuxedo was stained dark with sweat. The nervous grinding of his molars was drowned out by the thunderous music.

Far below the VIP box, Lee Matson waited calmly onstage, not a care in the world. Before him, a pair of breech-loading field guns aimed into the crowd. Only Tortilli and Matson knew that their explosive powder charges had been replaced with live shells.

In the box beside Tortilli, the President of the United States smiled and nodded to the music.

Thank God Tortilli had always been a generous contributor to the President and his party. There was no way he'd be there otherwise. It was a fat check drawn from the *Die Down IV* budget that had gotten Tortilli access to the White House layout, as well as a night in the Lincoln Bedroom thrown in for good measure.

Vanity drew the President there today. Eight cameras whirred around them at this very moment, catching the President's every blink, smile and itch.

Tortilli had told the President that he wanted realism for his latest film. His desire was to capture the real effect on a crowd when the Chief Executive was in attendance.

Of course, it wasn't vanity alone. A fresh, generous studio check to the President's legal-defense fund and—in spite of the previous day's unpleasantness—the Chief Executive had readily agreed.

Around the bowl, the rumbling music grew in intensity. Almost over.

Tortilli stood abruptly. A few eyes turned his way.

Sweating, the director patted his stomach.

"Gotta take care of business," he mouthed over the din.

As Tortilli slipped quickly from the box, the Secret Service entourage didn't give him a second glance.

Ears ringing, Tortilli hurried out into the enclosed hallway. To await the thunderous explosion that would be heard around the world *and* herald three hundred million, domestic, by Labor Day.

THE BURBANK BOWL WAS a half shell open-air amphitheater. Half-wall partitions near the stage separated the more expensive seats from the general-admission bleachers. A few VIP boxes lined the far back wall.

Remo and Chiun had taken a rear entrance, bursting into the main bleachers section at the midpoint. As soon as they were inside, they spotted the President. He was way back in the center box at the rear of the big stadium.

"Must have taken a cheerleader with a Milk-Bone to get him and Fido out of that closet," Remo commented.

Chiun was scanning the opposite direction. A long nail unfurled.

"There!" the Master of Sinanju exclaimed.

Following his teacher's extended finger, he spied the cannons at once. The tuxedo-clad figure behind them smiled with demented eagerness.

"I'll get Mr. Nutbar," Remo barked.

Chiun nodded. "I will attend the puppet President."

In a swirl of silken robes, Chiun headed for the

rear of the theater. Remo flew down the long flat steps toward the main stage.

The Secret Service protection thinned the farther he ran from the President, replaced by uniformed police officers.

Thanks to Remo, there weren't as many cops as there should have been. Every other police officer in California was doubtless waiting at the abandoned Long Beach shipyard for an attack that would never come. He avoided police all the way to the front of the stadium.

Down front, he hesitated.

He couldn't very well leap onstage. Wrists rotating absently, he tried to think of a way to take out the assassin without being seen.

Seen!

It was risky, but it might work. In any event, at least he had a plan. He only hoped he could implement it in time.

As the music swelled, Remo raced around the side of the stage, away from the cannons and the madman behind them.

QUINTLY TORTILLI LURKED anxiously in the hallway behind the closed-off VIP tier. Face a sheen of glistening sweat, he studied his watch. Mickey's hands moved with agonizing slowness.

He didn't know how far away he should be. He knew he wanted to be in San Diego when the cannon blasted the presidential box to smithereens. Or, better yet, Mexico. But he needed to be close enough to allay suspicion.

What if they linked him to Lee Matson?

What if they traced the Taurus prop cannons to him?

What if as a result of bad press, Lord help him, *Die Down IV* flopped?

He shook away the negative thoughts.

"Get a grip, Quint," he muttered to himself. "You're a Hollywood director. You're smarter than everyone in the world."

Feeling dizzy, he took a deep breath.

"*People* sez you're a genius," he panted, leaning against the wall for support. The cold sweat on his back made him shiver.

"Every kid in film school wants to be you," he insisted.

A rumble. Felt through the wall.

For an instant, he thought Matson had fired his cannons early. But before he could check his watch, his peripheral vision saw what his back had felt. A few yards away, one of the doors that led into the auditorium exploded inward.

Tortilli jumped back from the wall, expecting to glimpse a whistling artillery shell. But instead of a missile, the upside-down form of a blue-suited man soared in amid the splinters of wood.

The Secret Service agent slammed into the distant wall. As his unconscious body dropped to the floor, a tiny figure whirled like a miniature gold typhoon through the opening the unfortunate agent had made.

Chiun shot a single glance at Tortilli, eyes filled with the promise of vengeance.

Recognizing his famously vicious-tempered screenwriter, Tortilli sucked in a shocked gasp of air. But the old man didn't seem interested in him just yet. Chiun flew in the opposite direction, toward the restricted end of the corridor and the presidential box.

As the tiny Asian raced off, a sudden all-engulfing blackness consumed him. The racing dark cloud swallowed the rest of the corridor and the amphitheater beyond.

Tortilli didn't even seem to notice that the lights had gone out. As the first querulous shouts began to rise from the darkened stadium, the panicked young director was stumbling in blind fear down the pitch-black corridor. Away from the terrifying figure in gold.

BACKSTAGE, Remo spun from the sparking breaker panel. He had to hop over the bodies of three unconscious Burbank police officers.

"Work fast, Little Father," he muttered.

Swift feet moved in confident strides as he raced through the darkness toward the stage.

THE INSTANT the lights went out, alarm signals went off in the mind of the President of the United

States. Yesterday's frightening events were far too recent.

"What's going on?" he asked the nearest Secret Service agent, trying to mask the fear in his voice.

"Unknown, Mr. President," the agent replied tightly.

As soon as he had spoken, a cry rose from beyond the closed balcony door. The sounds of a scuffle ensued.

The Secret Service retinue reacted instinctively.

The President was yanked from his seat and thrown to the floor. A crush of dark-suited bodies— guns drawn—collapsed on top of him. Air rushed from his lungs.

Through his filter of living human flesh, the President heard muted shouts, then the sound of crashing wood.

More shouts. Louder. A single gunshot.

A yelp of pain.

The President felt the weight on his prone form lighten.

Another cry. Lighter still.

No time to even fire. In a panicked instant, his entire human shield was stripped away. He was naked. Exposed.

Looking up, frightened, the President saw the shadowy contours of a vaguely familiar face.

"Your life is in jeopardy, Your Majesty," the vision above him intoned urgently.

That voice. The President knew that voice.

It was one of Smith's men. The old Asian.

Before he could ask the Master of Sinanju what he was doing there, the old man pulled him off the floor, depositing the burly Chief Executive on his own bony shoulders.

As the Master of Sinanju raced to the door, there came a distant explosion. Through angled eyes, the President saw a brilliant flash of light from the stage.

And cutting through it all, the sound of a single shell whistling through the air.

The door was a million miles away.

The shell was coming in fast. *Too* fast.

A fiery impact. Explosion. Thunder and light.

The President felt the heat from the blast erupt around them, enveloping them. Obliterating them.

And the final, fatal burning fear consumed him.

REMO REACHED the stage too late.

Too late he heard the soft *foom* followed by an intense blast. The thunderous boom of a single cannon round being fired exploded from out the darkness.

An instant later came the sound of a distant impact. Then another explosion as the President's box burst apart in a brilliant flash of light.

Pandemonium instantly erupted all around the Burbank Bowl. In the darkness, terrified concert-goers screamed and shoved in a mad race for the exits.

The orchestra was fleeing, as well. Alone on the stage, Lee Matson was preparing to launch a second shell at the President's box just to make sure before joining the rest of the mass exodus.

Face hard, Remo sliced through the fleeing orchestra members and onto the stage.

THE PRESIDENT of the United States was dead.

He had to be.

The shell had struck. There was the crackle of impact. Splintering wood. Fire, heat and shrapnel racing toward his unprotected face.

But then something strange happened. The world seemed to freeze. The explosion, the fire, the hurtling debris—everything save the old Asian on whose shoulders he was perched appeared to lock in place.

Running seemingly apart from time, the Master of Sinanju zoomed out the balcony door.

Only when Smith's man had borne him to safety did the President realize this strange netherworld of slow motion was merely an illusion.

In the hallway, time tripped back to normal speed.

Flames belched out in the wake of the running Korean. The wall blew in, chunks of flesh-tearing debris screaming into the corridor in their wake.

Too late. The Master of Sinanju had already outrun the worst of the blast. He was halfway down the hall when he finally stopped. Chiun sat the shaken chief executive on the cool concrete floor. Behind them, fire burned. Fresh screams rose from the bowl through the shell-blasted opening.

"Twice," the President gasped. "Twice in two days."

Standing above the panting Chief Executive, the Master of Sinanju was impassive. "Do you still think to settle in this province once your reign has ended?" he asked.

"What?" the President sniffled, still trying to catch his breath. "Oh. I've got a few standing offers in Hollywood. If my wife doesn't follow through on her latest threat to run for the Senate out of Bangkok in 2004." He seemed shell-shocked. His eyes were ill as he looked down the corridor at the ragged wall.

"Heed my advice," Chiun instructed somberly. "Follow the Shrill Queen to some other province. If this kind of treachery unnerves you, you will not last a single day on the coast."

With that, the Master of Sinanju became a whirl of silk.

On bounding pipe-stem legs, he flounced away from the president and the burning VIP box. Fire in his eyes, he headed off in the direction Quintly Tortilli had gone.

32

The cannons were both pre-aimed. Even as Lee grabbed the cord that would fire the next shell, he marveled at the laxness of the Secret Service. He had read how this White House had at other times ordered agents to loosen security in certain situations—usually when the White House didn't want to be caught in something untoward.

Lee surmised their seeming dereliction of duty had something to do with the movie cameras he'd seen around the bowl. Quintly Tortilli must have convinced the President that too many agents would interfere with his shot.

Lee giggled at the irony.

"I can't wait till I have that kind of clout," he said.

Chuckling to himself, he fumbled in the darkness for the cord on the second cannon.

His hand brushed something warm.

Lee recoiled. The something he had touched had fingers.

In the dark, people still screamed. Succumbing to the contagion of their fear, Lee squinted at the blackness before him.

The blinding flash of the artillery explosion had splashed dancing splotches of light on his retinas. As the light-blindness receded, a figure resolved from out of the shadows. The cruel cast of the stranger's face jump-started Lee's waxing fear into full-blown panic.

"Tell me when this hurts," Remo said evenly.

Lee tried to jump back.

A firm hand gripped his throat, holding him in place.

"But I've got a development deal," Lee begged as Remo dragged him down to the business end of the cannon.

The maw stared at him. Lee gulped back.

As he watched in fear, the cannon seemed to launch forward like a hungry beast, swallowing Lee Matson's head all the way to his shaking soldier-of-fortune shoulders.

Outside, Remo gave the barrel a kick. The cannon twisted stage right, away from the thinning crowd. Lee Matson—head jammed too tightly to remove it—had to hop and skip sideways to keep up.

Remo slipped down the barrel to the small carriage. As Lee wiggled at the far end, Remo's fingers looped around the cord.

"If you didn't like him, you shouldn't have voted for Perot," he announced as he yanked the cord.

The instant he fired the cannon, Remo was already diving from the stage. He hit the aisle at a full sprint.

Behind him, the pressure built up along the interior of the cannon. With nowhere to go, the shell exploded inside the barrel, launching fragments of hot metal forward. Lee Matson was shredded to hamburg. Meaty red parts splattered like paint pellets against the backstage wall.

Remo wasn't there to see the aftermath. Wearing a tight expression, he was already halfway up the rear of the stadium. Beyond, the shattered presidential box belched smoke and flame into the starry California night sky.

BY THE TIME Remo caught up with Chiun in the hallway behind the row of VIP boxes, the stadium emergency lights had hummed to life. The Master of Sinanju was kicking in closed doors as he made his way up the corridor.

"The President?" Remo asked eagerly as he raced up beside Chiun.

"He will live to eat another day," the Master of Sinanju replied. His sandaled foot shot out, exploding a utility closet door. He peeked inside.

Chiun's face grew more dissatisfied. He went down to the next door. It, too, surrendered to his heel.

"Is this just wanton destruction or is there a point?" Remo asked once Chiun had emerged from this room, his face a scowl.

"The prevaricator Tortilli is here," the Master of Sinanju announced angrily.

"Why didn't you say so?"

Remo took one side of the corridor, Chiun the other. They kicked their way down to the distant wall.

After ducking inside the last door—which opened into an unused ladies' room—Remo emerged, dragging a yelping Quintly Tortilli by the ear.

"Hey, can't a guy take a leak in peace?" the director said, forcing injured innocence into his voice.

Chiun barged up to him. "Silence, liar."

The director cowered even as he tried to casually adjust his purple tux.

"Ohhh, that cutting-room floor thing, right?" he questioned. "No problemo. Next movie, I swear. You costar."

Remo couldn't believe what he was hearing.

"There isn't going to be a next movie, Tortilli," Remo said evenly. "You just tried to kill the President."

Tortilli nodded disagreement. "Sure, there is. I've already got my next five films sketched out. Chiun can be in one, two—hell, all *five* of them. Camera loves you, babe." He waved a wild arm down the hall. "But hey, how 'bout the whole John Wilkes Booth-Ford Theater thing here, though? President assassinated in VIP box. Pretty slick update, huh? Don't worry, no one'll notice the rip-off."

Remo had heard enough. "Let's go, Cecil B.

Dimwit." Grabbing the director by the ear once more, he began hustling Tortilli down the corridor.

The Master of Sinanju padded hastily behind them.

"Did you say costar or star?" Chiun asked cagily.

THE LONELY GUARD at Taurus Studios recognized Quintly Tortilli's red Jaguar as it drove up to the gates.

It was one o'clock in the morning.

The guard was used to such late arrivals. It wasn't unusual for the maverick director to keep odd hours. Quintly Tortilli was behind the wheel. Apparently alone.

The car was flagged inside.

Twenty minutes later, the Jaguar drove back off the lot, its taillights fading into anonymous red dots.

When Tortilli's body was discovered on Taurus grounds the next day, the guard shook his head, saying that he didn't notice who was driving the car as it left. He'd assumed it was Tortilli.

It clearly wasn't, he was told.

The body of the director had been found inside a private screening room. Someone had threaded the tongue of the young Hollywood genius into a film projector. Somehow—without any hope of a logical explanation—much of Tortilli's crushed and elongated head had trailed the tongue inside the machine.

When he learned of this new death, coming apparently just hours after the disemboweling of Taurus cochairs Hank Bindle and Bruce Marmelstein—who were found dead in their office around the same time as Tortilli—the guard had only one thing to say.

"Gee. Sounds like something out of one of his movies, don't it?"

33

Two days later, Remo was back at home in Massachusetts, sitting cross-legged on his living-room floor. He had just finished reading Chiun's script.

Whereas before he had only scanned parts of the screenplay, this time he had read it carefully from cover to cover. He was stunned.

"Unbelievable," he muttered.

Gathering the script up in one hand, he rose to his feet to go off in search of the Master of Sinanju. He got as far as the kitchen when the telephone rang.

"It's your dime."

"Remo, Smith. I thought you might like to know that I have just completed an exhaustive search of Stefan Schoenburg and the rest of the Cabbagehead backers. It appears as if Tortilli was the only one of them involved in this scheme."

Remo hopped to a sitting position on the counter, dropping Chiun's script beside him. "What about that family that was murdered in Maryland? Did you track down their killers yet?"

"Killer," Smith stressed. "The police found only one set of fingerprints in the home and on the

digging implements found in the tunnel. They were able to match them to those of the would-be presidential assassin in Burbank.''

"They must have picked them up with a sponge," Remo said dryly.

"He also had the items stolen from the Anderson home on his person. It appears as if all the loose ends are tied up." Smith's lemony voice sounded satisfied.

"What about the President?" Remo asked. "Is he ticked at us for icing his buddy Tortilli?"

"He may be," Smith replied with sincere indifference. "That is not a concern to this agency. We have neutralized a threat not only to his life, but to the safety of other Americans. *That* is our charter."

"You don't have to sell me, Smitty," Remo said.

"In any event, with Bindle and Marmelstein gone, Taurus Studios is in turmoil. Apparently, they converted a great deal of what is arguably Taurus property to their own use. From what I understand, their relatives are suing. The litigation will most likely drag on for years. It looks as if the legacy of Bindle, Marmelstein and Quintly Tortilli is the certain end of Taurus Studios."

From somewhere distant, Remo heard a horrified shriek. The Master of Sinanju. As he listened to Smith, Remo rolled his eyes to the kitchen door.

"That's great, Smitty," he said, trying to hurry things along. "If that's everything, I've got to get going."

"Is something wrong?"

"By the sounds of it," Remo said, still looking worriedly at the door. "And from what you just told me, I have a sneaking suspicion what it is."

Hanging up the phone, Remo grabbed Chiun's script from the counter. Hopping to the floor, he made his way into the hallway. He mounted the stairs to Chiun's special bell-tower meditation room.

The Master of Sinanju had gone out to collect the mail not long before the phone rang. Walking through the door to the glass-enclosed room, Remo found the tiny Korean seated on the floor, the day's mail spread out before him. Brilliant yellow sunlight spilled across a neatly typed letter that had been unfolded between Chiun's crossed knees.

"They are vultures!" the Master of Sinanju hissed as Remo came into the room.

"Bad news?" Remo asked. He noted the name of a California law firm at the top of the business letter.

"My movie is not to be released. All projects in that madhouse of a studio are being held captive by lawyers, the only creatures on earth lower than Hollywood executives."

Crouching beside Chiun, Remo scanned the letter.

"I've heard of stuff like this happening before."

Chiun looked at him, hope touching his hazel eyes. "How long will it take to resolve?"

Remo frowned somberly. "Beats me. Sometimes it's years. Sometimes never."

The Master of Sinanju's eyes became twin daggers of cold fury. "Even in death, they have lied to me," he fumed.

Remo straightened back up. "It's probably just as well," he said. He had been holding Chiun's script in his hand. He dropped it to the floor now. "I just finished reading this thing. Who'd you say wrote it?"

"I did," Chiun dismissed haughtily.

"You wrote *Assassin's Loves,* or whatever you called it. Who wrote that?" Remo pointed at the screenplay.

"I do not know. The lying Tortilli. Friends of the cretinous Bindle and Marmelstein. Why does it matter?"

"It matters because I spotted at least twenty other movies that were ripped off in yours. You've got elements of *Dirty Harry, Serpico, The French Connection, The Godfather, Batman,* the *Indiana Jones* movies and a ton more. And I don't even see that many movies. That was the most derivative piece of drivel I've ever read."

Chiun frowned. "This is a surprise," he said.

"Didn't you read it?" Remo asked.

"Of course I did," Chiun sniffed, annoyed. He rose delicately from the floor, bearing his script with him. "I am only surprised by your persistent jealousy. If you do not let it go, it will consume you, Remo." Tucking the script in the crook of his arm, he began marching to the door.

"I'm telling you, Little Father, someone would

have been sued over that thing. And *your* name is on the cover.''

''It is disgraceful that you are so envious,'' Chiun said. ''As punishment, I will not mention your name when I receive my Academy Award.'' He breezed from the room.

''*If* the movie is ever released,'' Remo called out.

''It would already *be* out if this industry was not teeming with vipers,'' Chiun shouted back.

Remo smiled sadly at the empty room. Warm sunlight touched the dusty corners.

''That's showbiz, sweetheart.''

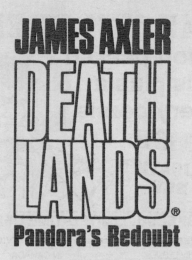

JAMES AXLER

DEATH LANDS®

Pandora's Redoubt

Ryan Cawdor and his fellow survivalists emerge in a
redoubt in which they discover a sleek superarmored
personnel carrier bristling with weapons from predark
days. As the companions leave the redoubt, a sudden
beeping makes them realize why the builders were
constructing a supermachine in the first place.

James Axler

OUTLANDERS™

SHADOW
SCOURGE

The bayous of Louisiana, steeped in magic and voodoo, are
the new epicenter of a dark, ancient evil. Kane, a renegade
enforcer of the new order, is now a freedom fighter
dedicated with fellow insurrectionists to free the future from
the yoke of Archon power.